Silencing the
Blues Man

Praise for Novels by Sherman Smith

The Honeysuckle Rose Hotel

"Full disclosure: I did not buy the book, it was given to me by the author. I was with my family in Bellingham WA eating Christmas dinner at a hotel. I didn't notice the gentleman eating alone at the next table until he arose and introduced himself. "I couldn't help but overhear your discussion about historical fiction. Perhaps you would do me the honor of reading my latest book." There was no quid pro quo, I didn't even tell him I'd written a historical fiction book myself. I assured him that yes, the subject was intriguing and I would be happy to read it. Now, writers are the most severe literary critics, at least until they can afford to be generous, which I cannot. So when I say this book is well written, that I found myself immersed to the point where I was no longer editing as I read, then you can trust me that it's a good read. The Honeysuckle Rose Hotel is especially delightful for those of us with connections to both San Francisco and musicians. I learned something, I felt something. I never did see Mr. Sherman again, I'm sure he's not usually alone at Christmas, but I am happy that he had the chuzpah to introduce himself. Thank you, Sherman Smith, wherever you are, and happy writing."

~*5 Star Amazon Review*

Silencing the Blues Man

"Wow – finished it in one night. Mr. Smith's handling of the intricacies of each character shows personal depth. Feels like I know each of the characters like good acquaintances or really good friends. It made we want to be part of this ragtag family. The book made a run of my emotions and that, to me, signals awesome writing. The fact that it drew me in to the point that I couldn't put it down to sleep made me smile. He just keeps getting better and better, Well done."

~CJK

"Silencing the Blues Man is the third book in the Poets Can't Sing series featuring amazing characters including the Blues Man himself, Earl Crier and his Lady Stella. The story of a quirky set of misfits, mostly musicians, takes place in post WWII San Francisco. The story illuminates some of the racism and fanaticism of the time, challenging us to think about we face today. The story within the story and the characters are compelling. I wanted the group experiences at the Honeysuckle Rose Hotel to continue. The author's work helps keep our faith in humanity."

~RH

Novels by Sherman Smith

Previous Books in this Series

Poets Can't Sing
The Honeysuckle Rose Hotel

Other Titles by Sherman Smith

Golden City on Fire
Sausalito Night Music

For information on the author and all his writings go to:
Shermansmithauthor.com

Special thanks to the team at FPW Media
for the cover design and irreplaceable editing support.

01
Only a Dream

How does one prepare one's self to go to war for a second time; one that he knows with certainty will end his life?

Henry Akita had once saved Ivory's life—not on the battlefield, but from the nightmares that haunted his hospital bed pushing him to the edge of the suicide cliff. Ivory had suffered for three years, nine months, and two days as a prisoner of war of the Japanese Empire. Japan lost the war. Ivory lost his will to live. He was a defeated man physically, emotionally, and spiritually. Unless he somehow rediscovered the desire to live, no matter the nightmares and pain, the doctors could do nothing more.

Ivory was sent to the veteran's hospital in San Francisco as a wait and see patient. What the doctors could not do, an angel, a blind man, and a Jap did. Henry Akita had been the Jap—Japanese American, Nisei, war hero, and friend. Ivory had many nightmares. Surprisingly, the one that shook him the most was the memory of his first meeting Henry. Now it was Henry who was in trouble and Ivory had no choice but to try to help.

Ivory's nightmare always began the same way, waking on a hard, earthen floor, drenched in a fever sweat, exhausted, his joints aflame, and skin screaming from the fire ants that fed on the lice that swarmed across his flesh. This is the way Ivory Burch woke most of the days he had been a prisoner of war of the Japanese.

Now his nightmares ended with his screams as he struggled to wake, his heart pounding, remembering pain so great that he wished he were dead, fearing that on the other side of life, there is something so horrific, that he is afraid to die. There is no heaven, only hell for both the living and the dead. The Japanese had been the doormen.

The Jap soldier, outraged, smaller, though stronger than he, pinned him to the ground with a hobnailed boot, as he raised his bayonet above Ivory's heart. There was pure hatred in his enemy's eyes as the bayonet descended . . .

Ivory had thrashed wildly in his bedding.

"Wake up! It's only a dream," a voice from the other side of his nightmare said. "Wake Up!" Strong hands held him down as he fought for his life.

The bayonet raised, he could see his own reflection, his own terror, glistening in the blade. He tried to run, his amputated leg useless as he opened his eyes, his fear beyond measure. "Easy, fella, it's only a dream. I've got you." Henry Akita had said. Ivory's eyes went wide as he shrieked at the sight of Henry's Nisei face.

"Easy Ivory, it's only a dream."

The terror slowly faded from Ivory's eyes as he began to remember that he was a patient at the veteran's hospital. He was no longer a China Marine. He was the sole survivor of his outfit. The Japanese had been right, he had surrendered and did not deserve to live. The only sounds Ivory had heard were the words "it's only a dream," the pounding of his own heart, the babble of other men imprisoned by their wounds in the same hospital ward. In the distance someone singing sweet and low while playing a piano, whose music sounded as pretty as a spring waterfall.

The war had ended five years prior and Ivory was still a frail survivor of everything he had been through. The strong hands that had woken him from that dream belonged to Henry, a former Nisei army corpsman whose face he still had trouble looking into. Now, he and Ivory had become more than friends; if necessary, Ivory would lay down his life to protect Henry Akita from harm.

Feminine intuition defies reasonable explanation, it is some-times right, even when it is wrong, creating in its own mind-set a reality that few men will even understand. That was the way it began the moment that Stella woke. She knew that something would happen this day that would change her life as nothing had since the first moment, she had heard her Earl sing.

Something had come in the morning mail.

Ivory knew that Henry was troubled; why he did not know. Nor where he had gone. Ivory left the Honeysuckle Rose Hotel to find his friend and to see that he came to no harm. Whatever troubled him, Ivory wished he could say: "It's Okay, Henry, it's only a dream." But it wasn't a dream, and there was nothing he could do to change the wind that blew in bad news.

02
The Road Once Traveled

June 1950. The news was not all bad, but one had to work hard at finding the good.

There had been hope after the end of the Second World War that things would get better. Now, hope was becoming lost in the headlines: "Hear Ye, Hear Ye, it is 1950, and dark clouds are gathering." War clouds loomed over Korea. The Communist Chinese invading Tibet. U.S. Troops going to Vietnam to aid the French. McCarthyism. President Truman ordering the development of the Hydrogen Bomb, while Albert Einstein warns that nuclear war will lead to mutual destruction. The cost of living continues to go up. The average house now costs $8420. A new car costs $1500, and a gallon of gas 15 cents. A top sirloin steak, a whopping 53 cents a pound. And in San Francisco a person of color still isn't allowed to work or earn a livable wage.

It is June, one of the most pleasant of times to be in San Francisco. With its warm spring days, the city stands out bright with its crisscrossed cable car hills, the Coit Tower reaching up into a rich blue sky pointing towards the cosmos where time began. Today was just that kind of day, with a slight breeze chasing whitecaps beneath the Golden Gate. The whitecaps glistening like so many sparkling rubies and diamonds that lift romance from the heart to the imagination, and back again.

The sky never failed to amaze Stella, filled with its mysteries and endless amounts of space. The sky was ever-changing, its various colors of navy blue, black, lavender, robin's egg blue, turquoise, with fiery tangerine, painted glass, a window to the vastness above. Sometimes the clouds are puffy and tall, other times they were no more than mere wisps, dashed across the sky by some divine paintbrush. While spring had come and gone, today the flowers sprout a blue field of loveliness.

If Earl, her husband could see her here, he would swear that she was an angel visiting from heaven above—and no blind piano playing crooner deserves an angel like her.

The Grotto, once an old Speakeasy beneath the Honeysuckle Rose Hotel, never felt the warmth of the sun. Never-the-less, it was where Stella spent most of her days listening to her husband Earl sing and play the blues, mixed with jazz, his touch velvety across the ivory keys of his piano. To Stella, the Grotto always seemed cold as the basement of an old Tenderloin hotel ought to. While at the same time it was warm and welcoming as Earl and his family of musicians create a warm fire of memories, emotions and dreams. Their music drawing people to a place that has become symbolic with good music and friends.

She sighed, her heart fulfilled, content, and sadly alone. The sigh fluttered in the breeze like a butterfly decorated with a chimera of color. There was one thing that brought her more joy than the vastness of the sky, and the clouds teasing her imagination. What brought a song to her heart when everything else seemed wrong, that there still might be some right in this crazy world, was her Earl.

Stella had taken the trolley to Golden Gate Park, walking to the Japanese Garden, a place she especially enjoyed when the cherry and plum blossoms bloomed—that had been late April. Her walks in the park were her private moments reserved for bringing some order to the chaos that was her life. A few minutes of simple peace and quiet; her me time. Earl, and her extended family back at the hotel, took all the rest.

A quirky bunch, these musicians and oddball friends who made the Honeysuckle Rose Hotel their home. Each has his or her problems, secrets, addictions, sins of their own making, traumatic issues the world has seen fit to weigh down upon their shoulders, nightmares from the past, or dreams of things the way they ought to be. Most were broken in one way or another, each with their own special gift God had given them to hopefully make this world a better place. Stella keeps a place in her heart for each of them, as if they were her own sons and daughters. Without qualms, or reservations, she holds tight to their gifts and imperfections. When they play their music, they put their problems aside until such time that their issues outweigh the music; then they play with a musician's passionate blind eye—Earl heart guiding them as they try to put their problems away. Is there any doubt on why Stella has so little time for herself?

No one is perfect, especially Earl, her husband who can be

cantankerous, argumentative, self-centered, wise beyond his years, and child—like, all at the same time.

Stella hadn't changed much since the dark days of WWII back at the veteran's hospital. She was still a petite bottle-blonde, deliciously curvy, with a haughty, sultry, heart—shaped face, who looked far younger than her forty-one years. Of course, she had added a few pounds to her hips, a fuller neck, just below her chin, along with a smoker's dark shadow below her eyes, that hid the worry lines her husband would never see.

She had gone into nursing with the heart and aspirations of Florence Nightingale. The life of a nurse was her life's calling. Then the war came. She buried her emotions and any dreams for her own future in the white uniform that camouflaged the real woman hidden beneath. She never thought about marriage; the war bringing to her too many broken men. These were the men whose injuries were too grievous to ever return home again. The sad eyes and broken hearts of the women who visited them were just as painful to her as the pain and despair of the patients she cared for. The war taught her to be afraid of love and all the heartbreak it brought beyond reasonable measure.

Then one day within the gloomy white-washed institutional walls came a new sound:

> *'Bye bye blues . . . I'm sayin bye bye blues*
> *Bells will ring and birds all sing*
> *Stop your mope-in,' keep on hope-in . . . '*

Stella pushed her hair back as she starred down the long hospital corridor where she saw a blind man, white cane tapping, a spring in his step, a jaunt to his stride, and he was singing:

> *'Now don't you sigh . . . and don't you cry*
> *Bye bye blues . . . '*

This blind man seemed terribly out of place compared to all of the bedridden patients surrounding her. But oh, he could sing. He did not have the gravelly voice of Louis Armstrong. But from that moment on Stella's world changed as Earl Crier reminded her on a daily basis that it was indeed a wonderful world.

His music helped heal and bring peace to men where her nursing fell cruelly short. With Earl she found a place where the cruel winds cease to blow. Where for every sunset there will be a sunrise, a place where the sun may set with no fear of the darkness to come. Where one soul can whisper to another in a language only one's mate can truly understand. A place where togetherness means it's possible. Earl was her life, her breath, her reason, and she loved the fact that he was an imperfect man.

Earl is blind, a casualty of the war, and he is terrified of the dark. When he sleeps, he remembers color and light. When he wakes, he finds himself trapped in his own worst nightmare. He sleeps as little as possible because waking is too traumatic. He finds his way in his darkness, chasing away his terrors, with his music—which is the reason he cannot stop singing his own personal blues.

Earl was the patient who could and would not be silent. When he wasn't at the piano he sang; time and place meant nothing to him. When you have a hospital full of seriously ill, dysfunctional patients, that can be a problem.

There was no medical reason for his admission to the hospital. There was nothing wrong with him besides his being blind as a bat. Fear of the dark in itself is not a qualifying event. He had been in the merchant marine whose members did not qualify for veteran's benefits. Yet, at the bequest of the United States Navy, the bequest coming from the highest levels, he was given an officer's room.

Victor Mann, the hospital's administrator could not stand Earl, swore daily that he would give up six month's wages to see Earl banned from the hospital. Earl's private room was signed, sealed, and permanent for as long as the United States Navy said so. Earl had all the privileges of an Admiral, his secret guarded from as high as the Director of Veteran's Affairs. There was nothing the administrator could do about it.

One day a new patient was assigned to Stella's ward. Like Earl, he was blind. The hospital was not designed for the blind, especially obnoxious pain-in-the-butt ones. Stella was not about to book him into the ward. Brooks Weingarden III was mean, nasty, unpleasant, and irritated everyone around him.

Finding out that Brooks had been with the ARMY USO and had played the piano, she moved Brooks out of the ward and into Earl's room. From their first moment Earl and Brooks could not stand the sight of each other. Earl could out sing Sinatra, his fingers magic on the ivories, there wasn't anything he could not play or sing, as long as it wasn't long haired classical. It wasn't that he could not play Mozart or Tchaikovsky, long hair did not cause his heart and fingers to dance.

Compared to Earl, Brooks was a rank amateur on the piano, his singing voice, wishful thinking. What came out of his mouth was mostly self-centered pomposity. Buried beneath his vainglory, shallow and cancerous, was a suicidal wish that ate away at what was left of his soul. He would argue that left is right, that right is left, and never meet you in the middle. It did not matter if he was right as long as you were wrong. Both, newly blind, competed against each other for attention— Stella's in particular. In his abject misery Brooks had a small advantage. Earl did not know it at the time but his pompous ass for a roommate wore a gauze mask which covered his entire head with barely a hole for breathing or eating through. Brooks had suffered more than the loss of his sight, he had lost most of his face, the damage too severe to repair, destined to be buried beneath a mask forever. Their feud, bitter, vicious, and unkind, continued until more important issues outweighed them. In time lady luck, and brother mis- fortune, cast them apart, with no love lost from either.

Three years had passed since Earl and Stella married. It was also three years since Earl and Brooks had been in the same room together. And two years since they had taken over and made The Honeysuckle Rose Hotel their home. It wasn't long after that that Earl shook up their entire universe, turning it upside down for good measure, by asking Brooks to come back and live with them at the Rose. Earl had sworn that before he would be in the same room with that god-damned SOB the fat lady would be singing opera in a hell frozen over. Well, hell froze over, and here they were. God, he detested opera.

Stella had expected World War Three when Brooks and Earl first came together; only Brooks had changed. He was no longer the angry blind suicidal drunk that loathed Earl more than his own disability. He was now a mild-mannered poet who called himself Oscar Katz. His deep rich soulful voice brought life to his poetry as Earl's piano playing brought life to the old hotel. As each day passed Stella wondered when their truce would end and their bitterness towards each other would rise again.

For friends, and music sake, Earl had acquired an old hotel in the Tenderloin District of San Francisco. The hotel had fallen into hard times, which became harder when Earl chose to fight against the corrupt and bullying musician's union to save their home, The price, if lost, the Honeysuckle Rose Hotel would be closed, and if the president of the union had his way, torched and burned to the ground. That was when the fat lady sang, when hell froze over, when Earl called upon his old nemesis, Oscar Katz, the former Brooks Wingarden, to put aside the past, their acrimony, and join he and Stella in their battle to save the old Honeysuckle Rose Hotel.

Oscar, having over-come his own suicidal quest, had found his dignity, and perhaps his character, stood with Earl, fires burning around them, union goons with rubber truncheons too near for comfort, their music and poetic verse winning the night.

That was two years ago.

There was still an edge to their voices that suggested that all was not forgotten, nor forgiven. It was for Stella's sake they each wore their truce as if it were a well-tailored suit. They were becoming friends, but they still felt anxious with each other's presence. Each morning when Stella woke, she prayed that her two blind men, men she loved dearly, would not trade their suits in for verbal boxing gloves, and start it all over again.

Stella needed her quiet walks in the park. While this day was lit by brilliant sunshine, she sensed a bitter cold wind coming from just over the horizon. It was a wind that would bring change, heartache, and trepidation. Being married to Earl Crier sometimes called on her to move both heaven and earth. She knew that she was helpless to change this coming wind.

03
Mail Call

'TAK! TAK! ACK!' "Wha . . .What is it," Stub asked? His Tourette syndrome his notable companion.

Stub always had trouble reading Henry Akita's face—the Japanese were always so stoic. At the moment Henry's was an open book reading of shock, anger, regret, disbelief, and resignation. "Tha . . . that's a . . . 'Tak—Tak' . . . a lot of emotion you 'Tak' . . . just pulled from that en . . . envelope," Stub stuttered, his concern evident in his voice.

Short, pudgy, and mostly bald, Stub was the hotel's food and beverage manager, everyone's—forty-year old—favorite uncle who wore his heart on his sleeve, always caring more for others than himself. This was even more remarkable because Stub suffers from Turrets Syndrome; a rare condition which burdened him with a pronounced stutter, with sharp and sudden outbursts of nonsensical—barking and yelping—uncontrollable twitches of the face and upper torso. There are certain pitches of sound that triggers his twitches. One is when Earl plays the first four notes of Stella's song which causes Stub's right arm to quickly fly up above his head; sometimes with a glass in hand. Earl usually opened up the first set with Stella's song, which is why Stub, when he waiters, wears a raincoat.

There are customers who at first thought Stub to be some sort of freak. Stub's openness, his heart, the twinkle in his eye, and his acceptance by the musicians, soon turned the harshest critic into an admirer of Stub's character.

—

Earl cocked his head to the left listening for Henry's answer as he slowed his piano playing down to the soft pitter-patter of a passing spring shower. Stub's tone of voice had indicated that something had come in today's mail that was causing Henry some unusual trepidation.

Henry had served as a medic with the all Japanese American Army Division during some of the worse fighting in Europe. He had become close with Stella when they had both worked at the veteran's hospital shortly after the war.

In 1946, San Francisco was still very unforgiving of the Japanese, as were many of the patients who had received their wounds in the war against the Empire of Japan. His short time employed as an orderly at the hospital had not been easy.

Music soothed the pain and sorrow he carried deep inside. Being accepted as member of Earl and Stella's musical family meant the world to him, and you could hear it when he played his clarinet. How could such a universe of beauty and emotion pour from such a small instrument?

"Henry?"

There was a long pause before Henry answered. He handed the letter to Stub. "Nothing to be concerned about," he said. His voice giving no clue as to the raw emotions he was struggling with just to breath. It's just a letter from my uncle. He says that it's been a long time since we have seen each other, and he would like me to come for a visit." Henry gently passed his hand over Earl's shoulder as he passed by. His touch saying, *it's okay, nothing to be worried about.*

By the concern in Stub's voice, Earl knew that Henry was deeply troubled. Earl, like Stella, considered his fellow musicians as if they were his sons and daughters. If this were true, then Henry was their first born.

Rosemary's bow slid across her cello before falling silent, the fading notes sounding like dark chocolate melting in your mouth. The room was silent except for the soft sounds of Henry's steps as he mounted the stairs leaving no more room for unwanted questions.

Stub looked at the letter, it was from Uncle Sam, Henry was being recalled to active duty with the army with orders within three days to report for duty for eighteen months, or for the duration of the hostilities. What few soldiers we had in South Korea were in desperate need of good infantry medics. Henry had three days to say his goodbyes.

"Tak! Henry wait, I . . .Tak!" Henry had already left.

Thaddeus Mohler, the hotel's former owner and manager,

was sorting mail for the second time. He just wasn't sure if he had placed the mail in the right slots. "Henry, I think I saw something here for you." He had and had given it to him a few minutes prior.

Les Moore, on his way to rehearsal, picked up his mail at the hotel's reception desk. He immediately recognized the official logo on the envelope and did not have to guess what it meant. The great, benevolent, white men in Washington D.C, had decided that it couldn't throw one more war without inviting good old Les to the party.

Les was Negro, black ebony with a natural dark mocha sheen. He eyes, eggshell white, took on their own brilliance whenever he played his trombone. He was tall, thin, his movements waxed with a graceful elegance. He was from a family of sharecroppers, born and raised in poverty south of the Mason-Dixon line; Broussard, Louisiana, to be more precise.

He had served in the war in Europe with an all negro transportation company. Compared to Henry, as a truck driver his war experience had been relatively easy. He never saw the enemy in battle, the fighting always a distant flash. He had followed the war, his truck one of thousands moving supplies to the front via the Red Ball Express with everything the advancing Allied armies needed to advance. Daily consumption of motor fuel was exceeding eight hundred thousand gallons a day. If the trucks stopped rolling so did the fighting men. While the Luftwaffe still flew, the fuel trucks were prime targets for strafing raids. Les lost two trucks the first month the Red Ball Express began rolling. After that the Luftwaffe seemed to disappear. Just because he had never come face to face with a German foot soldier did not mean that he did not know the gut-cramping feeling that came when you faced the possibility of sudden violent death. Being cremated alive in an exploding fuel truck was a fear that gripped you every mile that truck rolled towards the front lines.

As the war wound down, General Eisenhower held back the Allied troops, letting Stalin's boys take Berlin. Les' transportation company was lucky enough to be stationed just outside Paris—and for a poor colored man from Louisiana that had been quite the time. The good people of Paris welcomed him as a hero, because he wore the American uniform, taking little notice of the color of his skin; while the white G.I.'s looked down on him because he was black.

Back home he had played the trombone since he was old enough to hold one. Old Deacon Jones got mouth cancer from smoking a pipe for sixty some years and given the horn to him. It was hard for the old man to give it up, but the look of awe and aspiration in Les' eyes told him that it was better to give the horn to the boy than to lose it to the secondhand store down the way. Les never took a lesson, but he had a good ear, and in time playing became second nature to him. Once Paris was liberated the music—Jazz—quickly returned—with an added G.I. influence, and Armed Forces Radio. In Paris he learned to play the trombone at a level that left everyone around him astounded. He had a non-directional dark round buttery sound that filled the room similar to a French horn. He had a dark, singing fluidity, often taking the quality of a human voice; his soul, his story. His horn made you want to sing—just try to resist. Les could no more stop breathing than he could stop making his music.

Les was the most gifted of all the musicians at the Rose; including Earl. What held him back was San Francisco. The city was not a welcoming place to people of color. He had learned early on that the city's beauty was flawed; that what lay beneath beat a bigoted heart. The Fillmore was the only neighborhood in town where Negroes were allowed to live, to work, to raise their children, to express their community through their music.

The Honeysuckle Rose had its roots in the Tenderloin, a neighborhood close to, but far away, from the Fillmore.

—

"Aren't you going to open it?" Thaddeus asked; meaning the envelope. Thaddeus was annoyingly curious and repetitive. This was mostly forgiven because Thaddeus often forgot whatever he had said in an increasingly shorter period of time. Thaddeus was well into his sixties, and old father time liked to play games with his aging mind.

Les had first lifted his trombone in Stella's Lounge in the small piano bar next to the lobby of the hotel. At the time, Thaddeus had fumed and sputtered that he couldn't have a black in his hotel. What would the neighbor's think? "Why, I'll be run out of town tarred and feathered." Now, two years later, the immediate neighbors had become patrons of their musical arts, while Les and Thaddeus had developed an arm's length respect for each other.

Thaddeus struggled to change his way of thinking. He had never thought of himself as a bigot—the races were not supposed to mix, that segregation wasn't fair, but it was just the way things were; and mostly had always been. Now, Thaddeus didn't say much about it; it helped that he quickly forgot that there was an issue.

Les did not trust most white people. Thaddeus being who he was and, what he was, gave Les cause to be cautious. The old white man wasn't much of a threat, but Les had been born and raised in a city with a long history of bigotry.

This morning Les woke up in a good mood. The prior night he and Michael O'Dea had been working on their own version of the Tennessee Waltz, a tune recently made popular by Patti Page. Between his trombone, Michael's tenor sax, Rosemary's cello, and Earl's piano, they were going to knock it out of the park.

In his dreams Les had found the right improvisation to make it their own. It was midmorning, the city was up and humming, while the residents of the musician's hotel were just beginning to rise from their musician's caves.

A letter from the government rarely brought good news, and Les didn't have to guess what that bad news was. He folded the envelope and tucked it in his pocket. Later there be time for anger, regret, and all the whoa-is-me sorrow. Not because he was being called back into the army, but because it would take him away from Earl, Stella, and the Honeysuckle Rose.

Michael, Les, and Henry all understood the weight and personal hurt caused by prejudice. Les was black, Henry was Nisei, and Michael was white . . . and an uglier man would be hard to find.

Michael O'Dea, thirty-five, was their resident tenor sax player. He was barely five feet three, with large pendulous pointed 'elfin' earlobes, and a long stretched out leprechaun-like face that ended with a sharp lantern jaw. He had smallpox as a boy which left his face scarred and pocked, leaving some places hard to shave. He was mostly bald except for an auburn patch that he greased and combed into a ludicrous quaff. Much of his life he had carried the nickname 'Beauty' because he was so extraordinarily ugly. His pain could be heard whenever he played his horn, a sad majestic beauty that revealed his inner soulful true heart. Until he had come upon The Rose, he had been a solitary man full of self-pity and anger with an over-boiling need to be liked, overshadowed by the fear of being seen. Stella and Earl had helped take the ugly away from Beauty so Michael could find his own.

Les Moore hummed *'The Tennessee Waltz'* to himself as he imagined Imogene singing the lyrics: *'I remember the night and the Tennessee . . .'*

When he had first come to San Francisco to be part of the bebop scene in the Fillmore he had never thought that he would make a beat-up old hotel in the Tenderloin his home. Nor had he imagined that he would ever fall in love with a gorgeous, twenty-something, light brown songbird who was the vocalist for the Earl Crier Quintet. Imogene. It was love at first sight. Those words he could not speak because he did not understand them. His mama had loved him, but that was different. Imogene was a woman. He had been with some women in France, but that wasn't love; at least he hoped not, for fear that he would be in for some sizable disappointment. Back then he had just been sowing some wild oats. Imogene, she was a different kind of woman. He did not know it, but the truth being what it is, it was Imogene who had caused him to choose the Honeysuckle Rose over the Fillmore.

Les' mood slowly slide downhill as regret began to still his heart. He was being called back to war and there was nothing he could do about it. Yes, he was going to miss everyone at the Rose—but how could he leave without telling Imogene what he truly felt in his heart—that he loved her? She was hard to read, sometimes he thought she might feel the same; at other times she could care less.

Imogene loved Les' horn playing. His was a gift from God, and every note he blew made her want to sing. She knew, or at least it was a good guess, that he was smitten with her. He was a handsome man, a good catch, for someone else. She was too young to settle down. She had seen too many of her black sisters saddled with so many babies they never had time to live their own lives. They never even saw the possibilities. Then, all of a sudden that good man became a good for nothing, and all they had was their kids—God bless them. But what about the dreams, don't a girl get a chance to latch onto that lucky star?

Sure, Les was a good man, but what about tomorrow, will he still be?

—

Oscar Katz counted his steps from the elevator to the first bar stool nearest Earl. Both are blind. Earl deplores a cane. Oscar taps his way into everyone's attention. When he enters a room his first impression is one of dignified mystery. He is tall, a little on the reedy side. His upright posture drawing your eyes to his silken mask. Today he is wearing a white tux, his silk face mask scarlet, beneath a white top hat. The silk mask slips over his entire head coming to a loose fit on his shoulders. There are no holes for his mouth or nose, the loose-fitting mask allowing for easy breathing. The mask covers a face that had been damaged well beyond repair. His bearing and dress ties his appearance together leaving you with a sense of dignified mystery. The hospital style gauze mummy mask he had been given back at the veteran's hospital had left one with a sense of pity, and perhaps a little frightened of what must lie beneath; and for good reason. It had been Stella who had made these amazing masks of different colors to meet with differing situations.

There had been a time when Oscar thought he could sing. He had tried to go one on one with Earl and had only made himself a pompous fool whose singing was a joke. His piano playing was average, neither good nor bad, without personality or gift. Not one to be silent he had to find a way to draw attention to the man that lived beneath that mask. His voice, rich and melodic, was perfect for reciting verse. With his voice, and appearance, he had become the Honeysuckle Rose's popular and respected resident poet.

Oscar interrupted as he found his seat. "I like this new song, Earl. I've been working on it for much of the night." He had memorized the lyrics. The song Imogene would sing accompanied by the quintet's music, he would recite without need of musical accompaniment.

"I remember the night and the Tennessee Waltz.

Now I know just how much . . . "

He expected Earl to interrupt his moment by throwing in some unwanted background music. Earl didn't, which suggested to Oscar that something was wrong. He stopped his recital and asked.

"I don't know," Earl replied. "Stub?"

"Tak . . . Not my plah . . . place to say, Mr. C."

Ray Rexwickle, their drummer, filled in for Earl with light drumming. Earl did his best to stifle a laugh because while Ray was a good drummer, he was not by nature a spontaneous man. Most drummers love their time in the spotlight with a long energetic solo. Not Ray. He did not care much for the attention.

04
Playing From The Heart

War had come again, this time to Korea. It was not an accident. Newspaper headlines, dark and foreboding, fell short of telling the truth that there was no nobility to this new war so far away from home.

The division of Korea into South Korea and North Korea was the result of the 1945 Allied victory in World War II, ending the Empire of Japan's 35-year colonial rule of Korea by General Order No. 1. The United States and the Soviet Union agreed to temporarily occupy the country as a trusteeship with the zone of control along the 38th parallel.

Japan capitulated in August 1945. An effort to construct an independent government for the entire Korea was made in September 1945. An initiative to hold general and free elections in the entire Korea came up in the United Nations in the fall of 1947. However, this initiative did not materialize because of disagreement between the United States and the Soviet Union: During this period of two years, between the fall of 1945 and the fall of 1947, in the absence of the opportunity to set up a unified government, two separate governments began evolving and consolidating in the south and in the north. A Communist state was permanently established under soviet auspices in the north and a pro-western state was set up in the south. The two superpowers backed different leaders and two States were effectively established, each of which claimed sovereignty over the whole Korean peninsula. With both Soviet and Communist China's support North Korea Invaded South Korea in June 1950. The North Korean army caught the South Korean army, and what few American servicemen we had stationed there, by almost complete surprise conquering much of the South before any reinforcements could be sent. There was no time to train recruits causing the active reservist to be called up first. Thus, it was decided that Henry and Les had not served enough time in hell and were now to be shipped off to Korea and a war they did want, nor understand.

The headlines in the newspapers ran nothing but bad news. North Korea had invaded South Korea on June 25th, and in a matter of days had driven South Korean and American troops to the tip of the Korean Peninsula. If help did not arrive soon American troops faced their own Dunkirk on the beaches off the Sea of Japan. The most frightening news was that General MacArthur was asking for use of the atomic bomb. President Truman remained quiet, which meant that he was thinking about it.

The Second World War had not brought peace. The defeat of Nazi Germany and the Empire of Japan led to the release of new tyrants, with deadlier weapons, who wanted to conquer the world, no matter the cost. Stalin needed a war in Korea to draw America's attention away from Europe where he was intent on extending Soviet influence. Stalin also needed this war to keep Chairman Mao and the Chinese occupied. He had learned all too well with his former pact with Hitler not to trust anyone; especially his Communist brethren.

—

Stella's blond hair turned a light shade of gray when she heard the news. She reached out for Henry and Les but was politely rebuffed. She was more scared for them than they were for themselves.

Difficult as it was, Stella and Earl gave them the space they needed. They were both grown men, not boys. If they felt the need to talk, Stella and Earl were there for them—though Stella's heart was breaking as each hour passed before their departure. Earl shared her concern but dwelled on another. What would the Earl Crier Quintet be without Henry's clarinet, and Les' trombone? Losing them was a huge hit, and so far, none of the musician's that had sat in, or rehearsed around the hotel, had the sound or the talent needed. Les and Henry were music personified. Their leaving was going to be felt, when Earl had bought the Rose he had reached for the moon, and now he was looking at stardust.

—

With only a few days left before Les was to report back to the army he rehearsed and played as if he would never play again. He would suffer no discussion of his leaving. His sound had never been better, which told Earl how much he was hurting inside.

When Les had enlisted in the army back in 1942 he had thought of it as a grand adventure, a chance to see the world. A chance to get out of the heat and poverty he had grown up in. As a truck driver with the Red Ball Express he had made a meaningful contribution to the collapse of Nazis Germany. This time it was different. Korea was not a place he wanted to be. His heart belonged to the Honeysuckle Rose, and to Imogene—the woman he loved—though he lacked the courage to find the words his heart ached to say. Each time he looked at her his courage slipped farther away. He was possessed by his thoughts of her, confused, even missing a note here and there. She was so beautiful, and he was just a son of a dirt-poor sharecropper.

Henry spent less time rehearsing, less time with friends and family, as he prepared himself for another war. He increasingly dwelled on the thought that this time his luck would run out. Like so many of the Nisei soldiers he had tended on the battlefield he most likely he would not be coming back. As an army medic he seen to many men maimed, had not saved enough lives. He had seen the absurd nightmare of the Dachau Concentration Camp. He knew the awfulness of war and the memories of what he had seen put ice in his bones chilling him to his marrow. He worried that he might not be strong enough to emotionally handle going back into combat again.

Now, as the clock ticked against his recall, he filled his time by taking long walks alone. Where he went in a city still hostile to those of Japanese heritage no one could guess. They just let him go.

Except for Ivory.

Ivory took it upon himself to follow Henry. He knew that the Japanese believed in ritual suicide, and he feared the worse having been that close to that dark door himself. At the moment when he and Henry met, he had been caught again in the nightmare of his escape—the memory of a Japanese soldier poised with a long bayonet inches from his heart. It was at that moment that caring hands woke him saying 'Easy son, it's only a dream.' Ivory, woke, terrified, as he stared into Henry's Nisei face. That was the beginning of a tumultuous relationship. If Ivory could have put a knife in Henry's heart he would have. Now their relationship was like two brothers, tied together by hard struggles, who against the odds were bound together for all the right reasons. It was Henry, Earl, and Stella that had helped him find the will to live again. He had been saved by a blind man, a Jap, and a nightingale.

Ivory was no musician and carried the deepest psychological wounds of anyone calling the Honeysuckle Rose Hotel home. Unable to make any musical contributions Ivory took on the role of being the house guard dog; protector of the realm, guarding against threats, both external and internal. There was no threat too small to not get caught in his critical gaze.

He had a hard, raw-boned face with a sharp cleft chin, finished by a marine haircut, and a 'take no prisoner's' attitude of a man whose survivor's guilt tore at his soul. His external hardness was softened by an awkward gait, impossible to hide, because of his artificial leg.

Smelling trouble, Ivory followed Henry to protect the man he once hated.

"Ivory, I've been meaning to ask you," Thaddeus called out as the door to the hotel swung shut behind him. "Oh, Well, never mind." Thaddeus had seen a woman on the third floor he had not recognized. The fourth floor was mostly reserved for men, which is why it gave Thaddeus some concern. Musicians brought with them a basket full of addictions and problems, but hookers working the rooms of the hotel was one place where he drew the line. Could she have been a guest? He hadn't registered her, which is why he wanted to check with Ivory. Ivory kept his room behind the registration desk serving as their night and security manager. The key boxes for the fourth-floor rooms did not show that a new guest had checked in. Perhaps the housekeeping supervisor might know something? He wrote himself a note to remind himself to ask the next time he saw her. He put the note where it could easily be found.

The postman found quite a few of Thaddeus's notes when he picked up the outgoing mail. These were random notes from Thaddeus reminding himself to do something he had already clearly forgotten. The postman said nothing placing them on the counter when Thaddeus wasn't looking so as not to embarrass him. Later, when Thaddeus found them, he would carefully file them away where he would know where to find them again.

Henry followed his heart when he took his walks. When he had returned to San Francisco after the war he was unwelcome, and alone. His family had been taken away to the camps in 1942 as had most of the Japanese residents in California. Shortly after his arrival he had been chased off a city bus by a gang of street toughs and had run by business after business which still had signs in their windows reading *'No Japs Allowed.'*

The door to an old neighborhood bar was open, his pursuers, wielding chains and clubs were not far behind. He was desperate for refuge. There was no sign in the window saying that he was not wanted. Glancing behind him he saw that he had a brief moment where his pursuers had not yet rounded the street corner. He sprinted inside and took refuge in a booth in a dark corner farthest from the windows hoping that no one would see him, including the bartender. At the time, he was not sure if it was more dangerous on the street or going into that bar.

Adam's Place was named after the owner's son. A Nisei medic had once saved Adam's life in Europe. Neither Gibby, the owner, or Henry, knew if it had been Henry who had saved Adam's life. It could have been, and that was enough for Gibby.

Gibby opened his doors, as well as his heart, allowing Henry sanctuary, a room, a fatherly mentor, and in time a job when no one else would hire a Jap.

As the veteran's hospital had spun out of control through its own corruption anyone who tried to speak out against the administrator was removed, staff or patient, it didn't matter. Henry had been the first to be fired. His last paycheck, a promise never meant to be fulfilled. Gibby gave him a job as a bartender. The bar could not afford another, but Gibby wouldn't have it any other way.

Sometimes fate brings things on—without warning—in threes.

Stella was fired.

Earl was kicked out of the hospital for leading a patient

rebellion. His back pay stolen by the senior orderly, Earl followed Henry to Adam's place, where the two soon changed the bar into a successful piano bar; jazz and blues.

Stella followed Earl, bringing Brooks, who begged for a second chance from the man he most despised, Earl.

By the time the hospital closed Ivory had healed enough psychologically to have the rest of his infected leg amputated and fitted with a prosthesis at Oak Knoll Naval Hospital.

The relationship between Henry and Earl ran deep, and Henry's silence was like a vice squeezing Earl's love and devotion to the man.

Henry followed his heart . . .

After Gibby had died of a heart attack the bar closed, and shortly thereafter it burned to the ground. A Greek couple built a small, over-priced grocery in the vacant lot. The prices were too high, and no one in the neighborhood wanted to buy stuffed grape leaves or salted bonito. The doors were padlocked, the shelves inside bare, nothing left to say that Adam's Place had ever existed.

Fighting his desperate fears, Henry returned to where the music had begun; where Adam's Place had once been. He stood on the street curb and played his clarinet for hours on end. No one complained. No one seemed to care that he was Nisei. Windows opened to let his music in.

Ivory watched from a distance, listened, staying just close

enough to take care of his old friend should someone take offense to his music or the fact that he was Nisei in a city still unforgiving of the Japanese and the harm their quest for empire had brought.

Just as he was about to gather the loneliness of his thoughts as a protective cloak around him and return to the Honeysuckle Rose, Henry heard the clicking of a cane against the sidewalk.

He had been playing a slightly deep noted Johnny Mercer tune, *Tangerine,* with a touch of soulful inspiration. The old man stopped in front of him, nodded towards the empty space next to him as he took out a well-worn violin, leaving the case open for donated change. Henry nodded back, although he would not take any of the change for himself, it was obvious the old man needed every dime.

He studied the old man; he was, if anything old. How can he still play with those arthritic hands, Henry wondered? Many years ago, the old man might have been tall, now the stoop of his back drew him closer to the grave that wasn't far off. He had a strange appearance, almost as if it was contrived. His hair was wizened and straw-like, nearly fossilized it was so dry. He had crinkly way-worn rheumy eyes, buried deep within was a glint that suggested he had collected a lot of wisdom along the way. His beard was distinctive. It wasn't a thick beard but rather something a lunatic might have, straggly, unkempt and spittle flecked. His face was a sea of toil-worn wrinkles mottled with brown age spots, his nose pitted and webbed with thin blue veins. He stood on unsteady feet with a weary, lethargic air. His fingers were gnarled and knobby. The clothes he wore were musty and threadbare, suggesting that in another time they had been proper attire for a gentleman. "You choose son, I'll jump in where I can." The old man said with a crackled gravel and syrup voice. Henry looked at the old man's gnarled fingers, wondering if he could still play. He chose *The Tennessee Waltz,* a tune rich for the violin.

The old man smiled and began to play as if he had done it a thousand times reaching perfection as easily as the sun rises on a morning whose beauty one can never forget.

Ivory kept his distance allowing Henry his privacy. There was nothing about his music that suggested that he was about to do any harm to himself. His solitary clarinet sounded moody and introspective, a lost soul grasping for hope and meaning, asking the universe to answer his plea.

If God meant there to be a miracle on this day, at this moment, then it began with their first shared notes. Their music soared through the air like an eagle on an up draft, taking with it their very souls. They ascended together in a magical flight to the heavens, a breathtaking melody of musical exuberance. Then they dived back down until all that was left was the same silence there had been at the beginning. It was a shared journey that held Ivory spellbound in rapt silence.

Slowly bringing his violin's bow down the old man contemplated Henry; an old man impressed by a much younger musician's skill. It was a long silent observation, as if he were trying to unravel some complex puzzle—then with a slight nod and a wide blink that suggested that perhaps he had nodded off for a brief moment and just woken up. "Sy Jacobi," he said, his voice a dry rasp. He let out a brittle chuckle that came from deep within and had taken a long time to come out. "Son, I am honored to have had a chance to play by your side." Without further comment he positioned his violin and played the *Fascination Waltz*.

When the old man finished the waltz, he looked up at the blue sky as if his music had peeled the morning fog away.

"Henry Akita," Henry answered as he extended his hand. The old man, barely able to stand, extended his ancient, gnarled hand in return. How the hell had he done that? Henry wondered, as if the old man had pulled a flock of exotic birds from his violin.

Henry and Sy played without exchanging anything but their music for another twenty minutes. Henry sensed that the old man was tiring and brought the music to a rest. "I take it you live around here, Mr. Jacobi?"

"Just plain Sy will do, Henry. I used to live over in the Cow's Hollow area, near the Presidio." He sighed without knowing it. "I swore that when Judith, my wife, became ill, and I could still be by her side, I would stay awhile longer on this here good earth. Judith passed on nearly nine months ago, come August." His eyes slowly settled on his violin. "I made a separate promise, and that was to Elsie." He tapped his violin tenderly. "I asked her to continue to play sweetly, to help keep me whole, while I tended to my first love, Judith. My wife, she was never jealous. This one, Elsie, I am afraid, her strings are jealous through and through. My Elsie, she still sings sweetly, but won't let me go, though I'm well past my time. I've outlived any money I'd ever managed to save. She sings like an angel while I stand on a street corner, an old man begging for coins. God, she has a sense of humor, yes?"

He shared a thin slice of a smile. "The landlord, I don't think he likes Jews, demanded rent I did not have. I was forced to leave behind my home where Judith and I shared so many wonderful years. Oh, I still have my memories, but they too are struggling. I stayed at the Mission for a while, until someone stole my shoes."

"I found shelter in this here abandoned building and have been playing for what few coins folks might drop into my case. As you can see this is a hard place to earn a few pennies, a shekel, a little something for a simple meal. A boiled onion bagel, with lox and cream cheese, if only . . ." The old man fell silent, there wasn't much else to say, as Elsie spoke for him as he once again began to play *'And The Angels Sing,'* a tune that had not been written for the violin but sounded hauntingly rich with emotion as the bow caressed Elsie in all the right places.

Henry had not noticed his shoeless, tattered sock covered feet, until the old man brought it up. "Sy, I'm sorry to hear about your wife. It sounds as if you had a good long life together." It did not take Henry long to promise Sy what he hadn't to give; but promise he did. "Sy, I live in a hotel over in the Tenderloin that is a private residency for musicians. And I do believe you qualify. You continue playing your violin—Elsie—the way you do, and they'll give you free room and board. You have my word on that."

A string of pearl tears moistened the old man's left cheek

as he thanked God for this day and the generosity of a lone Nisei clarinet player to an old Jew who stood there clutching his fancy fiddle—Elsie—in filthy, shoeless feet that barely supported him.

Ivory sensed the spontaneous release of tension as Henry momentarily stopped being afraid for himself. His music came from a heartfelt place, the very notes settling like myriad song-birds on the old man's shoulders. He did not know who this old man was, or why he had touched Henry so. Whatever it was, Ivory left his distant post and introduced himself.

Both Henry and Sy brought their music to a gentle pause as Ivory approached. "Sy," Henry said, "this is my friend and brother, Ivory Burch." Henry was not the least bit surprised by Ivory's sudden appearance.

Ivory was not sure what to say. The old man seemed to possess an inner strength, a life force, far greater than his own.

The only person he had ever met who seemed to have this same radiance was Earl Crier. He also had never met some-one who looked this old, who by all rights should have been dead, but somehow had been forgotten, and somehow lived on. Instead of being on death's door his watery rheumy eyes were lit by curiosity, wisdom, and a special knowledge rare to most humans regardless of their years on earth. Ivory hesitated to reach out his hand, afraid that he might hurt the old man's gnarled hands.

"It's all right son, they're not pretty, but you won't do any harm by shaking my hand. Sy Jacobi," he said as he extended his hand to Ivory as he shifted Elsie to his left.

"Ivory . . . Ivory Burch," Ivory answered. "You're playing, it's . . . it's . . ."

"I've had lots of practice."

Henry relieved Ivory of his awkward moment. "Ivory is one of residents of The Honeysuckle Rose Hotel. He's not a musician, but that doesn't matter, he's more like our rough and tumbled guardian angel."

Ivory winched at the term Angel used in his introduction. Not one to easily meet strangers, Ivory accepted Sy's hand. The old man had surprising strength in his grip. There was also a slight tingle as if he had been shocked with a very slight amount of electricity.

Sy gave Ivory a careful reflective look. "You don't have to worry about Henry, he'll be coming home again. Your sergeant, he has finally found his peace. With luck, you shouldn't be seeing him anymore. However, I'm afraid your troubled dreams will be with you for some time to come. Pleased to meet you, Ivory."

The tiny buzz in Ivory's hand was nothing compared to the mental and emotional shock that came with the old man's revelations. There was no way a stranger would know these things. Henry would not have revealed them.

Both Ivory and Henry were blindsided by the old man's uncanny, somewhat frightening insight. While their curiosity was bubbling over, neither asked any questions, at least for the moment. Henry had second thoughts about his invitation. Sy Jacobi had just scared a year's growth from him. That his revelations brought good news . . .well. How was he going to explain this to Earl and Stella?

05
Sy

Mollie and Rosemary had started bickering about three months prior. Rosemary had started it with deliberate unwanted, catty remarks, that were meant to be subtly or indirectly insulting. Different from bitchy in that bitchiness is just mean, while cattiness is often clever and witty, and isn't always completely mean. Rosemary's comments were working towards mean: "Did Oscar do your hair this morning?" or "I thought I saw you walking down the street, but it turned out to be the chubby girl who works at the bakery. You look so much alike."

Mollie responded with hurtful silence; a silence that often can be more powerful than ill-spoken words.

They really weren't angry or hostile; they had just grown apart. Two young women from the Mid-West who had gone west to experience the big city. Rosemary had come for an audition with the San Francisco Symphony, which she never got to because they got caught up with Earl Crier and the Rose. Her world changed as she easily slid into the jazz and bebop with her tenor bass and cello.

Mollie, who had been best friends with Rosemary for as long as she could remember, tagged along. She played the piano, strictly classical, lacking the ability to step out of her comfort zone. Under Earl's charismatic guidance the quintet became a tightly bound group, which left Mollie on the outside. Two years had come and gone, and while the girls shared a room, they had become strangers sharing the same space—that they had come from the same small town, going trick or treating and Easter egg hunting together as kids no longer relevant.

Mollie loved the Honeysuckle Rose, but it was becoming claustrophobic. She needed her own space—more importantly a sense of being valued. Her room and board taken care of she helped out where she could; but it was not enough.

When the hotel had been struggling there had been plenty to do—everyone lent a hand. Now that it was sitting fat and sassy with the hotel rooms mostly booked, the Grotto filled to capacity most nights, with a loyal kitchen, bar, and house-keeping staff, she had less and less to do. With little money she couldn't just up and leave; besides where would she go—certainly not back to the small hometown which she had fled so eagerly. Mollie loved the Rose and thought of Stella as the mother she lost when she had been only seven. She spent much of her time playing the piano in the lounge, whether it was open or not. She was rarely alone, because Oscar spent more time there than his own room. She avoided her room afraid that her once upon a time best friend might come in. When Rosemary was there it was her room, Mollie was in the way—even when she wasn't. In the Grotto she usually sat in the back. Occasionally, Thaddeus, Ivory, or Stub would join her. If asked why she didn't sit closer up she just replied that she thought, they sounded better from there.

When Michael O'Dea first arrived, she had found him a sorrowful man who lived alone with his music. In his own way he lived in a kind of darkness greater than Oscar's or Earl's. Everything was sad about the man. He was pitifully disfigured, awkward and clumsy. Beauty was an unkind name someone had cruelly labeled him with—that was a cruel joke with a certain truth to it. Michel's hygiene wasn't the best leaving him with an unpleasant smell which drove as many people away as did his appearance. His taste in clothing was that of someone who most likely might be colorblind. He had no sense of style, did not give a damn, because he was ugly, and he knew it.

Never in his life had Michael O'Dea found acceptance as he did with the Earl Crier Quintet. Like Michael they all had their wounds, some profoundly tragic; others, their wounds evident enough to make one uncomfortable as might the sun beating down on a sweltering August day; there was just no getting away from it.

Mollie soon saw that Michael's music, and beautiful soul made up for all his shortcomings. He was the type of man who would run out in front of a fast-moving car to save a kitten that had become spellbound and terrified as the motorized beast bore down on it. The driver had not seen the kitten, but he sure got a scare when Michael gave him an angry glare. Beneath all the ugly she was finding the beauty within the man. Now, she took it upon herself to see that Michael was properly bathed, groomed, shaved, and as well dressed as one could be with a face like his.

Seeing what Mollie was doing Stella stepped back from the daily care of Oscar leaving that to Mollie. Mollie laid out his clothes in exactly the same way and place each day. She saw to his laundry and sewed him a rainbow of colored face masks. He delighted in her attention. She helped him memorize his poetry and accompanied him at *'Oscar's At the Rose,'* the name having been changed from Stella's Piano Bar. Downstairs, Stella's Grotto, was where the music was made. The lobby bar was where Oscar touched the poetic heart. Mollie took to calling him Uncle Oscar, and he called her 'Darling' because she was.

Yet, with all this, her tensions with Rosemary worsened each day. Rosemary seemed to go out of her way to make sure of that.

Stella saw the unfriendly breach growing between the girls but could find no remedy. Rosemary had become one of the boys, their music a higher calling. Darling Mollie was losing the awe and wonder of living at the Rose. No longer as beautiful and innocent as she had once been, she was lonely, just this side of despair. Recently she had taken to drinking, just a little; then a little bit more.

Rosemary did not have time or patience for Mollie's issues, her emotional up and downs. If Mollie wanted to drink that was her business. The opportunity Mr. C. had given Rosemary two years before had been like winning the lottery. She was becoming a jazz musician in her own right; as good as any of the male musicians she played with. Well, almost, she would never be as good as Les or Earl.

The Earl Crier Quintet was beginning to get national attention. Ella Fitzgerald herself, dropped in for a look-see in late May. She had high praise for the Earl Crier Quintet, in particular Imogene. The Earl Crier Quintet with Imogene Wick—*she is billboard.* From Ella Fitzgerald that was high praise indeed.

Rosemary was furiously jealous of Imogene. As long as Imogene grabbed all the attention: The Earl Crier Quintet, featuring the vocals of Miss Imogene Wick, Rosemary, as the only female musician, was still a background musician. She knew that she was better than Beauty, or Henry. Earl and Les, never. Ray was just a rhythm and stick man, good on the drums, but he was a timid little mouse, never meant for center stage. With Les and Henry leaving there was going to be a big hole in the quintet's sound. It was Rosemary's time, and she would be damned if she would let Imogene steal that from her.

Henry and Sy bopped, at least Henry did. Their music, open and unrestricted, ran the gambit of styles. It was amazing what the old man could do with his violin. "I think you will like this one Henry," Sy said. "It doesn't have a name, it doesn't need one, the music has its own free spirit that I have never played twice the same way. Join in when and where you hear where I'm taking it." His violin began soft, opening up into a sonata style recalling the Brahma's Trio, then uplifting it to the 20th Century. It was obvious that a piano was needed to even everything out. A shift brought in a Benny Goodman touch that allowed Henry's clarinet to take the lead. The violin and clarinet moved joyfully into abstract reflections like so many leaves dancing together in a whirlwind. Then they slowed, as Henry heard in his mind where a deep bass, the piano, and a moody horn would follow the violin into a poetic sunset. His clarinet filling in the moody finish the best he could. The last was a long extended note, voiced by both instruments, fading to a brilliant silence.

Sy, had been right, Henry thought, the sound never could be duplicated twice. Its direction set by the violin, the rest would come from the interpretations of the musicians, their mood at the moment, and their musical experience. It was perfect for the Earl Crier Quintet.

Ivory did a quick forced march back to the Honeysuckle Rose. A taxi would not pick up anyone with Henry's Japanese features. The streetcar, with two bus changes, could prove to be too much for Sy's unsteady feet. So, Ivory hoofed it back to the hotel to find Stub, who would borrow Stella's car, to bring them all home. For the time being Sy could share Henry's room.

Henry had only two days before the winds of war would sweep him away to a grim and far place. He guessed that the old man was psychic, or something like that, and believed him when Sy had told him that he would come home again.

Ivory had no choice but to tell Stub about Sy, who then told Stella, the story changing with each breath. While she agreed to have them bring Sy in, she wasn't sure what exactly they were asking. In the end Earl, would make the decision. As far as she could tell, Sy was older than God, played the violin, and was some kind of homeless gypsy fortune teller.

"Oh, my," Sy uttered as the car pulled up in front of the Rose.

Henry's spirit had been lifted from down and out depressed

to walking on thin air. In the back of his mind he still knew that he was going off to war. The thought occurred to him that when he got back Sy most likely would not be there, his time was short, and even shorter for their being able to make music together.

06
Bye-Bye Beulah

The growth of the hotel, Stella's Grotto and Oscar's Lounge, outpaced all expectations and staffing needs. The musicians no longer did double duty as bartenders and waiters; rehearsals and creative sessions trumped everything else. The Earl Crier Quintet was developing a reputation, and the transition from big band to bebop, finding their own unique style, pushed some to the edge—especially Earl who was a blues and jazz guy. Earl knew talent, and if he couldn't lead, he would step aside until he learned his way.

Stub had taken over as manager for both bars as well as food service. Beulah agreed to sell the cafe to Earl. It hadn't been doing that well. The asking price was too high. Finally, they agreed on a salary plus a percentage of the profits made off the food service for her to take over the management of the kitchen, which created instant conflict with Stub. She was used to doing things her way. Stub had never run a kitchen. That she was paid more than Stub was a bone of contention.

Despite his handicap, Stub had a knack with people, he had good eyes and good ears, the customers liked him easily sharing their likes and dislikes. Stub quickly learned that the menu evolved around the customer, not Beulah's comfort zone.

The staff had trouble figuring out who was the boss, often steering their frustrations to Stella who ran frequent peace missions between stuttering Stub, and hot-tempered Beulah, who was quickly becoming known as the Iron Maiden. The cafe remained open for breakfast only. While Stub was responsible for the over-all profit and loss of all food and beverages, ordering, and staffing, Beulah acted as if she still owned the cafe and would brook no interference from Stub.

Finally, Earl stepped in as a self-appointed ombudsman to broker a thin peace agreement. It was agreed that Beulah's name had to come off the cafe. Bab's cafe almost became the no name cafe until Earl decided it would be named after its most popular breakfast dish: Hangtown Fried Oysters.

Hangtown Fry could possibly be the first original California cuisine. It consisted of fried breaded oysters, eggs, and fried bacon, cooked together like an omelet. In the gold-mining camps of the late 1800s, Hangtown Fry was a one-skillet meal for hungry miners who struck it rich and had plenty of gold to spend. Live oysters would be brought to the gold fields in barrels of sea water after being gathered in and around San Francisco Bay. Such a meal cost six or more bucks, a fortune in those days.

The Hangtown Fry at the Rose developed a small plate menu, featuring fried oysters, done three ways, that was prepared and served from the small kitchen behind Oscars to customers of Oscar's poetry den. This small kitchen became another bone for contention between Beulah and Stub, whose stutter became more pronounced when she wanted to turn a stuttered word into a wicked tongue of abuse. Beulah contested the management of food and beverage services on a daily basis, pushing easy-going Stub towards a heart-attack waiting to happen.

Stella decided that it was time for Beulah to go, while Thaddeus pointed out that as long as she had a percentage of the profits as payments due for the cafe, they were stuck with her until they found a way to pay her off.

Stub, with his Tourette's stuttering and twitches, would have a hard time finding employment elsewhere. The harder he tried to find a way to work with her the more she pushed to get him to quit. What Beulah didn't understand was that Stub was family, and she had made herself into just a pain in the—starting at the neck and working down.

07
A Yiddish King Lear

"Thad . . . Thaddeus meet Sy . . . Sy Jacobi." Stub said as they entered the lobby. His stuttering from Tourette's Syndrome, which usually became worse usually worse when meeting strangers. Stub had only known the old man for as long as the car ride, but it was obvious they were both developing a keen liking for each other. "He . . . NAK . . . he's . . ."

"Son," Sy said, "if you'll put a plum pit in your left cheek, you'll have an easier time with that stutter." Sy's speech was long and drawn-out, a dry wind taking its time stirring up the leaves. "Now, a peach pit is too large, folks will think you might have the mumps. A cherry pit is more likely to be swallowed."

Sy's uninvited wisdom drew awe-struck smiles. He appeared to be so old and invalid, his voice raspy and dry, each word carefully chosen. Dressed in rags for clothing, finished with shoeless feet, one almost expected him to keel over with his next breath, rather than sharing his wisdom and psychic insight. The sparkle in his eyes said otherwise. "Mr. Mohler, pleased to meet you, Sir." Sy finished.

Ivory and Henry, who had both experienced Sy's psychic abilities, were once again caught off guard. Stub had not used Thaddeus's full name in the introduction. No one had, there was no reason for Sy knowing it.

Sy chuckled. "Fellas, it says right there on the plaque by the mailboxes: Thaddeus Mohler—General Manager."

"Sy, pleased to meet you. Are you checking in?" Thaddeus asked, the tone in his voice a bit snooty, suggesting that perhaps the Rose would not be that welcoming for a dirty old Jew off the street. "Our elevator is frequently out of order. There is a nice place you might find more suitable a few blocks from here near the synagogue. No stairs to burden your way."

Ivory did not like the tone in Thaddeus's voice and was about to call him on it.

"Earl is DAH . . . down in the GAH . . . Grotto, Sy. I'll take you down and introduce you. NAK." Stub said. He knew that Thaddeus meant no harm. Sometimes he was rude and hurtful, never vindictive. Most everyone put it off to old age. After meeting Sy, that was no longer an excuse. He motioned towards the elevator. "I'll take Sy down," offered Henry. You had best park Stella's car before she gets a ticket."

"Hold the elevator, gentlemen," Sy said. "Please allow me a private word with Mr. Mohler."

Henry was tempted to suggestively take Sy by the elbow. If there were an altercation between the two older men Earl would take Thaddeus's side just for loyalty reasons; admonishing him in private later.

If rheumy eyes could smile, Sy's did. He had taken Thaddeus's insult with a grain of salt. His turn was made with cautious deliberation, his balance unsure, as he edged himself to within whispering distance of the aging hotelier. "I hope you don't mind my wardrobe; I am an old vaudeville man and was trying out for a role in the revised off-Broadway play 'The Yiddish King Lear.' Perhaps you know it. It's a parody of the Jewish theater from a bygone era. It's terribly overacted—without overdoing the ethnic stereotypes at the same time. Ultimately, it's no harder to do a cheesy, overacted, funny-on-purpose production of The Yiddish King Lear, than it would be to do one of Shakespeare's King Lear itself. I like a good laugh as much as the next fellow, and there are plenty to be had here, but I guess I'm still groping for the point." He looked eyes with Thaddeus for an eternal minute. "You have a point . . . ?"

Thaddeus stared back, not sure what to say.

"Perhaps, it comes with age, those annoying memory failings. Though I have not found it to be a problem; yet. You have taken to writing notes to remind yourself of various things you think you ought to remember. Try sticking your notes on the wall right over there in the corner where no one but you can see them. Try it, you might like it." With a knowing wink, Sy left to join Henry and Ivory at the elevator. A few steps away he stopped, and turned back towards Thaddeus and nodded, his right hand up just above the brow as if he were tipping a hat, bidding him good day.

Stub left the hotel trying his best to hold back a mirthful laugh.

Thaddeus did not understand Sy's comment, his mind was wrapped around Sy's suggestion regarding his notes. It was a good idea; however, he was too embarrassed at first to recognize that. Growing old is not for the timid, of the many challenges, losing one's memory is on the top of the list—if one can find the list. Thaddeus had thought that no one besides himself knew about his memory dilemma. Maybe he had told someone but couldn't recall—still Sy's comment was puzzling. He looked back at the corner where Sy had suggested he post his notes. That just might work. Rubbing his chin, his eyes followed Sy to the elevator. The old man in tattered filthy socks was a paradox. "You stupid, old fool" he muttered, "that old bigot I have been trying to boot out, had gotten the worse of me yet again."

Tomorrow night, Saturday, usually their busiest night, was to be Les Moore's last engagement. It should have been Henry's too, but since Henry had opted to be mostly AWOL it was to be Les' night—held open for Henry should he decide to make an appearance. Earl had wanted to have a heart to heart talk with Henry; however, Henry was spending most of his time away from the hotel. Stepping outside the Rose was something Earl just didn't do.

"Mr. C.," Ivory started.

"Earl," Henry interceded, "I'd . . . we would like you to meet Sy Jacobi. He plays the violin."

08
Old Age Hasn't Bent His Bow

Earl knew that when one of the band members introduced a musician, he or she would be good enough to try out for the Earl Crier Quintet. If he and Stella could have it all their way none of these musicians, friends and family all, would ever leave. However, life is inconsistent, friends do come and go, as did the need for new passions and heart that made up the music that was so much their heart and soul. Earl was always on the lookout for exceptional musicians. They were hard to find because being just good enough to join the quintet was below his standard. One had to be exceptional, a blazing star in their own right, so bright that those who were privileged enough to hear them would fear that they might burn out leaving a trail of their music as fading stardust echoing clear and brilliant until the end of time. That, and they had to be willing to work on the cheap.

Earl always chuckled at that. Yes, he was picky. There were plenty of bands around town with more than enough second-rate talent. The Quintet was made up of exceptionally talented musicians, each better than the other, phenomenal talent that came around one in a lifetime. Gifted musicians who usually couldn't make it anywhere else—like Les being black, Henry being Nisei, or Michael being ugly. Imogene was the exception. She was very light brown, had the voice of a sexy angel, and was knock-out gorgeous. She had come to them by accident, or perhaps as a gift. She was their magical songbird.

So, this is what it has all come to? Sy thought. *From homeless to this . . . I am blessed.*

The bone chilling fog that had been building behind the great Golden Gate Bridge had been creeping closer each day and Sy knew that if he would have stayed in that abandoned building for too many more days the cold, damp, white billowing fluff would have silenced his violin's voice for evermore.

Sy caught his own reflection in the oversized mirror behind the bar as they had gotten off the elevator. He knew he was going through one of the lowest periods of his long life but— mercy—mercy—he looked like the cover photo for a rogue's gallery of the destitute. He was tired, hungry, needing to pee in an old man way, and ached in places he didn't know ached until he had passed the age where it didn't matter anymore.

It was Michael that caught Sy's curiosity. Sy had seen ugly in his lifetime, but Michael drew the grand prize. The saxophonist's unusual tuft of hair had fallen out of place. Comb in hand, a young woman doted over him as if he were the cat's meow; not roadkill. This one had the eyes of a gentle doe suggesting the innocence and joy of life of a small-town girl where the corn or wheat grew taller than she.

The young woman with the bass he somehow knew had once

been her dearest friend. Now, the frown she wore, said nothing nice about her once-upon-a-time best girlfriend. This one had the fever, and while she had come from the same small town as the first, she had developed a taste for the big city, men with thick wallets, and most of all, attention. But men did not matter to her, it was music that made her sway, caused her heart to palpitate, her tongue to wet her lips, to toss her hair back, as she caressed the strings of her bass. Her eyes were blue; not like the sky which would let the sun rise in it, and let it scatter its light, nor like the sea which could reflect the moonlight, and shine like a diamond. They were like ice; transparent. Sy could see that the ice held what appeared to be frozen tears. Her fears, sadness, weakness, everything was trapped in those eyes. And they looked so cold, like her stare could freeze the whole world in a moment. She had the fever, and nothing, no one would keep her from that. When she played, her music touched her in a way no man's touch, or kiss ever could. What she touched she had to own. She could never own the music, her heart too cold to give it true life.

When she looked at him, Sy had to turn his own eyes away least he let her know that what he saw in her future was an ugly passing filled with envy, violent rage, and in the end a deep, deep soul wrenching loneliness. That she would never understand that it wasn't her music that wasn't good enough—it was her vanity that would steal her stars away, leaving behind a bleak desert of scorched dreams.

Sy looked around the room taking notes of the various person-alities and instruments. *The blind piano-man had to be Earl. He is as charismatic as the day is long, blind, and terrified of the darkness that he must wear as a cloak until the days he dies, and then with God's mercy he will once again see light,* Sy thought. Drums, saxophone, bass—*it looks like the one with ice for eyes also plays the cello.*

The third young woman was perhaps the loveliest young woman he had seen in a very, very long time. She was grace in high heels. She wasn't beautiful in the classical way; no flowing golden curls or ivory skin, no piercing eyes of green. She was shorter than average, and certainly larger than a catwalk model, but in her ordinariness she was stunning. Something radiated from within that rendered her irresistible to both genders. Men desired her and women courted her friendship. She had a kind of understated beauty, perhaps it was because she was so disarmingly unaware of her prettiness. Her skin, a light delicate mocha, was completely flawless. She was all about simplicity, making things easy, helping those around her to relax and be happy with what they have. Perhaps that is why her skin glowed so, it was her inner beauty that lit her eyes and softened her features. When she smiled and laughed you couldn't help but smile along too, even if it was just on the inside. To be in her company was to feel that you to were someone, that you had been warmed in summer rays regardless of the season. He had not heard her speak yet, but he instinctively knew that when she parted her lips to sing, all the birds on earth stopped to listen and learn.

She looked up from a sheet of music and smiled, not at an old man dressed in rags, who looked as if God might have forgotten him. No, she saw an old man, with special gifts, whom God was allowing to live just a little longer, his gifts too great to be taken away from this earth one second too early. She whispered one word. It was please and was as welcoming as the best dawn he had ever risen to, and as hopeful as the first moment he had first seen his wife, the love of his life, and she him.

When Henry Akita had first invited Sy to come with him to The Honeysuckle Rose Hotel, the best he had hoped for was a place that was dry and warm, where he could end his homelessness, and live out his last days with a little dignity. Elsie, his beloved violin was almost as old as him. Until his last breath he would never put her down. It was almost as if the old instrument knew that here some special music was played and it warmed in his hands, her cat-gut strings almost purring to be allowed to sing. When he had first stepped off the elevator it had worried him that his old violin might not bring enough to make a difference. With the trombone and clarinet leaving the quintet they would be challenged on a number of good pieces. "Well, old girl," he said with a ghost whisper, as he lightly patted his violin's aged wood, "let's see if we can find a way to earn our keep."

"Earl," Henry said, "with Les and me leaving, you are going to need some new musicians. There are plenty here in the hotel, but from what I've heard, not one of them is good enough. Sy here is. Like a fine wine, if a musician gets better with age, Sy here is priceless. Whether or not a violin can fit in . . . I don't know. Being that I'm leaving, my parting gift to you all is Sy. I hope you will give old Sy here a chance—despite his looks."

"Isn't one Michael enough?" Earl said, with a touch of friendly humor to his voice.

"Age before beauty Earl." Henry responded.

"I see. How old are you, Sy," Earl asked?"

Sy took a second before answering. When the call to pee comes to an old man it is usually urgent, and rarely eventful. *Could he wait? Yes, a short while.* He glanced slowly around the room until he saw a sign and an arrow that pointed down the hallway past the elevator. "Sometimes I tell folks I'm seventy-six, sometimes seventy-eight. The truth is I'm a spry eighty-three."

Half the room let out a surprised whistle, including Earl, as each took in Sy's remarkable age. "Eighty-three, you say. My, oh my . . . and still standing. Still playing too, so Henry says."

Stella had just entered the room through the stairway. She looked expectantly for someone to introduce her to this vagabond as he unpacked his violin. "Perhaps, you might feel better sitting," she offered, seeing that the old man's legs were visibly shaking.

"I would indeed, but not until I can show you that my advanced age has not bent my bow any."

Mollie giggled.

Stella went over and whispered in Earl's ear.

"Les, tomorrow night's gig is yours. You call the tune. Sy, you go ahead and jump in whenever you're comfortable. If you don't know it, or can't play it, say so. Les will have a second one ready to go."

"Please allow an old man moment to warm up," Sy asked as he brought up his violin testing it lightly with his bow; his gnarled fingers flexing.

Les and the other musicians stood ready.

Sy did not wait, with a slight wink towards Stella, whom he had not been introduced to, yet, he began to play a gorgeous solo directed specifically towards her. It was a light, imaginative, if not a playful rendition of 'Stella By Starlight.' Everyone marveled at the beauty that poured from the elderly musician, his bow, and violin.

Henry and Ivory knew that there was more to Sy's music as he introduced himself to the grand lady of the manor.

Stub, who was about to push the elevator button on the lobby floor withheld his finger not wanting the sound of the creaky old elevator to interfere with this magical moment. Until that moment he had not heard Sy play. "That is the grandest damn thing I've ever heard," He whispered, without any stutter.

Thaddeus left his place behind the reception desk and stood next to Stub, tears easily flowing as he too, listened to the violin sing. In the rooms above, doors slowly opened, as the hotel's guests—musicians all—listened to the distant music and followed the sound as it called to each of them with its magical string voice.

Rosemary stood, fingers ready, just barely touching the stronger strings of her mahogany colored bass. A few moments before the old man had come into the Grotto, she had barked at Mollie to get out of the way. Inside she raged, not against Mollie—she was no threat and did no harm, it was Henry, Les, and Michael. They were all better musicians than her. With Henry and Les gone Earl would finally see that her bass had been in the background far too long. Sit back Michael and let some real beauty onto center stage. Now that this old man had come, she knew that Earl would make him their first violin, and she would still be second fiddle. Deep down, dreadful thoughts began to rise, harboring secret wishes for the old man's quick demise.

—

Curious, the hotel's guests filtered in making an impromptu and appreciative audience. None carried their instruments for it was known amongst them that one did not join in on one of Earl's rehearsals without an invitation.

Sy was about to sit when he saw a man sitting just out of the limelight. He was wearing a tux, top hat, and most unusually some kind of cloth face mask. He sat with a bearing of dignity. Sy instantly knew that, not that long ago, this man had lost most of his dignity, not much in life had sustained him other than what came out of a whiskey bottle. A faceless derelict of a human being who could have been found sitting in a filthy gutter in any big city's bowery. Faceless because people looked away preferring not to see how far a fellow human being could fall. How he had gotten to this marvelous ballroom Sy could not even guess. His intuition told him that he was there because of a most unusual and hard-won friendship. The mask that covered his head left him faceless, his emotional and physical scars now covered with the finest silk.

A young woman sitting by his side dusted some lint from his shoulder. She whispered into his ear that the violinist was looking directly at him. "Oscar Brandt is my name. May I call you Sy?" his voice clear and firm without having to shout to be heard from across the room.

Sy nodded to the affirmative. The man was not looking at anyone in particular. The mask had no holes for the eyes; that was when Sy knew that like Earl, he too, was blind.

The young woman again whispered into his silken mask.

"Do you know the Tennessee Waltz?" The blind man asked.

"I do," Sy answered, his feet telling him that he should have sat while he had the chance.

Stella, who was now standing by Earl, put her hands on his shoulder, whispering into his ear. "Why do I think that this is going to be one of those moments that is going to change everything?" She did not remember that had been her first thought as she got out of bed this morning.

Earl gently tapped one of Stella's hands. "Sy, Oscar once thought himself a musician, and found out otherwise. The Tennessee Waltz, please, in the tempo it is written in."

Sy glanced at the other musician's, seeing that none were bringing their instruments forward. He stretched the fingers of his bow hand, and then his other fingers as he brought the bow to the violin's strings. As he slid the bow into the first note Oscar rose and began to speak.

'I was dancing with my darlin'
to the Tennessee Waltz . . .'

This was not the way Patti Page sang it on the radio, not the way Leonard Cohen wrote it. This wasn't music but a poem recited well.

'The beautiful . . .'

Midway through Oscar slowly sat, his last word a brief flutter beneath his mask.

"Imogene," Earl whispered.

Imogene stepped a little closer to the mike. Everyone knew exactly what was to happen next. Sy's last note held long because the only conductor seemed to be a blind poet speaking from within a silken mask which showed no emotions. His voice taking you to the memory of that dance within his heart.

The very air seems to change as Imogene sang *The Tennessee Waltz,* her voice as beautiful as her smile, the tune carried the song as the composer could only have wished. Sy kept the violin as the lead instrument, second only to Imogene's interpretation as she kept a watchful eye on Oscar. The bass telling, the horns a low infatuating refrain. Earl's piano fireflies on a warm Tennessee night. Towards the end of the last stanza Oscar rose again. Imogene's voice faded away as did all of the instruments leaving only Sy's violin.

Oscar finished his poem. Sy's violin soft, low, as rich as a lover's dream, matching Oscar word for word.

" . . . the night and *The Tennessee Waltz.*"

Until that moment Oscar's poetry had always been separate from the music. Occasionally Mollie had dusted his words with her piano notes as soft as tiny raindrops on a forest floor. When

Oscar first heard Sy's violin he heard each note and knew if done right the poet in him would finally sing. He would do it his way, and Imogene and the Earl Crier Quintet, would do it theirs.

Tears ran down Stella's face, as Stub quickly brought up a chair for the old man to sit. "Sy," she said, "welcome to our home."

"And I wouldn't have it any other way." said Earl.

Rosemary was the only one not smiling.

Sy gently placed Elsie on the offered chair and excused himself towards the door down the hall.

09

Dry Martini, Stirred, Not Shaken

Rusty Mayer was a bartender's bartender. He had a champagne smile capped beneath a full head of unruly auburn hair streaked through with feathers of white, his bushy eyebrows more white than red, highlighting Irish green eyes set against a face that seemed to be flushed with enough color that everyone called him Rusty; his given name being George. Rusty is five foot six, not quite burly, and at age thirty-nine worked with confidence and an energy that challenged his younger contemporaries.

Rusty had been on staff at the Honeysuckle Rose just over a month, four paycheck's worth of effort, and all disappointing. He had been hired as the bartender for the lobby lounge. Oscar's place, a poetry den, where booze is sipped, rarely guzzled.

The lounge is open from eleven in the morning until sometimes eleven at night. It is open on Sunday afternoons from noon until six when there are few if any customers, but being that Oscar is blind he had little else to do. Oscar demanded that there be a bartender on duty: "What if someone comes in wanting something? Never turn down a happy customer, because if you do, they won't stay happy very long." Monday through Friday, after the usual lunch crowd have come and gone, it is mostly quiet until close to five. Saturday night is the big night of the week down in the Grotto and Oscar likes to sit in on the rehearsals to see where there might be a good place to mix his poetry in with the music. The Poetry Den opens at four. Oscar rarely shows until five when he will have two full hours to strut his stuff.

—

These are his busiest two hours of the week as the place filled with folks waiting for the real show to begin downstairs.

As soon as the doors to the Grotto open at seven there was always a steady flow of customers vying for the best tables downstairs. After trial and error, and complaints that there wasn't enough room, they found that The Grotto could seat one hundred and twenty-seven. The floor was divided into five sections, each with a friendly waiter who knows exactly where to seat the customers so few if any seats went empty wasted. Six additional seats could each be found at two full bars located on the far sides of the room. Few sat there because of the lack of view of the stage.

There is an underused commercial kitchen located behind the Poetry Den—underused because they only served small plates and fresh oysters done five ways. There wasn't much profit in the food, and serving it added extra time and effort on the waitstaff. The waiter's motto always guarded with a smile: Don't walk the walk unless it puts another buck in your pocket. The waiters in the Grotto never worked the Poetry Den; the tips too thin.

Stella's Grotto is packed most nights. The Grotto is where everyone had a good time, and never complains about the price. The Grotto was tip city—and Rusty didn't waste a moment in closing the Poetry Den down, so he could get to waiting tables downstairs. Saturday night he had section 3, which was closest to the stage. The other waiters would pocket a tip for seating customers in his section, but no drink orders or service were provided until Rusty came flying in. Stub had wanted him to bartend, but Rusty would have nothing to do with it. He needed the tip money and that came with the table service, and his section was a gold mine.

First Saturday night he served as waiter his tips were well beyond his expectations. He had never seen people eat so many oysters, nor had he walked so far since he had served in North Africa. Personally, he could not stand the sight of oysters, let alone eating them. There were plenty of drink orders, causing Stub to rethink letting one of his best bartenders work the floor. Still, Rusty knew how to sell the champagne and upgrade the brands of whiskey and scotch, making his section the most profitable of the night. Rusty had his one good night in the Grotto, the rest of the time his job was to take care of Oscar's Poetry Den.

By comparison the lunch crowd at the Den drank mostly beers while stuffing themselves with Hangtown Fries. Most of the tips were scooped up as soon as the tables were cleared by the one waitress—who kept the oysters coming. She had to account for each and every dime with Beulah, the kitchen manager. Stub managed the lounge, but that made little difference to Beulah, who could spot a dime left on a table from ten feet away. Bar tips were thin.

Rusty learned from day one that if you wanted to keep your job—and your balls—you did not cross Beulah. There had been three lunch shift waitresses since he had begun working there. The wages were not worth the aggravation. Beulah piled on like sour cream on herring. She was a bitch through and through glorifying herself in the role.

His immediate boss was Stub Wilcox, a nice guy with a stutter, and a case of the shakes that could mix any drink in the house. He was the food and beverage manager, but he rarely showed his face around the Hangtown Fry, or the Poetry den. It was plain to see that Beulah had Stub by the short hairs and he would turn and run whenever Beulah came into the same room. He almost felt sorry for the guy.

What Rusty needed was a boss he could go to when another superior was stealing his tips. The pay was not great, and he needed the god-damned money to get his marimba out of hock—more than once he had sworn never to gamble again. What he needed was to be transferred full time to Stella's Grotto where a waiter could make a pretty fair living. Not so at the Den. Oscar's Poetry Den drew its own crowd, mostly educated folks, who drank too much coffee and tea. A few threw some whiskey in their coffee. It was a poor place to earn your keep as a bartender or waiter.

It didn't take Rusty but a couple of days to change the atmosphere at Oscar's—with Stub and Oscar's full support martinis became the word, and the drink of the day. It was promoted as the only place in the great city of San Francisco where one could get the perfect martini: "Gin, stirred for twelve seconds exactly, not shaken, while glancing for five seconds—not one second more—at a sealed bottle of vermouth." The vermouth was placed strategically on the third shelf above the bar. Cobwebs and dust covered the bottle for theatrical purposes.

Seeing the profit and sales go up Stub made a certified effort to turning the Poetry Den into a Martini Bar. Poetry and martinis; a perfect mix. Oscar did his own promoting, promoting the elixir before and during his poetry recitals. "There's no cocktail more distinctly American than the martini. It's strong, sophisticated and sexy. It's everything we hope to project while ordering one. Some famous writer had once said that the martini is 'The only American invention as perfect as the sonnet.' The consumption of martinis rose so fast that within a few days those immortal words now hung above the bar between two over-sized martini glass-shaped neon signs. The place had a new name—Oscar's Martini Bar.

The former Brooks Weingarden had once been a full-time lush, everyone's pal, throwing decency and caution over the rail as yet another drink was poured.

"I don't drink to get drunk; I drink because I can see someone's reflection looking up at me from the bottom of the glass, and I want to get acquainted with the son-of-a-bitch. You pour me champagne and I become giddy with all the possible accomplishments and great things I have never done. When my glass is filled with whiskey, I stop being a sweet old tabby offering my best purrs and glancing snuggles. With each tip of the glass, and clink—clink of the ice, I become a lion in heat who is no longer housebroken, and hell on the furniture. You pour me a martini and I become sophisticated, humorous, wise, a ladies' man, who every man respects, and every woman lusts for; while my friend who winks at me from the bottom of that shallow glass promises that I can remain a happy drunk, blessed and befriended by all, with just one more—lightly stirred, not shaken."

Brooks had had more than his share of martinis in Hollywood before the war. While he would drink most anything, the martini was his elixir of choice. The war brought him to London, where rationing and a shortage of gin, brought him to cheap whiskey and rye.

Then one tragic night a Nazis V-II Rocket found him at a favorite pub, playing the piano, the RAF aircrews gathered around, with the ghosts of too many men standing somberly nearby. *Bless 'em all, Bless 'em all. The long and the short and the tall* . . . It had been a whiskey kind of night, the pending hangover waiting to scream with a lion's roar—no more . . . no more. The Nazis rocket killed all but four, leaving Brooks blind and angry, desperately searching in that pitch-dark glass or bottomless bottle for that the face of the happy drunk, finding only pity and scorn. In the end Brooks did not survive.

His drinking pals Mr. Pity, Mr. Dark, Mr. Despair, and his best pal, Mr. Loneliness promised him peace, and some much-needed rest as soon as he had consumed enough of death's elixir to no longer care. In that bleak place, where there was never enough drink to deliver him to death's door, he had stronger friends, that at first, he could not see, who with patience and understanding tried to guide him out of his personal hell. An angel, a blind man, an old bar keep, and a Jap caught him before he could touch the bottom of that abyss. Their music and combined hearts beat back the lion's roar letting Brooks go, while giving life to Oscar and the poet within.

Now, when Oscar appears at his own lounge, not to play the piano or sing, but to quote poetry, he will usually start out by toasting the audience with a water- filled martini glass, tipping it slowly beneath his silken face mask, then after a long deep sigh of appreciation he would share a little history to gather in the crowd's attention. With his rich voice he will start out: "Is everyone happy? Good. Allow an old martini man to share a few words of wisdom with you. The history of the martini is a murky one. As is the case with many alcoholic concoctions. Through time, things weren't always written down, and memories got fuzzy from drinking a few of them. Throughout most of its history beer has always been the working man's drink here in San Francisco.

There have been many a saloon or bar whose purpose has been to take every dime of those hard-earned wages. During the gold rush champagne became known as the gentleman's drink. The rich, they needed something more.

As the story goes, a miner walked into a bar and asked for a special drink to celebrate his new fortune. The bartender threw together what he had on hand—fortified wine (vermouth) and gin, and a few other goodies—and called it a Martinez, after the town in which the bar was located. The Martinez was a hit, and word soon spread about the new drink. It was published in the Bartender's Manual in the 1880s.

"Author Barnaby Conrad III, who wrote a book on the drink's history, asserts that San Francisco is the martini's true birthplace. Then there's the claim that a New York bartender created it in 1911. Some are adamant that the martini may have gotten its name because of Martini & Rossi vermouth. A customer asks for a 'Martini' cocktail because it utilized that product. Over the years, the drink's fame has grown, as for its ingredients." He shook his hooded head humorously. "No, no, no . . . Butterscotch? Seriously?" A short pause where he would hold the glass up for everyone to see. "The shape of the martini's glass, the ratio of spirits to vermouth, and even its name changed . . . try saying Martinez three times fast. It seems that everyone wants to take credit for this famous cocktail."

Then he would take another drink and raise it one more time as either Mollie or Stella sat next to him as he slid over on the piano's bench to accompany his verse. "Here is to the martini, it is a gentleman's drink, and as we all know a gentleman never . . . ever . . . mistreats a lady. And so, ladies, have one yourselves, and perhaps that bum by your side will in time start looking like a gentleman."

The tips were good while Oscar was on stage, the martinis always brought in good tips, but as it happened far too often the band would start up downstairs in Stella's Grotto. The crowd would pay their tabs, carrying their martinis with them to where the real show began. Oscar would continue to recite his poetic verse as long as there was one hand still left applauding.

Regardless of the success of Rusty's martinis the flow of traffic was always to the grotto. When the music moved into full swing, Rusty stood behind the bar for the rest of the night, listening to Oscar drone on, and pouring a few more martinis; a few, his tips as dry as his martinis.

When he was first hired Rusty had said nothing to Stub about being a musician. Now he found it damned hard to listen to the music pouring up from the Grotto when he could practically smell, taste, and touch the musical notes as they called to him—alluring mystical sirens beckoning from the mystical Grotto below.

Rusty polished the bar glasses while Oscar, his voice and choice of verse intoxicating, continued on. "This one, my friends comes from the poet, Sidney Keyes, and I sense its heart rises once again as another war comes to us in Asia." He cocked his head to show that he was thinking. "Korea, I think, I'm not really sure where that is. Is it worth making a war over? The appropriate title is War Poet.

> *'I am the man who looked for peace and found
> My own eyes barbed.'*

Rusty knew the poem. While he had not heard it until after the war, it was written during the time he was with the U.S. Army (Tanks) in Tunisia. His had been a thankless war; hot, deadly, bleak, and as far as he had been concerned, not worth the dust that coated his mouth and throat each hour of each day he had been there. He glanced around the room, outside of Mollie and Oscar, there was one couple and an old well-dressed lady listening to the poetry. Pouring himself a martini was the first thing he was not supposed to do. The second was to not leave the bar unattended to listen to the music from the stairwell that led down to where heads were bopping, and where there was room enough people were dancing. This was a full house night.

Thaddeus gave him a grumpy old man's scowl as he ignored the rule and deserted his post. As long as no one else saw him he'd be okay.

The Earl Crier Sextet was good, very good, and he ached to play with them. But that was his kick in the pants, his marimba was in hock, and he hadn't the money to bail it out. The second kick, the one that hurt the most, was that his martinis were doubling, perhaps tripling the lounge's cash sales, and he wasn't benefiting from an extra dime of it.

10
Cracked Crab Meltdown

Saturday night was the busiest night of the week—and this one promised to be the biggest yet. Word had gotten out that The Earl Crier Sextet's sound was about to change, for good or bad, no one knew, but everyone wanted to be there. If the Fire Marshall dropped by, he would have no choice but to close the show down. There were too many people and Stella's Grotto, located in the basement of the old hotel, was a dangerous place to be should there be a fire.

Oscar closed the Martini Bar early and settled himself into a seat just left of stage where he could be led to a seat near the piano. He only had four poems to recite during the evening, the last, their closing number was to be *The Tennessee Waltz,* just as he had done it with Sy.

In Earl's mind Sy was going to be a big part of the new sound, as the clarinet and trombone were laid down. However, tonight was to be about their old sound, friends and family, who might—perhaps—never play together again.

The sextet with Earl's piano, Les' horn, Henry's clarinet,

Rosemary's bass, Michael's saxophone, and Ray on drums would be reduced to the piano, saxophone, Sy's violin and Imogene's golden voice would have to carry the show. There was no question that their character was about to change. It would become less vibrant, and mellower. Michael played a mellow moody sax. He was not a strong bebop man. Without the trombone or clarinet, a number of their best tunes would have to be sidelined. There would be more poetry from Oscar until Earl figured out just what their new voice might be. One thing he had determined was that they would not bring on any new musicians who were not up to snuff just because they played an instrument that was needed. A piccolo could never replace Les' trombone.

One mistake that Earl was already making was in under-estimating Sy because of his age. Sy knew his music, and it was the music that energized him. The vibrancy of his violin would bring a new voice to the character of the music that was at the heart of San Francisco. Earl didn't get that, and worried if the old man was up to it.

Sy sat with Stella and Oscar with Mollie and Ivory seated just behind. When the time came Mollie would escort Uncle Oscar up onto stage and back again. It had been agreed that Oscar would be off stage when he wasn't performing. He had a tendency to rock and bop to the music as only a blind man can do—which was distractive to Earl's own gyrations at the piano. Ivory had a seat, which he rarely used, because as usual he took his job as head of security to an over reacting zeal state.

As the months passed, Thaddeus had become more and more uncomfortable, if not neurotic, in a crowd. He preferred to stay at the front desk to check guests in, and to tell others there were no vacancies. On a busy show night, he just told anyone who asked that they were booked up. More than a few of the gentlemen dusting off the dance floor were not with their wives, and regardless of Ivory's zeal, Thaddeus did not want a jealous husband shooting any of the guests.

Stub ran the food and beverage, and tonight his game was off. Beulah had not been able to get the number of oyster's they needed and hadn't planned on a change in the menu for a crowd this large.

After his argument with Beulah, Stub had a row with Rusty. With Oscar's Martini Bar closed early the orders for Rusty's magical elixir were backing up. The other bar tenders were not nearly as fast, and no one could make them like Rusty. On what might be their busiest night of the year, Stub had ordered Rusty off the floor and behind the bar, which meant he would be missing out on their busiest tip night ever.

Stub had called every fish monger in town and hadn't come up with enough oysters to make a difference. Abalone was his second choice, but hard to cook for a large crowd; over-cooked it was inedible.

Beulah saved the kitchen by getting in a last-minute truckload of Dungeness crab. It was too late to do anything else. She soon discovered that the prep work and cooking of the crabs was a lot more work than she expected. It was time to start serving the food and they were nowhere ready. One mistake after another slowed things down. Finally, Beulah's stressed-out rages brought everything in the kitchen to an incompetent stand-still.

The messy cleanup from the cracked crab and drawn butter slowed down the waiters. Many plates were returned because the boiled crab was too messy for people dressed in fine evening clothes to deal with. The kitchen hadn't planned on enough entrées to replace the crab.

The waiters were taking it on their chins, their grumblings silent and rumbling. It seemed like everyone had a beef with the waiters, or about the food. The back-up of the drink orders didn't help, and the music hadn't even started yet.

Earl had Stella take him on stage twenty minutes before the music was to start. The crowd was getting surly, needing drinks and entertainment. The room was already hot and smoky. Food was another matter. The tiff between Stub and Beulah had been going on far too long. Earl had had enough and made a mental note that it was time for Beulah to go—that was the easy part, buying her out was going to cost a pretty penny.

"Ladies and Gentlemen," he crooned before Stella had the mike positioned, "while the rest of the quintet is setting up, how about some good old fashioned bluuues!" His fingers danced, his voice not quite ready, as he rolled into a spirited, crowd-catching rendition of:

> *'Oh, here's a dance you should know*
> *Oh, baby when the lights are down low . . . '*

Adjusting the standup mike, Michael added his sax. Imogene, who had been finishing her hair, practically ran across the dance floor added her voice . . .

'. . . Ah do the Hucklebuck . . .'

Imogene could see that the crowd was not simmering down, no champagne laughter, unexplained angst just below the smoky haze.

Stella noted the same.

Towards the back of the room a loud oath was sworn, a woman's voice changed to a startled scream as a cork pulled from a champagne bottle popped out explosively, splattering the couple with half the contents of the bottle, the cork flying through the glowing tip of gentleman's cigar at the next table, leaving behind a brief flash of sparks as it sailed across the room. That would cost them free drinks for both tables, a dry-cleaning bill, and whatever damage the sparks might have done to the evening jacket.

Stub was on his way to calm the situation with a broad smile, apologies, and extra stutters to hopefully change their frowns to smiles; everyone loves a clown.

Imogene took over on stage: "Now here is one of my personal favorites," she cooed into the microphone.

Earl lifted his fingers from the piano keys as he cocked an ear. He had been seconds away from stepping into 'Messing Around' by Memphis Slim. He knew that Imogene was reading the audience and knew what she was doing.

"Long About Midnight, as recorded by Mr. Cab Calloway." Her voice, almost a bedroom whisper, purrs into the microphone.

The bass came in on the second note.

'Just take a look at Harlem after sundown
Any time you choose . . .'

Rusty had four martinis and a manhattan up and ready noting that he was nine orders behind with the waiters working the tables as best they could without tripping over each other. The ice sink was down to the last inch of cubes. That wasn't his job, the bar and serve area was bogging down into slow moving chaos. Somebody needed to fill the ice buckets before chaos became a calamity. He waved at Wiggy—Dominic Villa—the bartender working the station at the bar's far end. Wiggy waved him off, he was too far behind. The bartender who usually covered the middle bar had called in sick, which meant that both end bartenders were picking up the extra load. It was going to be a long night—and it hadn't really started yet.

Rusty needed ice and would have to scrounge for himself. He stopped at the kitchen door where he heard Beulah 'out-swearing a sailor' at some unfortunate soul. He wasn't about to get caught up in that.

Stella added her own cigarette smoke to the pall as she stepped off stage motioning to Mollie that she is needed elsewhere. Her gaze momentarily settled back on the service bar where for some reason there was one bartender when there should have been three.

With Beulah out of control there was no way Rusty was going to go through the kitchen. The next best way was to take the back stairs up to the Martini Bar and bring back as many buckets of ice as he could carry. He slammed through the swinging doors to a storage room then stopped dead in his tracks. He had gone the wrong way. The stairs up to the Martini Bar were located off the service way on the other side of the kitchen.

What he had blundered into was the storage room where the second piano was now kept and all of the instruments that had been gathering dust in the old speakeasy until it had reopened as the Grotto. What kept him from turning and running for the badly needed ice was the same thing that made his heart skip a beat or two; a Marimba. It was much like the one that sat silently in a pawn shop, with a price pinned to it he couldn't afford to pay. He thought about the tips he was missing tonight. The drink orders that are piling up with every wasted second.

The marimba was his instrument and this one was a beauty; almost new. He played both the xylophone and the marimba, the marimba he played the sweetest. The marimba is similar to the xylophone, with wooden, pitched rosewood bars that are struck with a mallet. The wider bars are suspended above a tubular metal resonator, giving the marimba a full, resonant tone. His had been a 4 1/3-octave rosewood marimba. This one had a four octave range from C3 to C7. It was a newer instrument, and finer than anything he had ever played. It had six styles of mallets, ranging from hard rubber to soft yarn, in addition to a bow. Wetting his lips, he quietly tested the bars finding the instrument remarkably in tune. While constrained, he found himself drawn . . .

He shook his head as he started to put the mallet back where he had found it. No, he thought, not tonight. He had many a martini to make; stirred, not shaken. His way. That was a damned hard decision and he wanted to kick himself for having made it. Wiggy was the chief bartender. He could make just about every drink invented. He could make a good martini, but not Rusty's way. He glanced back at the Marimba, with loving eyes, and whispered. "Don't you go nowhere, baby, you stay right here. I'll be back, that I can promise you." *They will fire me for sure if I don't get back to the bar quick.*

—

There were two bars. The one nearest the kitchen was the only one used. Sure, there had been nights where they had wished that they had the second bar up and running. It was a pride issue. The night had not come when everyone threw up their hands saying, "We give, open the second bar, we can't handle the load." As long as the waiters carried the load that day would never come; the heavier the load, the bigger the tips. Each waiter had his territory, a set number of tables. Opening up the second bar would ultimately mean hiring some drinks only waiters; that meant splitting the tips.

Stella took in the chaos, glancing wishfully at the closed bar across the room. The waiters were practically on roller skates. Piecemeal, food was finally coming out of the kitchen. She quickly noticed that just as many plates were going back to the kitchen full. It was the crab. On any other night they would serve drinks and food together, seeing that all orders to a single table were delivered at the same time. Not tonight, and that would cost the waiters a bundle. "The show had better be damn good tonight, honey," she said through tight lips, "folks can be very unforgiving."

She reached Wiggy's end of the bar addressing him almost accusatory. "Where's Rusty, what the hell happened?"

"Stub said that tonight no one makes martinis except Rusty. He went to get some ice, and ain't back yet." Not seeing the waiter whose order was up, Wiggy bellowed; "Table 16 up, minus two."

"Minus two?" Stella asked.

"Yeah, minus two martinis. We ain't getting nothing out until Rusty gets back."

"How long . . .?"

"If you want me on Rusty watch, you're going to have to pay me double."

Ready to bite someone's head off Stella slid behind the bar. "No more yelling. I'll dispatch, put the ticket on the tray and slide them down to me. We'll match up the tickets with the martinis if I have to make them myself." That was an idle threat, she had never made a martini in her life. She eyed the waiters, most of them off the floor waiting for food and drinks to run out to their restless customers. They were getting pushed to their limits and she was now becoming concerned that a few might throw off their aprons and walk off the job.

    'That's Stella by Starlight . . . .'

That was her song, and this was usually where she would come on stage, light a cigarette, lean up against the piano, as

Earl sang to his woman. Only this was not her night, and she could not remember a time when Earl had sung their song that she hadn't been there. Earl was long to anger, when he heard about tonight someone was going to be sacked. She looked at the growing stack of martini orders, and then back at the kitchen door.

The kitchen was chaos, and, as far she was concerned Beulah would be the first to go. There was no excuse for their kitchen to be this non-functioning. All of the waiter's eyes were on her—they had reached gridlock. "Can any of you boys make a fair martini?" She knew there would be no volunteers, moving behind the bar would mean no tips, and plenty of abuse because they wouldn't be Rusty's martinis.

Biting her lower lip, she thought about moving Wiggy over until Rusty got back with the ice. Wiggy saw her look, guessed what was going on in her female head, and shook his head no. Against all the stress and chaos she couldn't help but to stifle a secret smile—Wiggy's hair piece, which was bad enough in the first place, had slid out of place making him look like Groucho Marx with a dead rat on his head.

"Make a hole, make a hole," Rusty grumbled vociferously as he pushed his way through the waiters porting four heavy buckets of ice. "Wiggy, take two and then pass the buckets back." He grabbed ahold of the shoulder of Wally Cox, the largest of the waiters. "I know you have half of my turf tonight, so you're raking in a few bucks. I've got a shitload of martinis to mix and we need more ice. Take all four buckets and fill them, when you get back your orders will be ready. You've got priority because you are such a . . . pal."

Rusty didn't give Wally a chance to argue.

Stub finally made it over to the bar after being badgered by impatient, and disgruntled customers every step of the way.

Stella wagged a finger at Stub that it was time for a quick Pow-Wow. It only took a moment before Stub came back around the bar. "Okay you gah . . . guys . . . Nak—Nak . . . I'll dis . . . dispatch."

Drink trays slid down the bar as Wiggy worked his end. Rusty mixed four, five, six, martinis at a time, placing one martini from each batch on a tray set aside for Wally.

Stella spotted Ivory and waved him over. Beulah was a hot-tempered bitch who might easily turn violent when told that she was fired. She was going to need Ivory to escort Beulah as quietly as possible from the building.

The tricky part was getting the kitchen staff back and working as a team. No doubt firing Beulah in front of them would be a moral boost. Stella did not want to spend the night holding the kitchen staff's hands, she had too many other fires to put out. Someone needed to start matching up the food with the drink orders and get them to the waiters who desperately wanted to deliver both food and drink together.

Earl elected to pass up on Oscar's first poem sensing that no one was in the mood for poetry. He needed Stella to tell Oscar, otherwise he would be one more problem added to their list. He was just finishing up their song when he realized she wasn't there.

Les Moore was going to get an extra solo tonight, and it was going to be as much a surprise to him, as everyone else.

11

Stub's Dilemma

Stella paused. She had to be certain in her mind as to where the blame belonged before she fired Beulah. Nothing was going to change about firing the kitchen bitch; it needed to happen. She did not want to get into a hissing fit with Beulah because she was a master at being nasty. She would turn it around making it Stella or Stub's fault—they were conspiring against her. She was being blamed for something that was none of her doing. A few mistakes had quickly compounded into a dozen, that dozen into more—so many mistakes that it no longer mattered where it began, or who was responsible for what, or how many screw-ups there had been. The reality was that little could be done to correct everything that had gone askew. Stella had to cut the lifeline to the problems—Beulah—wipe the slate clean and then start fixing it.

How bad things had become was most evident in the kitchen. Stub was responsible for the food and beverage service. It was his job to make sure that the kitchen's needs were met, the orders placed on a timely basis, and the right questions and decisions were made should there be a glitch in the system. The list of items and amounts needed had to match the menu and had been ordered on Wednesday for delivery on Friday.

Things were right on Wednesday.

Deliveries were made on Friday.

It was Beulah's responsibility to match the deliveries with the orders, and if they were short, to find out when the missing items would be delivered, and to adjust the menu accordingly. Oysters, fish, and produce were always required to be same day fresh.

Stub ordered the fresh fish and produce needed for delivery first thing Saturday morning. Beulah paid any attention when none were delivered on Saturday—until it was too late. Then, and only then, did Beulah get on the phone and screech at the fish monger who told her there were no oysters to be had at this late date. He quickly made her a good price and a quick delivery on one-hundred and fifty live Dungeness crabs laughing to himself as he hung up the phone.

The crabs arrived as promised. Live? The joke was on her. All of the crabs needed to be boiled, cracked, and cleaned. The kitchen wasn't designed for that and the staff hadn't a clue as to how to go about it; at least with that volume. Beulah should have paid an extra charge to have the fish monger cook, clean, and crack the crab, before delivery. She hadn't even asked.

Instead of resolving the issue Beulah yelled, and screamed at everyone within ear shot. The crabs were boiled and cracked to clean; but not to serve. The crab, when delivered to hungry customers who were disappointed with the menu change in the first place, now had to be cracked and pulled apart by hand. The drawn butter dipping bowls were too small and too full. There were no crab crackers or extra plates for the shells, and no extra napkins for messy hands and spilt butter. Although comical when matched with fine evening cloths, crab bibs would have been ideal. They hadn't any.

The waiters caught the flack for this.

The smarter customers turned the unmanageable crab away without even letting the plates dust the table.

The steaks were always good at the Grotto. The waiters, returning the crab, quickly found out that what steaks they had were gone. The entrees were limited. As more and more of the crab plates were being returned the options for their replacement were growing slimmer by the minute Beulah demanded that since there were no other options the crab be sent back to the tables—if the dinners didn't like it, they were just being crabby and difficult.

Nothing could be done until they got Beulah out of the way. As food and beverage manager, Stub was beyond frustration. Tears glistened in his eyes as he struggled to find any words of conciliation for the waiters. There were no words. His handicap only accentuated that he was a bartender, not a manager, and out of his league at that. What business did he have pretending to be a manager? Stub felt deeply for Earl and Stella, and The Honeysuckle Rose. This night was ruined and would be remembered for a long time as the night Stub brought shame to the Rose. His head down, he thought seriously about leaving, even though he had nowhere else to go.

Leave? The Honeysuckle Rose was more than a job; it was his home . . . and family.

Rusty stopped pouring mid-martini and put his hand on Stub's shoulder. "We'll get through this. If anyone's at fault it's that bitch Beulah. Soon as Stella finishes with her, the two of you will figure out how to get the kitchen turned around." Rusty finished pouring the martini adding it to a tray that was now ready to be delivered. "Here is an idea for you to chew on. Stop trying to serve the crab whole unless someone wants it that way. For right now cancel all food orders and get the drinks out. Figure out what the kitchen can put out quicker than right now and do it. Stub, it's not up for me to say, you're the Food and Beverage Manager, but whatever you come up with is on the house. Get the booze out there and we're half-way home on fixing this thing."

Stella overheard. *Now here is a guy who can think on his feet.* She thought, making a mental note to find out more about him.

Stub blinked back his tears as he tried to straighten up his shoulders as he thought about what Rusty had just said. *The only way to get ahead of this screw up is to stop wading through the muck and find some dry land. We've got to shift gears and find something that works. Whatever comes out of the kitchen has got to be quick, tasty, and free. Happy customers will come back another night. With the sextet and their music changing we cannot afford to lose this crowd. The hotel is on good financial feet, the loss of one night's profits will be tough, but not the end of the world.*

He took in the unhappy faces across the bar from him. *Right now, it looked like about half the waiters are ready to quit. It won't take much more before a few of these guys take off their waiter aprons and walk out of here. Free booze and free food; this might turn around the tips.*

He glanced over at Stella who had one hand on the kitchen door. Ivory was flexing his fingers as if he expected a fight.

Stella had waited just long enough for Stub to decide. She smiled as she nodded yes and blew him a kiss that said: *do what you have to, you have my support.*

"Come on Ivory, we've got some garbage to throw out and a kitchen to clean up." The door swung shut behind Ivory as Stub swallowed his hurt pride, willed his stutter away the best he could, as he grabbed an ice mallet banging it hard three times on the bar. "O . . . kah . . . Kay, listen up. Here is how we are go . . . going to fix this thing. All food orders are cancelled. Get the the booze flowing out there. Drinks—first two—are on the house. Champ . . .path . . . pane, the first bottle is on the house, the second at half price. We just ran out of the premium stuff. Give me and Stella a mo . . . moment to straighten out the kay . . . kitchen and I'll tell you wah . . . what food we can puh . . . put out lickety-split."

Wiggy gave Stub a broad smile and a full thumbs up.

Earl smiled as he heard a male cheer rise up from the other side of the room. *That must be where Stella is,* he thought, as he rolled into a song that wasn't on the night's agenda. Tonight, was supposed to be Henry's night. Sorry pal, but tonight we are all going to have to play by the seats of our pants until we find what, if anything, is going to grab this crowd. Earl reached out to where he knew the mike to be and brought it in a little closer. "This is the song that launched Miss Patti Page into her first one million records—*With My Eyes Wide Open I'm Dreaming,* sung by our own Miss Imogene Wick." The truth was that he wasn't sure if Imogene even knew this one. He paused for a brief moment before playing the intro a second time to allow her to adjust to the sudden change. Rosemary snuggled into her some more time as she brought in her bass on the third note.

Ready as she would ever be Imogene nodded at Rosemary who guided everyone back to where Imogene should come in.

> 'Dreaming, dreaming of you
> With my eyes wide open I'm dreaming . . .'

Imogene left no doubt that she owned this song though she changed the lyrics because she couldn't remember exactly how the lyrics went. It still wasn't good enough to draw the crowd into the music.

At least the drinks were beginning to reach the floor. Those who had already received theirs earlier were waving down waiters for more. Voices throughout the room had risen making it hard for the musicians to hear their own music—they brought up their own volume, the voices escalating. While the drinks were being served the quintet was still losing ground. At this point Earl almost quit playing mid-tune. The musicians were not getting any respect. He wasn't about to call the audience on their rudeness, the lack of food and drink hadn't been their fault. Rarely had Earl played before such an inattentive audience. Perhaps it was time to call for a break until things quieted down?

"Earl."

He softened his playing, lifting his fingers quietly off the keys as Stub whispered in his left ear. Stub never interrupted a performance. Earl cocked his head in Stub's direction. The mike was hot, and he did not want what Stub had to say broadcasted. His fingers hung motionlessly while he tried to hear what urgent matter Stub was bringing to his attention. At Stella's request he had made a quick trip to tell him about Stella and Beulah, their solution to the food and drink problem, and that someone needed to announce that the food and drinks were going to be on the house."

"On the house?" Earl grimaced at the price they were about to pay. "Everything?" He asked, thinking it might be cheaper to just say there had been a small fire in the kitchen and it was closed for the rest of the evening.

"Jah . . . just the first few drinks and the first bottle of cham . . .pa . . .pagne." Stub answered. He rarely stuttered when he whispered. He did when he was nervous, or tense and this evening was a bit on the tense side.

"Well, hells bells," Earl replied after thinking about it. "I don't want this to be a complete disaster on Henry and Les' last night. Push the booze and let's get the party going."

"Ladies and gentlemen, our very own Miss Imogene Wick." His fingers came to life as he began to play *Singing the Blues* a song made recently popular by Frankie Laine. Imogene took the chorus. Without missing a note Earl turned his head away from the mike telling Stub to get both Oscar and Sy up on stage ready to do *The Tennessee Waltz*. Tell Oscar that he's to make the announcement, and to consider this a command performance. If he can break the back of a crooked union, he can turn this house around." Earl chuckled to himself as he thought: *Who would have thunk that the day would come when I would have to trust the fate of our fame and fortune to a blind poet. Well, I did once before, so let's do it again.*

"On second thought, tell Oscar to be ready to do a poem or two. We're going to take a break and rethink the next session."

"Sy?" Stub inquired.

"I've got a feeling the old boy can improvise while taking a nap."

Stub told Mollie what Earl wanted from Oscar and Sy, then skedaddled back towards the kitchen.

12
Bouncing Beulah

The only thing moving in the kitchen was Beulah's mouth. The waiters were not even bringing in the returned crab entrées—these were stacked into a shaky pile on a rolling dish cart parked just outside the kitchen door. Inside, the kitchen staff huddled in small groups trying desperately to blend in with the pots and pans as Beulah tongue-lashed a young female prep worker who shook as if she were a miniature schnauzer who had just been whacked on the nose with a rolled newspaper. Her lips quivered, nose dripped, her round blue speckled eyes were becoming bloodshot as Beulah chastised her for every problem known to mankind because she had cut her finger while slicing a lemon. The cut was barely in need of a bandage, but the damage to the young woman's ego and self-esteem needed emergency room treatment.

—

"That is enough!"

The prep worker covered her mouth in terror as she stumbled back three steps afraid that she was going to get a double blistering for her heinous crime.

"Beulah, I said that that is enough. Your days of playing Eris, the Greek Goddess of Chaos, Strife and Discord are over." Arms crossed across her bosom; Stella had spoken with an owner's determination. She turned to Roane, the over worked, and overweight Sous Chef. "Roane, Beulah is no longer running this kitchen, you are now the Head Kitchen Chef. Please take the staff out of here and up to the Martini Bar." She looked at the poor prep worker who had been the main focus of Beulah's wrath. She knew most of the employee's names, and to her regret she did not know this girl's name.

Stella took her by the hand, leading her over to Roane. "I'm sorry, I don't know your name?"

"Beth," the still shaking prep-worker answered. She whimpered rather than whispered her reply.

Stella passed the girl into Roane's pudgy hands. "You all go up and take a break. You can have a beer if you want one." She accented the 'a.' "I'll be up in about fifteen minutes and we'll get this kitchen back into a happier place."

"Well, I Never . . ." a look of bitter rage engulfed Beulah's face, her eyes wide and flickering as would a ferret cornered by the meanest bear in the forest. "You all stay right here. I am the Chef of this kitchen." The word 'I' was said in a way that its very utterance might drive that dreadful bear away. "I own this kitchen, and no one is going to tell me what to do." Her face was now tight and red as a beet. "I . . . I . . ." She needed to validate her righteous wrath. "Beth, you stupid little cow, you're fired."

Several of the kitchen staff wanted to scream back at Beulah. None dared, her dictatorial sway still all powerful.

Stella put a finger to her lips shushing any response, then quietly waved them out the door that would lead to the stairs that would take them up to the Martini Bar.

Beulah did not notice Ivory as he stepped behind, he. He could see Beulah clinch her fist as she prepared to settle this her way.

Woman, or not, Ivory grabbed her by the wrist twisting her arm painfully behind her. Under no circumstances would he allow any harm to come to Stella.

Beulah squawked with surprise, and a touch of pain, as she tried to free herself. "Damn you, let go." Ivory's grip was too tight, the increasing pain shutting off the vindictive curses she tried to spit out.

Ivory could not believe what happened next. It was something he's be able tell with a guffaw over drinks with the boys for years to come—even if his drink now was a cold soda.

Stella brought her hand back, then delivered a loud tooth clinching slap to Beulah's right cheek. "You have nothing more to say that matters. You are no longer the kitchen chef and you are no longer employed here. You do not and never have owned any part of this kitchen or hotel. You sold us a small cafe that barely made a profit. Any pay due you will be mailed. Our attorney will be in contact with you regarding any money still due on the cafe. You are not to call, nor enter the Honeysuckle Rose Hotel, or the cafe again—if you do you will be arrested." Stella shook her head as if some sympathy was to be included here. "I do not bluff, if you want to try me Ivory will be glad to entertain you until the police get here."

Ivory gave her wrist an anticipatory twist.

"Now hand over all of your keys."

Beulah hissed that she couldn't as long as Ivory had a grip on her.

Stella searched the room with her eyes until she saw Beulah's sweater and purse on a shelf nearby. The keys were found.

"Ivory, please escort the lady out."

"Gladly."

"Oh, please remind her that she is not welcome here." Stella gave a slight smile as she rubbed the hand she had slapped her with. "But don't break anything."

"That won't be necessary," Beulah groaned as Ivory escorted her towards the service elevator.

Stub arrived just in time to see Beulah escorted out of their lives. "Are you all right?" He asked Stella, the glisten in her eyes evident of the emotions boiling just below the surface.

"No." She was not one to resort to physical force and was not happy with herself. "I would like nothing more than to go up to my apartment, lock the door behind me, leave all this god-damned crap on the outside, and have a good old-fashioned gut- wrenching cry. I don't have that luxury right now."

She lit a cigarette.

"I just need a moment. Would you be a dear and run back out to the bar a pour me a brandy; be generous. Then we have some work to do. The staff is upstairs taking a break. I didn't think it appropriate for them to see what happened with Beulah. If it is alright with you, Roane is our new head chef. Right now, we need to go upstairs and help paint some smiles on their faces so we can get things moving down here. We also need to figure out what we can afford to feed our guests, with what we have available.

While Stub went to get her brandy, Stella started to poke her head into the various fridges and storage rooms around the kitchen. There was salad enough for all, but it was humdrum, and doubtfully could be served as an entree. By the time Stub got back with her drink she knew that they did not have enough of any one thing to feed a hundred plus hungry people. Time was not on their side. She had not even found enough of the right kind of bread to serve everyone peanut butter and jelly sandwiches. They did have a whole lot of expensive crab that no one wanted.

Eve Marie, who managed the Hangtown Fry popped her head in right after Stub. The Hangtown Fry started serving breakfast at 6:30, her days often starting at four in the morning. She wasn't much of a night person, but with Les and Henry leaving, she wasn't about to let them leave without saying good-bye. When she peeked into the kitchen it was empty except for Stella and Stub. "My God, where is everyone, its chaos out there. What's with all the crab, did you get a bad batch? What happened to the oysters?" This was a real concern because the Hangtown Fry served oysters five ways for breakfast.

"Bu . . .Beulah messed up the order. We don . . . don't have any." Stuttered Stub.

This was bad news. After she said good-bye to Les and Henry, she was going to have to pull an all-nighter getting together a menu sans-oysters. It was then that she noticed that Beulah was not dominating the kitchen with her Hitlerian personality. "Where . . . ?"

"We just fired Beulah and had her escorted from the building. Roane is our new Head Chef. Everyone is taking a stress break up at the Martini Bar until we figure this thing out." Stella finished for Stub, followed by a long taste of the brandy.

"I saw the leftover crab outside." Eva said. "What are you planning on serving?"

"All I could find is some salad, we don't have enough of anything else to work with. You have any ideas, Eva?" Stella's eyes were earnest, they were in a jam, and not enough bread to smear it on.

Eva thought about the mountain of crab that was wasting just outside. She knew her own kitchen, and little about the capacity of this one. "Breakfast for dinner," she suggested.

"What?" Stella's curiosity peaked, as well as her sense of hope, if there was any.

Stub could see Eva's mind racing a mile a minute.

"It will mean closing the Hangtown for breakfast in the morning." She took a quick deep breath. She was thinking and talking so fast. "Two choices. Get some of the prep-workers to work shucking the crabs. We can do crab omelets with hollandaise, with a side salad with a blueberry vinaigrette. If they don't want the omelet, they can have a crab salad. For those who don't want the crab, its bacon, scrambled eggs and flapjacks. I've got enough of everything we need upstairs. It will go a lot faster if I cook everything there. What I don't have are enough dinner plates. We can haul up the hot plates on the elevator where they will have to be dispatched to the waiters. Keeping everything hot is going to be the tricky part." She let out a long slow breath as she waited for their response.

"I think it just might work."

Stub nodded his agreement as he tried to picture the logistics. This was above his pay grade and anything he had ever encountered.

Stella drank about half of her brandy, put the glass down, then patted her chest as the heat from the brandy settled in. "Whew." She tapped her cigarette out in the remaining brandy—not realizing that she had done—the glowing tip of the cigarette briefly igniting the alcohol. "Okay, it's the only option we've got, and a pretty damn good one. I'll go up and get the kitchen crew on board. We'll crack the crab here and bring it up quick as we can in big bowls. Roane, will see that everything you need, you get. Stub, tell the waiters what they need to know, and get the orders going. If Earl hasn't made the announcement yet, let him know; then get back here. Your job will be to see that the right plates go to the right waiter with no mix-ups. If there are more drinks to go out with the food Wiggy will match them up with the table numbers. I'll check the orders before they go down." Once again Stella promised more than she could deliver. She couldn't be up in the Cafe checking orders while heading off any new problems in the Grotto at the same time. She looked up at the clock at the same time as she reached for her cigarette." That brought on a much-needed laugh. She clapped her hands twice. "Okay, let's go, the clock is running faster than we are."

13
Dance Rusty, Dance

Rusty wasted no time catching up with the waiting martini orders and had mixed six back-up pitchers and put them on ice. Considering the way things had been going so far for the evening he should have offered to help out Wiggy—but that was not what he had on his mind.

Wally Cox would be taking home what should have been his tips, so Rusty figured that Wally owed him one god-damned big favor. They were in a momentary lull, the drink orders they had had been served. Not one of the waiters wanted to go back out onto the floor until the crowd was told the good news that food and booze was on the house. Good news for them, not so good—the news—for the waiters and kitchen staff were about to double time their services.

Rusty tapped Wally Cox on his shoulder. Wally, who leaned with his back up against the bar taking a smoke break, slowly turned until he locked eyes with Rusty. "What?" His eyes said this had better be good, pal, with a touch of menace and mirth mixed just enough you did not know which horse he was riding.

"I gotta take a break. Handle the bar for a couple of minutes, okay."

"No way pal." Wally's tobacco-stained teeth flashed their prominence as he chuckled.

"Look, I've got enough martinis mixed to last quite a while." Rusty's eyes remained locked with Wally's, their banter just short of friendly with a slight threat when one blinked. "I've gotta use the john and I don't want Stub to have a conniption fit when he sees the bar unmanned. You gonna help a pal out, or should I put your drink orders at the back of the line; way back if you get my drift."

Wally stubbed out his cigarette. "Shee . . . it, hurry your whiny ass up."

Mollie guided Oscar up onto the stage to his usual spot where he would lean with one arm for support on the piano. She pointed Sy towards the standup mike which Imogene had just turned off so the violin would not overshadow Oscar's poetry.

Sy tapped it lightly, then turned it back on.

Henry helped Earl off stage as the band headed towards the service elevator which would take them up to the Martini Bar for a much-needed break.

The crowd noticed little of the change on stage as Mollie took her seat at the piano after putting the mike in Oscar's hand.

Oscar deliberately caused the mike to let out a loud piercing shriek. When that did not get much notice, he did it again. Shreek! Piercing the eardrums usually broke-up the best of conversations.

"Now that's better." After the painful shrill Oscar's rich melodious voice was as welcome as a warming fire in one's own hearthside when sudden goosebumps have given you an uncomfortable chill. His silk face mask flutters with his every word. The mask had no holes to indicate where his eyes or mouth might be which was why the flutter became a central focus. The mask was a masterpiece in the old curiosity shop. "It appears that we have all gotten off on the wrong foot this evening. Well, not me, I've just been sitting down there listening to what has become a disenchanted evening. An evening here at the Grotto is not supposed to give you indigestion. You came here for some good old-fashioned blues, great jazz, good food, and drink, and to perhaps dance a little."

He tapped his fingers on the piano indicating to Mollie that few lively cords were needed here. "I'm told that you are not happy. Well, get over it, because Uncle Oscar is going to fix that right now." He turned his head from one side of the room to the other as if he could see everyone. He ended with his head turned in Sy's direction.

"Sy, if you please. Ladies and gentlemen, the newest member of our musical family, Mr. Sy Jacobi. Sy, did I say new? Hmmm." He waved a hand. "Sy, you have not been anywhere close to new since Ulysses S. Grant was President. Folks, it's true, Sy here is older than dirt, but you are about to find out why God has left him on this here good earth."

Sy and Mollie guessed that he wanted some up-tempo music. They started soft and built up tempo as he manipulated the crowd from a surly disgruntled mood towards that of fun and a party atmosphere. Sy's bow started softly then moved into a surprisingly gay rendition of *'On the Atchison, Topeka, And the Santa Fe.'*

Mollie followed Sy's lead.

Oscar knew better than to try and sing. He held everyone's attention by just tapping the beat on the piano, the mike on, allowing Sy's violin to sing.

When Oscar heard the first drunken voice break the audience's attention somewhere out there in the dark, he waved a hand, and the music softened to a whisper. "We don't want any of you to get crabby because you are not happy with the menu or the service tonight. Shhhh, I want you all to hear this. Who loves you? The Honeysuckle Rose does, and because we do, we just changed the menu to something more to your liking, and it is all on the house . . . as are the first two rounds of drinks." He cupped a hand to the left side of his head where the tattered remnants of an ear was hidden beneath his mask. Somehow, with God's grace, he had been left with most of his hearing intact. "I said, it's on the house. If have to say it again we just might change our minds."

The crowd roared their approval as the atmosphere in the room electrified. Even the fat cats love a freebie. At that moment all of the disappointments of the evening drifted away with the tobacco smoke as doors were opened to let in fresh air from upstairs. "Your waiters will be coming by with your menu and beverage choices as soon as they can get their roller skates on." Oscar fell silent, and with a snap of his fingers Mollie and Sy brought everyone back onboard *The Atchison, Topeka, And the Santa Fe.*

Getting Wally to sub for him behind the bar had been about as easy as drilling a tooth without Novocain, but it wasn't a pee break Rusty was asking for. While Oscar worked the crowd Rusty made a beeline for the marimba and wheeled it quickly out onto the dance floor bringing it to rest just in front of the stage. He had neither the time nor the strength to raise it to stage level.

The look on Wally Cox's face was incredulous. He was stuck bartending until Rusty returned and that did not appear to be any time soon.

A mumble of curiosity and a more noticeable drunken voice caused Oscar to repeat the high note of his announcement. "I said it's on the house."

When Sy and Mollie began to play again Rusty brought his mallets up making them dance across the keys as if it were a well-rehearsed part of the show. While Oscar, Sy, and Mollie were caught completely off guard, Rusty had gotten everyone's attention where so far, they had failed.

—

Stella and the kitchen crew scurried to their stations as Earl and the quintet came into the Martini Bar through the back stairs entrance. The musicians remained silent as they expected

Earl to give them all a half-time pep talk. They had all been off their game and they knew it. Henry and Les felt worse, their last gig had so far been bad enough to make the audience wonder why they had wasted their time coming to the Grotto which right now smelled far short of a rose.

In all brevity Stella had told the kitchen staff of Beulah's removal, what was happening in the Grotto, and what needed to be done to get the kitchen hopping again. The workers knew what they had to do, with three prep-workers settling in to picking the crabs as if there was a prize for the most crabs picked in the shortest amount of time. Roane showed himself to be a natural leader and a good communicator, which in a large food service environment, you had to be. Without Beulah fouling the air the help were quickly becoming an effective team.

"Hey, Stub," Wally bitched as soon as Stub pushed open the kitchen door. "That son-of-a-bitch Rusty left me holding down the bar while I should be working my tables."

The marimba sounded much like a waterfall. The rhythms both rolling and hypnotic, bringing joy, smiles, and the tapping of feet throughout the room. The violin sometimes demure, other times seductive, with warm highs. The piano dancing among the best notes, fireflies teasing the flickering flames. An experienced ear could tell that Mollie was having trouble keeping up.

What on earth is that? Stella asked herself as she poked her head out the kitchen door, quickly focusing her full attention on the marimba parked just in front of the stage. The marimba, violin, and piano made for an entirely new sound. *Where the hell did that come from? Earl must have . . .* She thought. Then she realized that Earl did not know a damn thing about it. Rusty Mayer had abandoned his post at the bar and was saving the evening with his brilliant playing. She hadn't even known that he was a musician, and here he was bringing life back to the party.

Oscar was practically dancing on stage.

She queried Stub with her eyes. His eyes answered back that he didn't know, as his body slowly began to move with the music, as did hers. She looked at Wally as the music began to sway her. "That so-called son-of-a-bitch just saved our collective asses." What to do with Rusty she would have to leave up to Earl. Right now, she was either short a waiter, or a bartender. There were martinis to make, and no one made them better than Rusty. Now here he is making this place sing. "Stella?" Wally was falling behind on his table by the minute. "Okay, I'll take the bar, you get to your tables. You got the menu down?" *What the hell,* she thought, *it is one of those days.* "You bet."

Stella did not know gin from vodka in making a martini.

"Stella, you get back in the kitchen. I'll handle the bar." Stub stepped behind the bar looking for orders to be filled. He spotted the ready-made martini pitchers and let out a long-relieved breath. He held up one of the pitchers for Stella to see.

Stella was needed in the kitchen. Stub had his assigned post. Each of them needed to make sure the dinner orders got out quick, hot, and without error. Both roles are too important to sub in at the bar.

—

Ivory followed Beulah two full blocks to make sure that she hadn't any plans on returning. Even though she was a woman, deep down Ivory really wanted to throttle her. She crossed the street going into O'Rielly's, a neighborhood dump, saving herself and Ivory from any further confrontations.

Ivory turned at the front door to the Rose for one last look; no Beulah. Thaddeus wanted him to take over behind the registration desk while he went down to check out the music. Ivory ignored him as he headed towards the stairs leading to the Grotto. He stopped at the top of the stairs mesmerized by the music.

It was hot, almost sexy. He rarely let his emotions roam free enough to enjoy the music, which was constant at the Rose. This was different and he could feel it in the coursing of his blood. He had never heard a marimba before. And that violin; whew.

It took several attempts for Stella to catch Ivory's attention and wave him over. She hated to put Ivory behind the bar, the temptation too close for an alcoholic who had come so far. Sometimes you just have to trust and hope, but never-the-less she asked Wiggy to keep an eye on him.

The elevator door whooshed open.

The sound of the marimba had drawn Earl, Henry and the rest

back with no real break, and no wise words from Earl. Stepping out of the elevator Earl paused, holding everyone back a moment. "What is that? Is that a Xylophone? Where did it come from? Who gave him permission . . . never mind, he's damn good? Who's playing?" *Is it a he or a she?* He listened for a moment. "Is Oscar up there?" He knew he was.

"Imogene, do you know what happiness is?" Earl asked as she guided him back towards the stage. "Happiness tastes like sunlight, smells like soft skin, feels like your favorite song, and melts in your mouth like the finest chocolate and champagne. This guy's music makes me happy." He cleared his throat theatrically. "However, he's cutting into Oscar' time. Hurry on over there and bring in Oscar's poem as close to when this guy finishes as you can. If he can back you up along with Sy and Rosemary, I think we can put a capital 'H' on Happy."

Henry took Earl's elbow as Imogene quickly stepped to the stage. "Earl, the marimba player is Rusty Mayer. He was instrumental in turning the Poetry lounge into the Martini Bar," advised Henry. "He knows about Oscar's Poetry, so he should have no problem sitting in."

"It keeps getting better and better." Earl said.

Imogene came up the back steps to the stage. She first whispered to Oscar that he was to go into the poem before Rusty could roll into another number. Like any musician, when you're playing solo, and hot, it's not easy to share the stage. She moved silently next to Sy, while Rosemary, who had followed Imogene, unfolded a chair as she moved her cello into playing position.

The only one out of the loop was Rusty.

It was doubtful that Oscar would introduce Rusty. No one had taken the time to tell him who was playing the marimba. He liked the sound, but the guy had stolen Oscar's moment—and Oscar did not get that many these days.

Rusty brought his mallets down on the final few notes preparing to switch mallets for the next number. His mind raced as he decided which number should be next.

Imogene spoke into the mike. "Ladies and gentlemen, now that we've got your attention, Mr. Oscar Katz, our resident poet."

Oscar brought the hand mike up to his mask and began to recite: *The Tennessee Waltz*.

> *"She comes dancing through . . ."*

The piano and violin slipped in with a quiet seductive massage of his words as he spoke them. Rusty knew that Imogene would take the verse on Oscar's last word and sing them as if she were God's meadowlark. Softer than the piano or violin, he brought in some soft transition tones from the marimba as Imogene began to sing the first note.

Rosemary's lips tightened as she thought, *this damn bartender is stealing the show.* She instinctively knew that with Les and Henry gone the marimba would become the lead sound reshaping their sound. The marimba added a joyful sound, like mahogany Christmas bells that helped enrich each word of the poem. The violin; a perfect match. The cello came in on the last verse. While the audience heard its beauty, she only felt threatened.

The audience applauded before Oscar finished. This was a new sound that elevated Oscar's act as nothing ever had before.

Oscar knew it. Imogene sang . . .

> *"She comes dancing through the darkness*
> *To the Tennessee Waltz . . ."*

Her voice a sensual siren that rode each note as the marimba, cello, violin, and piano married with her vocals. No one had heard anything quite like it. It was better than good. It made everyone want to dance.

None dared break the magic of the moment.

The dance floor was empty except for Rusty as he played his way into the heart of the song, stealing no one else's thunder as Imogene turned Oscar's poem in vocal magic.

Earl, Henry, Michael, Les, and Ray waited just off stage. The Earl Crier Quintet was about to, at least for the moment, become the Earl Crier Septet. Imogene brought the song to an intoxicating finish. The rest of the septet moved on stage quiet as cat paws as Rusty, Sy, Mollie, and Rosemary swept into silence. One could almost hear a feather land lightly on rose petals as Oscar spoke: "The night they were playing the beautiful Tennessee Waltz." The audience leapt to their feet with a roar of appreciation.

Mollie took Oscar by the elbow to lead him off stage while Earl was escorted to the piano. The musicians each taking their places as quickly as the applause would allow them.

Sy took a couple of steps to follow Mollie and Oscar off stage.

Imogene touched his hand. "Stay," she whispered.

She glanced down at Rusty expecting him to be hanging up his mallets. He wasn't. Instead he pointed at her, motioned for him to join her as he began to play a hot *Lidi Hop* version of *'In the Mood.'*

Earl realized that this was a big dance number where every instrument on stage was needed. It was a great number to follow Oscar and to make up for the flops they had started the evening with. He would take back control of his stage after that.

The marimba set the pace.

Earl brought in some of his best finger work on the ivories. They sounded as if they had rehearsed it to perfection. They were in the swing with everyone on the edge of their seats waiting for the vocal.

When Imogene heard what Rusty was playing, she turned back to the mike. *In the Mood* had great vocals, one of her favorites. Rusty deliberately missed two notes as he motioned for her to join him.

All eyes were on them.

She had no choice. When she reached him, he stopped play-ing, allowing the other musicians their moment as he took her in his arms saying—"I hope the hell you can swing dance, because here we go."

She did.

He led. His feet aware as good as his marimba playing.

She whisper-sang the lyrics as they glided effortlessly across the dance floor.

> 'I'll just tell him, "Baby, won't you swing it with me
> Hope he tells me maybe, what a wing it will be . . ."'

It was the sound everyone knew. It was the music during the darkest days of WWII that brought the impossible smile to your face while giving you a reason to dance.

Rusty guided her to the center of the dance floor where he showed everyone how the dance is done; including Imogene. Dancing effortlessly one full circle around the dance floor Rusty spotted his next dance partner. He released Imogene as he extended his hand to a fiery redhead in a sequined evening dress that showed just enough of her full almost feline beauty. She was with an old sugar-daddy, who looked like he enjoyed his cigar more than a token beautiful woman at his side. She did not turn down the invitation. She was a good dancer, almost as good as you might see in the movies. They danced, inviting all to fill the dance floor around them. Imogene quickly found her way back to the microphone. Slightly winded and blushing from a hot dance with a man who knew how to hold a woman, her sensual vocals made the moment . . . .

> '. . . In the mood, my heart was skippin'
> It didn't take me long to say . . .'

Rusty had made his point and when the dance tune ended, he returned fiery Sonia Galant to her escort—but not before memorizing her phone number. He returned to the bar where most of the martini pitchers were waiting empty and a nervous Ivory Burch anxiously waited to be rescued. Rusty knew what he had done and so did Earl. The smart thing was to not overplay his success. For the moment he focused his attention on another success pouring one well deserved martini for himself.

The kitchen had their act together. No one went hungry, the crab omelets were the hit of the evening. The tips left for the waiters showing that all the earlier fumbles and mistakes were both forgotten and forgiven.

At Earl's request Rusty returned to play with the band's last two numbers. The dance floor filled, including Stella and Earl. Mollie filled in at the piano the best she could.

That night, Thaddeus left himself a note that he needed to hire a night desk clerk. He was missing too much of the fun.

Sy found his way to bed both tired and happier than he could remember, and he had a long memory.

Rusty's marimba lifted Rosemary's bass to where it needed to be. That did not mean that she respected him.

Beulah got good and drunk at O'Reilly's Bar where she met and went home with the wrong type of guy.

In the early hours of the morning the Grotto emptied, the kitchen crew finished the clean-up, the waiters counted their tips as they left the hotel behind them. Rusty made his way back to his single room in a tenement hotel with no tips, confused—if not somewhat worried about where he fit in; but richer for the day. Stub had told him that Earl wanted to have a meeting with him in the morning.

Stella looked lovingly at her husband who had fallen asleep as soon as his head had touched the pillow. She knew that he would be awake and working through his thoughts back down in the grotto within a few hours. She was too exhausted to think about anything as she finished her last cigarette, then turned out the light.

Oscar found his way to the Martini Lounge. To him it was neither night nor day. It was just a quiet time where he could have his solitary thoughts, lightly play the piano when no one else could hear—and sometimes sing a duet with Brooks, who was sometimes still there, hidden deep behind that damned mask. Alone, in the quiet of the room, when the music finally settled from his mind, he would think of Mollie. It was the only time and place he dared.

Rosemary and Mollie returned to their shared room, neither speaking to the other.

Les slept, he had never been one to fret about the future; it took care of itself one way or another.

Henry neither slept, nor closed his eyes, the future coming at him like an unwanted freight train. Wrapped in a blanket he lay on the floor having given the bed to Sy. He listened to the old man quietly snore as he waited with worried thoughts for the sun to rise on his last day at The Honeysuckle Rose Hotel, his home.

Rex, did what he did most nights alone in his room, cried himself to sleep. He was a desperately lonely man who could not share his secret that was driving him deeper into the cold heart of his desperation. It was only when he played his drums that he rose—just slightly—above his pain.

Imogene had loved her night, it had so many surprises, she wished it had never ended. She had danced. She had danced with a white man and had liked it. As her mind settled towards sleep the white man melted away as the hands holding her became those of a tall black man. The single sound in her dreams his horn as it blew magically just for her.

Ivory closed the front door, putting up the sign 'Use the night bell for entrance' as he prepared to do one last security check of the hotel.

Half asleep, Thaddeus did a walk-through of each floor as he made his way to his suite on the top floor. There was something about a woman in a nightgown wandering the halls that he needed to check into.

One by one the lights went out for the night at the Rose.

14
The Hard Good-Bye

Earl slept an hour longer than he normally did. The prior day leaving him with umpteen puzzling questions. The sun was just peeping over the Oakland Hills and he could feel it's warmth as it dusted the bay waters with glittering sun diamonds as it slid purposely towards the crowded, not yet bustling city of San Francisco. It seemed that he had been a different man living a different life when he had last seen these marvelous sun diamonds—now he could only imagine them.

Though it wasn't much, he was comforted by the knowledge that another day had come and somehow, he had managed to keep his dragon away. The last few days it had seemed to him that the dragon was restless, hungry; if it couldn't find and devour him, it would do its best to ruin his day. This morning that was particularly true as he sat alone, outside the Honeysuckle Rose, perched the best he could against a street planter box. He thought he was facing the front door to the hotel, he wasn't sure, and wouldn't be until either Henry or Les came out.

One of these days, he lamented, *I'll step outside those doors and that bastard dragon will be there and,—chomp—that will be the end of me.* He had resisted bitterly, both tooth and nail, to the point of paralysis leaving the protective cocoon of the Rose—now here he was facing that same cloaking darkness that held his mortal fears and promises too awful to speak of. Now he was standing guard with his back to the dragon's lair.

He knew that both Les and Henry were afraid of going back to war—especially Henry—for good reason. Unfortunately, Uncle Sam was giving them no choice. Sometimes a man has to do what a man has to do, even if the fear of it chokes your breath away as it wraps cold hard ice around your backbone. Earl could feel that ice moving down his spine. He had come here to say good-bye and would be damned if he left before doing just that. He had put himself at risk so they would know that he understood the cold sweat that was coming to their own brows.

He had thought about waking Stella but knew that if she had to say this hard good-bye, she would cry for the better of two days. Then cry again a week later after she got her tears restocked.

"Shoo! Those are my feet, damn it, not a fire hydrant." He barked at a small hyper dog that now found his trouser cuffs of interest. "And you are too damned short to be a seeing-eye dog." He tipped his hat to the owner. "No offense, Ma'am." He could tell by her pungent perfume that she was an older woman. No self-respecting younger gal hoping on attracting or keeping a man would dare douse herself with that obnoxious over-powering concoction. "I'm not much of a dog fan. They have a nasty habit of leaving stinky surprises that I don't get the pleasure of stepping around."

"That's alright, Mr. Crier, Foggy May always holds her own until we reach the park. I hope she didn't startle you. English Toy Spaniels are always affectionate and curious. She wouldn't hurt a flea."

A Toy dog? Well hell, wind the nosy thing up, and find a car tire for it to pee on. Startup that car and roll, baby roll. "That's all right," Earl answered with a pasted-on smile. "No harm done." *Harm? The damn thing most likely has fleas. All it takes is two or three of the little buggers to hitchhike on my pant cuffs and the Rose will be infested. Blame might be placed on the stress of just being out here on the street*—the smell of the dragon clogged his sinuses as he waited to say good-bye to two men he thought of as his sons. The fact that he did not like dogs, especially small hyper ones with stupid names, was a small irritant. "Foggy May." He shook his head with heart felt exasperation as the woman took the dog for their sojourn to the park. Clickity- click, clickety-click, clickety-click. "Little paws, smaller brain," Earl grumbled as he turned his attention back towards the front doors of the hotel. The woman had known his name. He hadn't given any thought to hers, hoping that she and Foggy May would never brighten his day again. A siren shilled in the distance. Someone's morning was starting out far worse than his. His nose wrinkled as a noisy garbage truck passed by belching exhaust and the pungent stench of the offal of every kind of human waste.

The hotel's door made a clicking sound a second before the door swung open.

"I think you done killed the rooster before it had a chance to crow." The shock of seeing the great Mr. C. sitting out here in his lonesome is enough to give the rooster a heart attack. "You been walking in your sleep?" Les Moore asked, his voice evident of his surprise.

"You are up early for a wayward musician," Earl responded with obvious delight. "You did not think that you were going to leave the Rose without saying good-bye, did you?"

"No sir. Our orders are to report to the Presidio by 0900 hours. That's military time in case you have forgotten."

"Son, I was merchant marine. Without us you poor dog-faces wouldn't have even had K-rations." Earl lifted himself from the street planter, supporting himself on his cane, which he almost never used in the hotel. "Henry?"

"Oh, he'll be down by and by. The Nisei have their own concept of time, you know. Stub volunteered to drive us over in Stella's car."

"Dih . . . did some wah one say my name?" Stub's voice sounded from the open doorway just behind Les.

"Earl? What are you . . .?" Henry had come down with Stub. In all the years he had known Earl he had never dared ventured outdoors by himself.

Earl sensed Henry's puzzled, if not worrisome, facial expression. He would have dearly loved to have seen it.

Henry's father had declared his son dead when Henry had shamed him by joining the all Nisei Division at the beginning of the war. While his father had been born in America, he was traditional in many of the Japanese ways. He and his family had been humiliated by being incarcerated in one of the Japanese American concentration camps. America was at war with the Japanese Empire as well as the Nazis Axis. That his son would go to war against people of their own blood was unforgivable. Henry's all-Nisei Division had fought hard in Europe. That did not matter. When an honorable Japanese father declares his son dead because he has shamed the family—then he is dead—his name never to be uttered again. While Henry grieved daily for the loss of his father, Earl had become that wise and supporting figure.

Henry wanted to avoid a long emotional good-bye because he knew that if he were to be killed in Korea it would cause grievous pain to both Earl and Stella. Now, here he was, and there was no avoiding it. Facing this was worse than all of the nightmares from the last war combined. His eyes misted, as his chest tightened.

"There was a shitty little dog sniffing around my trousers a few minutes ago. Did it leave any nasty little piles for me to step in?"

"Nah . . . none that I cah . . . can see." Stub answered.

"Nothing personal Stub, but your eyesight isn't much better than Thaddeus.' Henry you take a look, these are my best shoes. Look really close."

Henry could see that there were no droppings anywhere nearby. Still, Earl had asked, so Henry stepped closer searching the sidewalk around and behind Earl.

Earl sensed when Henry was close enough, then reached out and gave him a sharp, almost painful, blow across his left shoulder chest with his cane.

"Hey, what was that for?" Henry jumped back a step then froze, his head bowed, eyes to the ground, in respect. Had he somehow offended his honorable adopted father?

This time it was Earl who stepped forward as he wrapped Henry in an embracing hug. Henry's breath slowly left him, his gratitude, and respect returning the love and embrace Earl was wrapped around him. "That was for thinking you could leave without saying good-bye."

The moment awkward. Stub whispered that he had best go get the car. As he jingled the car keys in his hand, he stopped a couple of yards down the sidewalk, looked back as he hiccupped, a common emotional tic, savoring the moment. A grown man, he wiped his tears on his coat sleeve as he hurried to fetch the car.

Henry slowly started to release his embrace.

Earl did not.

Henry's eyes, which had been closed, now beckoned towards Les. Help me out here, brother.

Les felt the same way as Henry. He had never been one to say good-bye. There was something that just didn't feel right about the word. It always made him feel sad and emotionally clumsy. Caught in an awkward moment, he cleared his throat.

Earl released Henry.

"Come here, tall dark, and handsome—or at least so I'm told. I'm going to miss the hell out of the both of you. Earl wrapped himself around Les as he had Henry. Les bent to accommodate him, he being two feet taller.

A car honked, the driver driving past expressing his displeasure at seeing a black man and a white man embracing on a public street, or anywhere else for that matter.

The honk got the attention of a police cruiser following close behind. The passenger side window rolled down, as the cruiser pulled up next to them, its red and blue flashing lighters switching on. The officer just inside the car reaching for his baton as he gave his partner a concerned look as he saw what appeared to be a blind white man being manhandled by a tall menacing nigger. He wrapped the baton firmly on the car door frame as he prepared to forcibly remove the white victim from any further harm while the officer behind the wheel called in an incident report requesting backup.

"Everything is all right, officer, we're family," Henry started to explain. The officer's eyes went wide, his bull-shit radar pinging away. He had fought four hard years in the Pacific against the nip bastards, and here was one telling him that everything was all right, when he could see that it obviously was not. He had never seen a nigger and a nip working together strong-arming someone. That was when he saw that the white man was blind. "God damn, Matt, these sons-ah-bitches are rolling a blind man."

Matt, the officer in the driver's seat, was now out of the car, his side-arm pulled and aimed squarely at Les as the first officer demanded, "Back off, nigger, I won't ask twice."

Les urgently released Earl as he quickstepped backwards, almost tripping over himself as his hands flew up and over his head to show that he was not armed, harmless, and contrite.

The officer with the baton swung the car door open separating Henry from Les and Earl. The officers were not interested in explanations. Things were happening fast, the officer, not certain that the black assailant was raising something to strike him with, brought his baton down in a fast swoop catching Les just above and straight down on his kneecap. Crack; that was his kneecap. His knee bent; his leg twisted unnaturally underneath him as he collapsed with an animal like shriek of pain.

Both enraged and helpless, Earl did not care if they were cops or not. They had assumed that Les was a criminal, a black one assaulting a white man. They were more likely to bash Les' head in than not. With no concern for himself Earl started to swing his cane out wildly. "These are my boys, you son-of-a-bitch!"

"You black bastards don't know when you got it good, about time someone taught you . . ." the officer swore as he brought his baton around aiming for the back of Les' neck.

The second officer's finger tightened down on his gun's trigger as he pointed it squarely at Henry's heart. "Drop to the ground, your hands behind your head, or the last thing you will feel is . . ."

Earl's cane swung wildly until it connected directly with the kidney of the cop who had struck Les, his baton flying free. The hit was both lucky and unfortunate.

Ivory, hearing the commotion, barreled out of the hotel, bare knuckled and ready to fight. All he saw was Earl fighting for his life with his white cane swinging wildly about fending off two lethally armed cops.

Henry had a gun aimed directly at him. He could look right up the barrel. If fired it would blow a hole in Henry, the size of a tennis ball.

Les rolled on the ground, his hands reaching back for a kneecap that looked like it was badly twisted if not shattered.

A second police cruiser, lights spinning, screeched to a stop just behind the first patrol car. They had been only three blocks away when the call for help had been made and had come to the rescue of their fellow officers. A call for back-up was standard procedure when arresting blacks, they were known to be unpredictable and sometimes pull a weapon when caught outside of the Fillmore. Few had any weapons and the cops tended to be heavy handed with their billy clubs even when no evident crime was being committed.

Blinded by anger and testosterone, Ivory did not see the officers as being police, just a bunch of uniforms taking it out on

Earl, Henry, and Les. That Henry and Les were a black and a Jap made it that more dangerous. He had seen plenty of that back in the Marine Corps when the dogfaces or swabs chose to say the wrong thing to a marine after one too many beers. When the shore patrol needed to bust a few skulls the coloreds always got the worst of it. The Nisei were under orders to not get into a fight under any circumstances—any. This was not the Marine Corps, and Earl, a man Ivory dearly respected and owed his life to, was in immediate harm's way. Ivory launched himself, tackling the officer that Earl had just clobbered with his cane, the two of them slammed back into the open door of the patrol car.

One of the arriving officers kicked Les in the stomach doubling him over when he thought that the black man was going for the other officer's baton. He took no notice that that the black was down and out suffering a serious leg injury. The fourth officer called in for more back-up, his free hand on his pistol, eyes on the participants.

Earl swung wildly hitting the officer who had just kicked Les. It was pure luck that his cane struck the officer's wrist as he was pulling his gun to take aim at Les. The cane flew free. Spinning around, the officer backhanded Earl. His dark glasses knocked free, slid beneath the patrol car. Earl fell back hitting his head hard against the rear door of the car. The gun fell to the sidewalk sliding a short distance towards the hotel, but still within reach of Les, who writhed in agony as he grasped his knee as if he was trying to hold the joint together.

At first, Earl had been overcome with anger, desperation, and fear that Henry and Les would be hurt. He knew that Les was, but not how bad. After striking his head on the rear door of the police cruiser Earl no longer knew his left from his right, up from down, or if it had been a man or the dragon's tail that had swatted him down. If it wasn't for Les' screams, he would have slid into panicked withdrawal back into that pitiless abandoned well he had fallen into as a boy. The darkness in his head swirled leaving him with no sense of balance. He tried to scream for help, but the words swirled around in the same vertigo never finding his vocal cords.

A hand reached down and cautiously picked up the officer's fallen gun.

The officer who had his gun pointed at Henry swung it towards the man who had picked up the weapon. His finger tightened on the trigger as . . .

A shot is fired. The recoil of sound is followed by a sudden frightening silence which ends the melee as everyone stopped, breaths held, as all of the officer's checked to see who if anyone had been hit—was there an officer down. Anyone else. The blind man is down and obviously injured. Had he been shot?

The silence is broken by Les and more police sirens speeding in their direction.

—

Old men nod off far more often than they actually get sleep; that is, baring other health issues until they get the final nod. This was true for Sy. While he had not slept much, the clock said that it was time for him to rise and go find something to eat.

He made his way down to the lobby to see what, if anything, he could find to stop his stomach's grumblings. He arrived just in time to witness the escalating conflict just outside the hotel's doors. Leaving his violin on the registration counter he called for Ivory. *That was stupid,* he thought as he saw that Ivory was punching, kicking, and wrestling with a police officer just inside a patrol car. "Oh my, this is not good." It reminded him of the rough and tumble union strikes that had rocked the city back in the 1930's. He stepped out of the front door and clapped his hands. "Here . . . stop this before I call the authorities." *What am I saying? These are the authorities.*

No one noticed.

"I must be getting a little feeble-minded he mumbled as he rubbed his jaw wondering how to put a stop to this thing. "I'm going to have to be a bit more persuasive." That was when he saw it. "That ought to be persuasive enough." He picked up the pistol a few seconds after it had been knocked from the officer's hand. He held it for a moment, feeling the cold metal in his hand as he thought: Now that was really stupid.

There was another gun pointed straight at Henry's heart. Sy knew that this had to be stopped now before someone was killed. Now he did a really stupid thing, but sometimes stupid is the right thing to do. He pointed the gun high above his aged shaking frame and fired it safely above everyone's head. His only intent to stop the fighting.

BLAM ... BLAM . . . BLAM . . . BLAM!

—

Stella was jolted from her sleep. She reached over for Earl finding his side of the bed empty. That was not unusual, the shots and their descending echoes were.

Thaddeus woke frightened and confused. Had that been a gunshot within the hotel? Had the mystery woman shot one of their guests—or they her? He threw on a robe, forgot his slippers, as he worried his way towards the elevator. Once the elevator's door closed behind him, he pushed the down button to the next floor.

—

Ray, whose window faced the alley, saw nothing out of the ordinary. On stage he was all energy, his drums his extension into the music, and their world; their, meaning people; normal people. He was a shy man who spoke little off stage. He never had visitors, male or female. Life was a cycle of giving his all to the Earl Crier Quintet, then returning to his room where he would listen to the radio and read his magazines. He never inquired about other's business and took care to never share his own. The shots had shattered the status-quo. After listening at the door, he decided that whatever had happened posed no threat to him. There was no need to leave his room, besides he wasn't dressed appropriately.

—

Oscar sat up in bed, a frightened morbid figure. He now slept without his mask, and anyone coming to his aid would find the hideous truth he so carefully tried to conceal. In the late hour as everyone had gone to bed Mollie had neglected to lay out his clothes. She was the only one besides Stella who had ever seen Uncle Oscar in his most vulnerable state. Even if a fire alarm were to sound, or another shot fired, he would wait for her to come for him. Sweet Mollie, what would he do without her?

Most everyone in the hotel was awake, their heads popping curiously out of many windows as they slid open. Voices babbled, as fingers pointed at the scene below.

The officer who had called in for backup ducked down behind the patrol car, both hands leveraging his weapon as he elbows extended across the hood. "Drop it." He demanded, with every intent on shooting to kill if the old man holding the police officer's lost gun didn't comply within the next blink of his eye.

A third and fourth police car pulled up further blocking the street, its doors flying open as four officers quickly jumped out dropping into firing positions—all guns pointed directly at Sy.

Sy did not drop the weapon. His eyes moved slowly from one officer to another. One wrong move, one second too late, and that would be the end of his many years. He carefully brought down the hand he had extended above his head, the pistol still in place. "Now that I have your attention," he said as he opened and closed his mouth a few times, at a loss of words. He began to extend his arms and out to his sides.

"I think we should all pause for a moment before something needlessly tragic happens here." *So, this is the difference between telling a story and being in one,* he thought numbly as the weight of the gun grew stronger than his fear. His aged clairvoyant inner self told him not to put the gun down. As his hand, still holding the gun, became level with his head, he leaned in towards the gun and brought the gun's barrel to his own temple. "The next shot fired here will be mine, unless you all holster your weapons and make common sense and peace the order of the moment. I do not know what started this, but I can assure you that no crime has been committed here."

"Sy, no!" Stella had come to the nearest window above the street just as Sy brought the pistol to his head.

Another police car arrived pulling up onto the sidewalk in front of the cafe giving the officers within a clear line of fire.

Officer Keith Killian drew his weapon as he dropped behind his now open car door., his weapon braced through the open window. "What the hell?" He uttered. Whatever had happened here there was far too much lethal force being inserted into it. There was an old man with a gun to his head, two civilians down—shot or what he did not know—an officer within a half breath of shooting a terrified Nip, someone scuffling with an officer inside a patrol car, and hotel's windows full of witnesses, with one woman screaming . . .

"Stella? He knew her.

His eyes quickly searched and found Earl. Killian stood as he holstered his weapon. There were six to eight policemen with guns aimed directly at an old man whose hands had been raised and now threatened to shoot himself. He quickly stepped towards the center of the confrontation. "Everyone holster your weapons. Now. Don't move old fellow. I don't want you hurt just as this thing is ending. He pointed towards Earl. "Someone for God's sake check him out and see if he needs medical attention. Who is that on the ground?" He could see that the Negro's leg was twisted unnaturally, pain etched firmly on his face. "Someone call an ambulance!" It was lucky the injured man was black, otherwise there would be a mountain of paperwork and incident reports to be written up.

All weapons were holstered.

Sy still had the gun touching his temple, his finger shaking but not tight on the trigger.

"It's all right Sy," Stella said, her voice just loud enough for him to hear.

Sy turned his head just enough to see her in the window above. He could see the glistening of tears as she shook her head frantically that everything would be okay.

Sy slowly lowered the gun.

Officer Killian carefully took it from Sy's hand as Sy's feet gave out beneath him. He abruptly sat on the edge of a step to the Honeysuckle Rose, his long thin legs causing him to look like a weeping scarecrow who had fallen off his cross. Officer Killian had been one of the officers on scene when Earl, Oscar, and Michael had brought down the mighty Musician's Union two years prior. He had never forgotten the courage of the poet hidden beneath his silk head mask.

Michael, who slept with ear plugs, curiously stuck his head out of his room's window. "Damn it, now what?" With no clue as to what had happened, he could see that none of it was good. He leaned out the window and looked up towards the window where Stella was sobbing. He could see Earl sitting, his back against a police car, his arms covering his head protectively.

He quickly dressed, then took the fire stairs two steps at a time up to the next floor to comfort Stella.

What the first officer had thought to be a mugging was quickly explained by Henry. Earl sat where he had fallen unresponsive. Two officers, neither of them who had hurt Les, aided the crippled black man the best they could as the sound of an ambulance grew nearer.

Ivory was pulled off the officer as he was pulled out of the police car and handcuffed. He had after all physically attacked a police officer.

Michael brought Stella down to Earl. It took her touch to get him out of the emotional pit he knew all too well as his dragon's lair.

Imogene, still in her nightgown, hurried off the elevator, out onto the street, shooing the officers away from Les as she took him in her arms. His eyes were red from tears, his lips tight with pain as she sang to him, and only to him, as the ambulance rounded the street corner.

Mollie's first thought was to go to Oscar. Instead, she sat next to Sy. She patted his arm saying that he had saved them all.

He just nodded his head. After a moment she rose and went back into the hotel.

The night shift Sergeant arrived, listened carefully to everything that had happened. Ivory's handcuffs were removed. There would be no charges for anyone. Sadly, there would be no further incident review of the officers who had taken it upon themselves to teach a lesson to a black man who had been caught where he shouldn't ought to be.

Stub arrived, having missed everything. He had had trouble getting Stella's car started.

Les was put on a stretcher and loaded into the ambulance. There was some discussion as to which hospital, the nearest one did not treat blacks. Imogene wouldn't leave Les, but neither could she go in the ambulance, especially dressed only in her nightgown. While Les was loaded into the ambulance she made a mad dash to her room, dressed in record time, returning just in time to see and hear the ambulance vanish around a street corner two blocks down. She was told that Les was being taken to a hospital over in the Fillmore.

Thaddeus searched the floors for the mysterious woman, found nothing but people up and stirring at too early an hour of the morning, and then went back to his suite and went back to bed. He hadn't bothered to go as far as the lobby. It had been a late night, and he wasn't ready for the day to begin.

Mollie returned with Sy's violin, which was just what he needed. While an odd tune to pick, Sy brought up the violin and began to play *'Laughing on the Outside, Crying on the Inside.'*

15
The Wind Becomes A Mighty Storm

Complaining of a headache, Earl retired to their room—
speaking little as Stella gave support. His head did not ache
as much as the vertigo that swirled around in his head left
him nauseous and confused. Stella knew that something was
wrong, but he couldn't tell her what.

He did not want to talk, couldn't find the words when he tried.
He became prone to spurts of sudden anger and anxiety when
he could not find the words or thoughts, he wanted in the swirling darkness. He should have gone to the hospital with Les,
but his adventure outside the Honeysuckle Rose had already
proved to be a grievous mistake. The vertigo had been mild
until he had reached his own bed. As Stella pulled back the
sheets and helped him take his shoes off, a sharp headache
followed by a sudden numbness that seemed to start in his left
jaw then seep down that side of his body. Before he could grasp
what was happening, he fell back onto the bed—then—*Holy
Jesus, Joseph, and what's her name someone put a coin in the
slot*—which began a mind-numbing trip even the Mad-Hatter
would declare too mad for even the insane to endure.

The numbness slept away just as suddenly as it had begun.
The headache lessoned but refused to leave him as the swirling

darkness took over control of almost everything. *Is this it, am I going to die?*

The events of the last two days left him with a lot of decisions to be made, most could wait a day or two, others not. He tried not to lose his temper with Stella. He knew that she loved and cared for him and was rightfully concerned. She kept asking questions it hurt him to answer. With each question the spinning got worse, the roaring of the wind blowing from deep within his subconscious deafening. He managed one answer, one she did not want to hear, but it had to be said while he still might be considered to being of sound mind.

Since he would not go to a hospital, she wanted to call a doctor and have him come to the Rose. "No!" Earl had snapped, "I don't need no damned doctor. All I need is some good old-fashioned peace and quiet and this will all blow over." With the roaring in his ears there could be no peace; no quiet. The effort of tying that many words together had left him with a light film of sweat on his brow.

In truth he was frightened almost to the breaking point. It was one thing to be blind. He had learned to live with that and may have evolved into a better man because of it. The vertigo was a whole other thing. When he lay quiet and tried to not think the dizziness fluttering in his darkness made it seem like he was on a flimsy boat caught in a churning sea of endless whitecaps.

Whitecaps? He had not seen light in years and now the sparking whitecaps were floating around everywhere. Everywhere. If I'm going to be blind than let me be. These little sparkles of light give me no promise that I will ever see again—it's more likely that I will never be at rest or own my own mind again. Earl thought with the bitter taste of anguish drying on his lips as the vertigo seized his thoughts as if they were hot embers from a sudden fire, each spark turning, turning, turning as it became a mighty wind that strengthened into a horrific storm. The waves below rising and falling, the whitecaps lost in a violent sea of churning froth. His thoughts were torn and tossed into a thousand separate parts of what had once been a complex, sacred, human mind. As a blind man, he had learned to depend on his other senses—they were beginning to fail him now. He had trouble hearing because of the shrill wind deep within his ears. The smell of burning toast overwhelmed him. The taste of cabbage; spoiled cabbage as he had eaten in that long winter in Murmansk.

His soul struggled to find a way back into his body of blood, flesh and bone that still drew a breath, and then another. No matter how hard he tried, his thoughts would not connect together leaving him lost within a boiling choppy madness far more dangerous than the threat of his dragon had ever been. Here even the dragon feared to tread. As the wind roared, the bright sparks swirled around him, he could not help but wonder if the door to hell had just opened and this storm, he was caught in about to hurl him into that final abyss.

Earl covered his eyes; his dark glasses having been lost in the scuffle. He had a second pair, had not been able to remember where they were, didn't care much either way. It all became too much for him to bear as he screamed a raging defiant, yet helpless, "NO, enough . . . No more . . . No," his words faded with a gasp followed by body and soul shaking sobs that seemed to find no bottom within his desolate pit of fright and despair. Music had always soothed his deepest anguishes; it caged his fears where they could do him no harm. Now he could not find his music . . . not one damned note.

—

As a nurse Stella had seen men traumatized by dreams and memories of such anguish that she could almost see their souls trying to leave their earthly burdens behind. Earl was close. She lay on the bed next to him and held him tight, her body rocking with her own quiet cries of anguish. She did not know why her life's love was hurting so. She had never been so afraid of anything in her life than this moment as she held her Earl for his very life. Dear God, she was afraid that he would leave her, that whatever horrific thing that now gripped him was so horrible that he would rather die than bear another moment of its soul-sucking presence.

His screams were heard throughout the Rose. No gunshot could have terrified them more. Life at the Rose slowed to an absurd silence.

—

Mollie was helping Oscar dress. Hearing Earl, he turned and drew her close and held on as his head lifted, still unmasked, and stared up into his own dark reality and listened to his best friend howl. He wondered if Earl had finally fell prey to his immortal dragon. He listened for the beast to howl back as his own heart broke for the fabulous Mr. C., whom he had played and toyed with, and now took great pity upon.

Henry raced to Stella and Earl's room. He did not knock as he burst into the room to find Stella struggling to keep her own sanity as she held onto her Earl.

While no longer working, Stella was still a registered nurse and through the quiet friendship of a semi-retired physician she had known at the Veteran's Hospital she had managed to discreetly put aside a few syrettes of morphine for a crisis just like this. There were other medications available, but right now Earl was in traumatic pain and needed relief that would put him into a deep enough sleep that whatever he was seeing in his mind's eye would spare him for a while. Her eyes told Henry that it had reached this point. He knew where she kept them, and as a battle-hardened medic knew how to deliver them.

One by one everyone gathered outside their room as Earl slowly quieted; then finally fell into a deep sleep. Stella held him and continued to hold him until Henry reached for and slowly pulled her away. "It's only a dream," he whispered as he now held her, her body trembling, weeping quietly as he repeated those haunting words: "It's only a dream."

"This is not a dream, Henry, it most certainly is not a dream." Her whisper a pained portrait of her own soul. "Nor is it a nightmare; to Earl it is real in all its ugliness." There was an anger in her voice that if it had been directed at him it would have chilled Henry to the bone. After a while she slowly pulled away from Henry, their eyes sharing each other's concern, each gathering some strength from the other. Silently, she fluffed Earl's pillow as she gently supported his head trying to make him more comfortable. She touched and held his hand. He did not squeeze back. Wherever he was he was beyond her reach.

She wanted to but would not call a doctor. She had promised Earl that she wouldn't as he struggled to keep his sanity. He was afraid that if he was taken away, he would never return to the Rose. With that promise made, he had told her that all of the decisions that were needed to keep the Honeysuckle Rose Hotel alive and well were now hers to make. The Rose, its family and friends, would have to live with that until such time as he recovered; if he recovered. Outside their door she choked back a deep welling sob which desperately needed to come out. But not now, not now.

First, she needed to have a talk with Thaddeus and then peel her apples—her decisions—one at a time as they fell from the tree. Her tear-glistened eyes met each of her friends and family. "He's resting now," is all she managed to say as she patted her hair as if that made a difference in bringing some normalcy back to the world. There is work to be done, so much, where do I begin? "After the doctor sees him, we'll know more." She added as she put her heart on hold. There would be no doctor, she had promised.

Henry promised to stay by Earl's side most of the day.

Stella peeked in as often as she could. More than anything else she wanted to hold Earl's hand, to be with him just as urgent a need as his to rest. It was his wish for the Rose to pull itself together and everyone continue with their lives—their music— while he recovered. And so, with an almost single-minded purpose she took on the world within the Rose and began to reshape it her way.

16
Hard Decisions Made Quickly

Rusty Mayer arrived at the Honeysuckle Rose around eleven in the morning. For those who worked late nights this was early. He was both excited and nervous because he had a promising meeting with Earl about a full-time job with the sextet. He was nervous because he needed to get paid and knew that the other band members were only being paid room and board plus a few bucks here and there on the side.

He knew nothing about the tragic events that had occurred earlier in the morning. Like everyone else he had his dream, and this might be his chance.

When he had been a young man starting out in the workaday world he had worked as a waiter, bartender, and musician at one too many illegal speakeasies. The cop car parked in front of the hotel made him wonder if he should go across the street for a cup of coffee. Pulling up the collar on his coat, tipping his hat to cover as much of his face as he could, he started to do just that.

He stopped and turned back to look into the lobby of the hotel.

Thaddeus was talking and gesturing to a cop who appeared to be taking notes. Standing next to the cop was a woman. He couldn't tell who. Over the years he had had more than his share of legal complaints from chastened women. This fortunately was not one of them, although he couldn't be sure until he saw her face. Opting to save the twenty cents for the coffee, he pulled his coat collar higher to help cover his face as he entered the hotel.

It was Beulah.

Curious, he did not hang around long enough to sniff out any information except that Beulah looked as if she had taken quite a beating; her face puffy, modeled black and blue, one eye swollen mostly shut. Her left arm in a sling, middle finger in a splint. As the door to the stairs leading to the Grotto closed behind him, he heard Ivory's name.

The Grotto was rarely quiet, but now it was drop dead silent.

Most days you would find Earl at his piano at most any hour of the night or day. His musicians always at his side making sweet music. This morning there was no Earl. No Henry. No, Les. No Stella. No Ivory.

The blues punctuated the silence, it did not come from a bow, a piano key, or a horn, but from their hearts. Imogene, Michael, Mollie, Oscar, Rosemary, Ray, and Sy all sat glumly around a table. No food, no drinks, no words spoken, no cheer. As Rusty drew nearer he saw a tear slide quietly from one of Imogene's eyes.

What the hell . . . what has happened? He wanted to ask; but it was not his place. He had barged into their world last night without so much as a please or a thank you. As he passed, he took off his hat, holding it as if he had come into a funeral parlor. He laid the hat down on the bar where Stub inventoried the liquor. The scratch of pencil on paper as loud as a ticking clock in an empty room in the wee hours past midnight. Technically, Stub was his boss, unless he was fired for abandoning his post as bartender the night before.

Stub saw Rusty's reflection in the mirror. "What are yu . . . you dah . . . doing here? There . . . there is no show to . . . to night."

After using a guest room to wash her face and tidy her hair—a moment to compose herself—Stella had come down to the Grotto where she knew everyone would be. She heard the silence of her piano man as she stepped into the room. They needed reassuring. She hadn't any news other than Earl was in trouble, his pain shaking the very bricks and beams that were the flesh and bones of the Rose.

"That's alright, Stub, Mr. Mayer was invited last night by Earl. Rusty, why don't we have a seat over here." She waved a welcoming hand towards a table away from everyone else. They walked over to the table. "Please give me a couple of moments, there are a few things I must do first."

Saying nothing about Earl she calmly walked over to the table where everyone sat silently; all eyes on her. "I know you all are concerned about Earl. I . . . I wish I could tell you something. I can't, I simply don't know. He's resting now. Henry is with him. All I know is that Earl hit his head on the police car and

145

must have some kind of concussion. I've called a doctor; he'll be here soon." She lied with all the best intentions, then cleared her throat as a sob tried to sneak out. "In the meantime, there are some changes that will have to be made, so bear with me."

She briefly glanced back at Stub.

"Mollie would you be kind enough to relieve Thaddeus at the reception desk and ask him to come down here. I have a need to speak with him."

Mollie dabbed her eyes, gave Oscar's wrist a reassuring squeeze, and then went up to reception with no questions asked.

Sy, sensing where everyone's heart was, reached down to the side of his chair and opened up his violin case. Searching the faces of each of his fellow musicians he began to play. It was soft, sweet, classical, neither joyful nor melancholy. It was something they all needed as they sat silently as the music wrapped their hearts and thoughts around Earl.

"Officer, look at this woman." Thaddeus insisted. "She looks like she's been run over by a runaway freight wagon. I've never liked her; can't say I feel much sympathy for her. She is a tough, nasty, cold—hearted bitch." He had come close to not using the word, but Beulah was a Bitch, no if's and but's about it, so in Ivory's defense the world was appropriate. "Look officer, Beulah is not one to hold back a punch. I suspect that whoever she tangled with is sporting some bruises and a few scratches wherever she could lay her claws. She was fired last night for good cause. Stella, one of the hotel's owners, had her escorted from the hotel by Ivory Burch, our Chief of

Security. Once out on the street he followed her to the end of the block to make sure she was gone. Mr. Burch was not gone long enough to do anyone any harm." Thaddeus shook his head at Beulah. "If he had gotten into a tussle with this . . . this woman, it would have showed on his person." He noticed that she was missing two fingernails. "It looks like whoever she tangled with will have some pretty fair scratches."

The officer noted the nails, something, to his embarrassment, he had missed on first inspection. "When Ivory returns from his rounds you can see for yourself. In the meantime, officer, would please see that this lying bitch . . ." his right eyebrow rose just a little to accent his meaning. "That the, uhmmm, lady would please wait outside. Her appearance and the smell of cheap whisky is disturbing to our guests."

"That's all right," replied the officer as he tucked his note pad in a shirt pocket. "You say that Mr. Burch was only doing his duty and shows no evidence of being in any form of a scrap is good enough for me."

"But? But, he did it, I told you," protested Beulah, her voice bringing a look of warning from the officer. When the officer started to take hold of her good arm to escort her from the building, she slapped him and stormed out of the building.

There hadn't been much spunk to the slap. The officer rubbed his cheek saying: "I see what you mean, I'll see that she doesn't bother you again."

Just as the door closed behind the officer, Mollie came up to relieve Thaddeus from the reception desk saying that Stella needed to see him.

Thaddeus figured that it had to be about Earl—worried to a frazzle he put the issue about Ivory and Beulah on the back burner and hurried down to the Grotto taking the elevator because he no longer trusted his balance on the stairs. The first thing he heard as he got off the elevator was the violin. What he saw was the gloomy musicians sitting around a barren table quietly waiting for the devil's postman to deliver more bad news.

Stella motioned for Thaddeus to take a seat at table on the opposite side of the room from where Rusty waited. She could see that Thaddeus was just as worried as everyone else. Thaddeus was a full partner—mostly silent by choice—in the hotel. He rarely gave any arguments regarding how the hotel was run, nor any of the profit-making schemes Earl came up with; even though some of them made him blanch. Everything always seemed to work out. Stella did not have her husband's insight and always tried to steer away from the business decisions. Now she was in charge and did not want to get ham-strung by a man who did not think women should have a voice in business—that—and he was stubbornly indecisive. She bit her lip as she struggled with her own indecisiveness. *This isn't going to be easy,* she thought as he approached the table. That was when she made the decision to just tell him what changes were going to be made, the decisions made, no further discussion needed.

With a determined stride, and a desperate yearning for a cigarette, she followed him to the table.

"Earl? How is . . ." Thaddeus asked as she sat across from him.

She touched his liver-spotted hand thanking him for asking. "He's asleep for right now. The doctor will be here a little later. Perhaps we'll know more then. Thaddeus, before Earl finally found some sleep, we had a talk. He asked me to see that things here at the Rose continue to run smoothly in his absence." The word absence was a hard one to hear let alone say. It sounded so permanent.

She glanced around the room at everyone anxiously watching her every move. We don't have time to debate or test out any of the changes needed. The decisions have been made. Okay?"

He nodded, having no idea as to what he was agreeing to.

"First, we are going to close The Martini Room, as well as the Hang-town Grill. All food and drink will be served here in the Grotto until we find better options. That will simplify things and save in labor costs. We will serve a light breakfast menu starting at . . . no, I take that back. We will no longer be open for breakfast; except of course for our musicians and hotel guests. They will get what the kitchen has prepared for them. Lunch will be served for the public with full bar service from 11:30 until 2:30. Oysters will still be the specialty of the house. Beer and well drinks, no mixed drinks including martinis."

"But we make a bundle on the martinis. How can we call it the martini room if we don't serve martinis?"

"As I said, The Martini Room will be closed, everything will be served in the Grotto. We will bring back the martinis for lunch service when we can."

It was a point worth discussion, but not today.

She took a breath. Why hadn't she brought any cigarettes?

"We will sell the Grill as soon as possible, hopefully for a little more than we still owe Beulah for it. Beulah has been fired and is to be arrested for trespass if she so much as opens the front door. We will not be paying her one thin dime until we sell the Grill. Agreed?"

Thaddeus opened his mouth, about to tell her about Beulah's recent visit with the policeman but was caught short.

"We are going to raise all of our room, food, and beverage rates by twelve percent starting as soon as we can get new menus printed." She did not know if twelve was the right percent; it could be less or more; she hadn't thought it out. It sounded good as she gave the number to Thaddeus.

"Next, we need to hire, or transfer someone on staff to the reception desk. You are going to be needed down here. I thought about Mollie, but without Earl we don't have a pianist. She is going to have to be a fast learner. For the time being Rusty's marimba will take lead, which means that he will become the leader. Everyone else is going to have to step it up. With Rusty on the marimba he can't bartend, which means someone is going to have to learn to make the martinis almost as good as he does—that's you. Okay?"

"I don't think . . ." It was a lot to take in and he was already having trouble wrapping his mind around it all.

"Good, now that is settled here comes the big one. We are going to have to pay Rusty a livable wage, which is one of the reasons we are raising all the prices. I don't know what that will be yet because if we pay Rusty, we are going to have to pay everyone else."

"Now wait a moment, we can't afford . . ."

She leaned forward and placed her finger across Thaddeus's lips to silence him. "Rusty can take part of his wages in room and board, same as everyone else. We will deduct the cost of room and board from everyone's paycheck. It will all work out, trust me."

All eyes were on Stella and Thaddeus. From the look on Thaddeus' face the question rose that they might be putting the hotel up for sale, or worse closing it.

Rosemary had other ideas. Rusty Mayer was not here to be part of any conversation about closing the Rose. And he sure wasn't here to buy it. Dark thunder silently raged across the room as she now saw Rusty as a personal threat her mind racing to do something about it; the thunder so loud she could not hear her own thoughts.

Thaddeus wanted to go back to bed, this was not the kind of day he had bought into. Earl was injured, how bad no one knew. Bad, he guessed. Now Stella was turning his world upside down. There was so much to take in—his worries about the money taking precedent over everything else.

"Thaddeus, look at me." Stella reached out placing her hand over his. "This is the way Earl wants it, and until he is back with all gears clicking, there will be no further discussion, the decisions have been made."

"All right Stella, until Earl gets better, then we'll take another look at everything." He did not know what else to say, he certainly did not want the responsibility; nor did he want to lose the Honeysuckle Rose. If they lost the hotel he might as well move into a coffin and wait to be lowered into the ground. He rose to take his leave before Stella tossed another bomb in his lap.

"Not yet, Thaddeus, we're not done yet. There is much, much, more." She waved for both Stub and Rusty to join them.

Seeing this, Rosemary guessed what everyone else missed. Rusty Mayer was not here to discuss martinis; especially after last night. Reacting to her intuition she excused herself to the powder room.

As food and beverage manager, Stella needed Stub's input on the tough decisions she was about to make. First, they had to know what kind of money they were talking about. If Rusty didn't agree to a reasonable wage, hopefully trading off part of that for room and board, they might not be able to afford to pay everyone else.

"What's going on?" Oscar asked from his seat at the barren table. He could hear the mumbled voices better than everyone else but couldn't quite make out what was being said. The tension around their table had risen, scaring him. When he had accepted Earl and Stella's invitation, he had taken it to mean that the Rose would be his home for as long as he remained standing. This was one of those times when he was glad that he could not see the storm clouds growing dark and threatening. Trouble, he could taste and smell it.

Ray grew noxious—unknown to everyone else he would have a harder time relocating; except for Oscar of course. He wasn't black, nor a Jap. He wasn't old and broke, at least not yet. He wasn't hideously ugly. He wasn't a woman—although he secretly liked to wear women's clothes. He wasn't a homosexual—at least he didn't think so. So far, he had been too afraid to find out. Having to move could be a dangerous thing—too dangerous to ponder. He glanced nervously at his drum set wanting desperately to lose himself in the rhythm and motion of the sticks.

Stella's smile was warm and quite remarkable considering the pain behind it. "Mr. Mayer, may I call you Rusty. We haven't actually met, but I heard you last night. Love your martinis. And . . . well, Earl thinks the world of you. Which is why he wanted to meet with you this morning." She hesitated, that sob she had checked earlier rearing its ugly head. Not now girl, you are doing just fine. Hang in there. Maybe one of his martinis will help. She thought as she almost lost it.

Stub knew that Stella was having a hard time keeping her emotions in check. He could see her struggle. He wanted to say something but couldn't—it wasn't his place.

"Earlier this morning," she continued, "we had an incident" She wanted to say a brutal, unprovoked, assault by bullying . . .

but she held back her anger. "Les Moore, our trombonist and Earl were injured. Les has a shattered knee-cap. Earl is resting, and for the moment I would prefer to say nothing more."

Her glistening eyes told him that Earl's condition was far worse than she was letting on. He took a slow glance at the rest of the musicians who looked like the Honeysuckle Rose were burning around them—caught in the terrifying headlights of the unknown. "For the time being I am the Captain and Master of the good ship Honeysuckle Rose." She did not waste a breath before adding "Rusty, I would very much like for you become a member of our musical family."

Rusty smiled wanting to shout out a jubilant 'Yippie,' however he was still afraid that they wouldn't offer him any kind of reasonable wage. He couldn't play for nothing. After last night he couldn't see coming back as a waiter or bartender.

"When we first took over the hotel, we had nothing coming in and put nothing down. It was all risk and Thaddeus took the most. For the last several years our musicians have taken their room and board here in exchange for their music. No one will give you an argument that we are all a bunch of odd-balls; talented odd-balls. Everyone here has sacrificed something to be part of Earl's vision." She looked at Thaddeus, her eyes cautioning him that he wasn't going to like what she was about to say. "Earl may not be returning to his piano anytime soon. Without his inspiration I'm not sure if we can continue—at least to draw the type of crowds we have been. We do have another pianist, but she is miles away from Earl. That leaves your marvelous marimba playing to take the lead, not just the sound, but the musical arrangements as Earl used to do. The blues, jazz, ballads, bebop they all had his signature. We're not going to try to compete with the blues Earl is feeling now. Here in the Grotto, for the time being, we are going to silence the blues, and it will be your job to give us a new voice for the Honeysuckle Rose Jazz Band. Can you do that?"

His answer was a carefully orchestrated nod; the *YIPPIE* harder to silence. He was being asked to take over, an opportunity he had never had before. Nothing yet had been said about money. It sounded like there might be more in this than he thought—if given the lead he would logically earn the bigger coin.

Stella passed a pencil and bar napkin to Stub. "Stub, would you write down for me the average wage your bartenders are getting as well as your own." Not being a musician Stub was compensated as their Food and Beverage Manager; minus an agreed upon amount for room and board. She then passed another napkin to Thaddeus. "Thaddeus, would you please write down the amount you and Earl agreed upon as being a fair exchange for the room and board." She had not been involved in that discussion and hadn't felt the need to know until now.

"Rusty, what is the union rate for working musicians now? Not for the leader, but for the average musician." She wasn't asking him to write it down, wanting Stub and Thaddeus to hear. The napkins were passed back after Rusty thought for a moment.

Rusty wondered if he was bargaining for his own wage. "Well, the union wage is a little better than average which is .75 cents an hour. Once you take away the union dues it often works out to be around .64 cents an hour. The union also regulates how many hours a musician can work." He stopped for a second and cocked his head curiously. "I heard you were all non-union here?"

"That's right," Stella answered, never giving a hint as to where she was going with this. She took a pencil to the numbers Stub and Thaddeus had given her. "0.75 an hour should average out to about $1,560 a year. The agreed upon rate for room and board is $45 a month. As food and beverage manager you are earning $150 a month, minus the $45 leaves you with $105 a month. Is that right?"

"Yes Mah . . . Mam, and a fair wage in . . . indeed considering that meals are included." Stub answered. It would be the best take home pay he had ever earned.

Stella did a quick check of her math. They had never paid any of their musicians. It had all been done on a handshake for room and board. Earl gave them each a ten-dollar bill for pocket money every few weeks. They also did not have a set number of hours to work; in truth if you counted rehearsals, they worked fifty to sixty hours a week. It was Earl's charisma, the sense of family, and their cutting edge of music that kept everyone here. That and they each had something like being black, Japanese, being a woman, or being Jewish that kept them from getting and keeping a regular paying job. The numbers, when added up, made her suck in her breath. If she paid them for what they did it would bankrupt the hotel. She made up her mind, based on Stubs earnings she would pay them each $125 a month which after a room and board deduction would give them each $80 a month. Counting Stub's and the wage she was prepared to offer Rusty that would make the average payroll week a whopping $350 to $400 a week. That was a lot of money, and it did not include kitchen, housekeeping, waiters, and the bartender's wages. The look on Thaddeus's face said it all. Would a ten percent price increase for food and beverage allow enough to make up for that? She didn't know.

Both Stub and Thaddeus shook their heads doubtfully. Without Earl, attendance might blow away like a piece of old newspaper in a squall. How much business could they afford to lose without losing it all? No one dared to think the thought that was nibbling on everyone's mind. *Earl? What if he never comes back? What if . . .?*

———

Imogene joined their death wake after having been on the telephone with the hospital. The silence, being what it was, she whispered the news. "Les' knee had been shattered and had just been taken into surgery. She had been reassured that he was not in any danger. His knee however would not. He would be needing three to four surgeries. He would be kept in the hospital for a couple of days and should be able to come home as soon as the swelling had reduced enough for his leg to be put into a full cast. The next surgery would be six to eight weeks out depending on how the injuries to his knee are responding. Never-the-less he would be in and out of that cast for the better part of a year. It was doubtful if his knee would ever function normally again." A stream of quiet tears followed each word. The good news was that Les would not being going to Korea. Further-more, being a veteran, his future surgeries could be transferred to Letterman Army Hospital where this type of surgery was now a well-honed art.

—

Rosemary didn't care that it was hard-hearted to be thinking the way she was. At the moment she could care less about Les. When Stella had told them that Earl wouldn't be with them for some time, she saw herself stepping into the number one spot. She would be the one to step into Earl's shoes; who else. It had not dawned on her until this morning that when Rusty had rolled out his marimba he had just aced her out of the job. That was why he was talking with Stella now. She was offering him her job.

She did not go to the powder room as she had said. With everyone's attention fully occupied she went behind the stage and took four of the wooden tone bars from the marimba back to the kitchen where she carefully split each one on their undersides with a sharp knife and a metal meat mallet. When she replaced them back on the marimba you could not see that the cracks were even there; they would never resonate anything but sour notes again. All of the tone bars would now need to be replaced in order for the instrument to resonate with any quality sound. Rusty would not be playing anytime soon.

Stella's mind flashed back to all the negatives. *What if? Earl had always taken care of things.* This side of the business was foreign territory for her. "Rusty would you please go and make me a large martini, the three of us need to discuss this for a moment."

Thaddeus was always scared about money; more like paranoid. Adapting to change wasn't easy and these days so much the worse. Being somewhat of a spendthrift he had trouble working with the numbers. He knew what their average take on a good night was. Dollars they did not have he couldn't add up in his mind. They could sit here all night and Thaddeus would not be able to envision the positive side of this.

"I know . . . I know, but guys, it's a fair deal. I'm afraid that if we do anything less than we will lose more than Henry." Henry, she had not added into the equation because Henry had gone into the army same as Les. Only that was all wrong. Les was in the hospital, and at least for the time being he would not be going into the army. She would have to adjust the numbers by one more because Les was still very much part of the Rose.

It dawned on her that Henry was upstairs with Earl. He had not reported into the army as he was supposed to. *Does that mean he is AWOL? Probably.* That added one more headache to her growing list. *Okay,* she thought, *Les is still in, and Henry is . . . is . . . What about Henry? Easy girl, one problem at a time.* She concentrated on the immediate issue. Where the hell was her martini? Her hand shook as she reached into her handbag for a cigarette she did not have. "If necessary, we can cut some of the housekeeping. Stub, can you find someone on the kitchen staff that might fit in at reception?"

"Oscar?" Stub asked.

"Are you kidding?" She almost laughed. She hadn't thought about Oscar in all of this. He was a poet, not a musician. Like Earl, he never left the hotel. He got free room and board. If he needed anything else Earl always found a way to keep him happy.

Thaddeus wasn't comfortable with the idea of paying out all that money. But he had to agree with Earl's thinking as conveyed by Stella. It was a good deal, everyone was family, and what choice did they have. Once you started losing people the whole gang might decide to take a hike—then what would we have. The Honeysuckle Rose would be forced to close without its music. Their music was the heart of it all. *The problem left was Rusty. Would he demand more money? Sure, he needed a job. He also had no loyalty and heart as everyone else had for Earl. Thaddeus was just beginning to see that. Would everyone accept Rusty as their new leader? Filling Earl's shoes was an almost impossible job.*

Rusty brought Stella one of the best martinis he had ever made. And a cigarette, which he lit. She lingered over it for a moment while she eyed the musicians across the room. After a couple of sips, she said. "Rusty, we would like to make you an offer. My offer is the same as what we are paying Stub including room and board; no more and no less."

Rusty embraced the opportunity full heartedly. He under-stood that they were taking a big gamble in taking him on. He really did not know Earl, which meant that in stepping into a blind man's shoes he was blind to the heart and soul of the man and his music. He looked over at the other musicians. "I'm not so sure these guys will accept me as their, well, hells bells, I'm no Earl Crier, that is for darned sure."

"I don't want you to even try to mimic my Earl, there is no one like him. If he does not return to his piano his greatest wish . . ." A sudden memory of the first time she had heard him play was followed by a sudden sickening panic. She flashed back to the day she had run away because she had been afraid of falling in love with him. When she had come to her senses he had disappeared. She had scoured San Francisco for months and had come up with only heartache. A tear teased the memory as she recalled the moment, he had come back to her and her mad frivolous race down the stairs dressed only in bubbles. She could not bear the thought of losing him again. She took two large sips of her martini as she tried to find her voice. The first word was a squeak which could be blamed on the martini. "His greatest wish... would be for the music to continue and flood the hallways of this grand old hotel with the music that is its life's blood. If . . . when . . . he returns to us he will understand that we had to create a whole new sound."

She looked at Thaddeus. "Now that that is settled, we are not going to let any dust settle on the top of our shoes." She took another sip. "This is one fine martini. Thaddeus, would you please go with Rusty to the bar where he will teach you how to make a martini as good as this. Stub, and I, are going over to where those anxious eyes are burning holes in my heart and share with them the news. If everyone is on board, we will all be over for a round of Thaddeus's martinis and you Mr. Mayer will have your first opportunity to bond with your band.

17
Handcuffed To A Nightmare

He was done running. Ivory stared across the street at the front door of the hotel. The scarred stub of his leg where it met his prosthesis had been rubbed raw. He was done running. With specks of powdered sugar and jam marking the edge of his mouth he took another bite of his jelly donut. It wasn't a bite, one finished off with a spot of tea, it was half of the donut which he chewed and swallowed as fast as he could manage. A chocolate one filled with sweet confectioner's cream tucked into a paper wrap waited in his free hand, the cream oozing through his fingers as he woofed down the first.

Being handcuffed by the police had brought out disturbing memories. The last time he had been handcuffed was by a Japanese soldier in a prison camp deep in the Philippine Highlands. Life had been horrific, as were the memories he now tucked deep within his subconscious, least they return and take the life of the camp's last survivor. Work had slowed in the tunnel the prisoners were being forced to dig; starvation the true cause. The Japanese said that it was sabotage.

Three prisoners were chosen at random—Ivory being one.

They had been handcuffed with their arms stretched to a breaking point from a beam at the top of what the prisoners called Tojo's Jungle Gym. No matter how hard they tried their feet, their toes, could not reach the ground. The pain, intense, as each man's weight stretched every muscle, the humerus threatening to pull away from the shallow ball-and-socket-style joint created by the humerus and scapula which allows the arm to rotate circularly and to move up and out from the body. Each man was whipped hard enough to draw blood, their wild thrashings ultimately too much for the soft tissue and fibrous ligaments. Two of the men became useless as slave labor as their arms were torn from their sockets. Mercifully, they passed out before an officer's sword decapitated them.

The message that the Japanese would not brook idleness or sabotage clear in its harsh reality to the rest of the shaken POW's who had been forced to witness their ordeal. Ivory, smaller, lighter, and stronger than the prisoners who had died on Tojo's Jungle Gym had suffered his agony in stoic silence. His arms had not yet detached from their sockets when the Japanese officer respected his stoicism and spared his life.

To be handcuffed again had been traumatic. The nightmares that raged deep within his mind he had buried deep, least the worst of them destroy his fragile hold on sanity. If he had been left in the handcuffs too long, beaten or man-handled, he might have lost that fragile grip. Once freed, his head down, eyes on the ground, never reaching any of the police officer's eyes, bowing in deference to an all-powerful authority, he slowly backed away. Once far enough away, mostly forgotten as other issues were being settled, he turned and walked away, his walk becoming faster until it became a mindless sprint, a race away from torturous memories to nowhere, anywhere safe. The ghost of Sergeant Ware ran beside him, watching each step, his hollow eyes beckoning him to run no matter how hard his heart pounded in his chest, his lungs laboring to find each breath. In his mind's eye he did not see the city streets, the buildings, people turning curious of his passing. He did not hear the distant clang of the cable cars. He saw the jungle path where he had once run only steps ahead of heavily armed Japanese soldiers who only wanted to kill him.

A man running with a limp is both curious and to be admired. A man running with an artificial leg is an oddity, courageous—if one knew of his burden, to be amazed.

San Francisco is a city of steep hills.

And still he ran . . .

The endless hard pounding on cement sidewalks up one hill then down another caused the metal of his artificial leg to tear at the scar tissue that allowed him to wear it. The scar tissue began to wear through as tiny patches of blood began to show on the exterior of his pants. Finally, at the top of the first hill, from which he could overlook the Golden Gate Bridge, he stopped. Rasping, his lungs sucking in air, sobs consuming him, he had run as far as he needed to as the Sarge turned and walked away leaving him one more time to be the last man standing. No one had promised that life would be easy.

It took a while for Ivory to regain control of his labored breathing, to realize what he had done, and how far he had come. He remembered that Les had been hurt, that Earl had fallen, but not that he had been injured. Finally, he rubbed his wrists where the handcuffs had been and began the long trek home.

His eyes searched the windows and doors of The Honeysuckle Rose Hotel as he stuffed the sugary donuts into his mouth. *Was he safe? Were the police waiting for him? What of Les? Earl?* He almost choked as a flickering memory of the handcuffs crossed his mind. Sucking the cream from his fingers he opened the door to the bakery and crossed the street to the Rose.

18

A Shrew's Revenge

Beulah is not the gentlewoman everyone thought they knew when she owned the neighborhood cafe next door to the Rose. Beneath her beloved June Allyson like smile she was a violent, overbearing personage, a bristling porcupine whose quills she has purposefully sharpened to inflict as much pain as she might wish on anyone who might dare to cross her. Relentless as she was angry, her venomous hostility now focused fully on Stub, who had been her immediate boss, and Stella who had dared to challenge her—and won.

After her attempt to bring assault charges against Ivory failed, she immediately focused her wrath on Stub who had the unpleasant responsibility of being the food and beverage manager and her former boss. Her vent on Ivory had been short lived. She now saw Ivory as an impotent little man, who had only been doing the Queen-bee's biddings. His strength as a male was the only thing, she was truly wary off. In her mind he was nothing more than a mental and physical cripple who by her standards deserved less pity than a mongrel dog. Stub, the stuh . . . stah . . . stuttering idiot had strutted his mousiness over her when he thought he had been her superior. He was not and now she planned on putting him in his proper place-unemployed and homeless on the streets.

She sat alone in a small house out on Collins Street, off Geary, she had inherited from her alcoholic mother. Not much had changed over the years, the furniture worn, floor rugs faded and torn, dust and cobwebs that had been there when her mother had sat in the same chair chain smoking while drinking cheap gin.

There had been a time in her life when Beulah had managed the booze. She had never quit drinking. AA—Alcoholics Anonymous - was not for her. There had been only one person who had had enough influence on her to keep the devil at bay; Archie. He was a no-good bum who went through jobs faster than a hummingbird sprinted through a field of nectar-sweet wildflowers. He didn't smoke, drink, or swear. He wasn't a Holy Roller by any means. Perhaps over the years, when others needed these vices, he had been too poor to waste money on tobacco or booze. What money he had in his pocket came from Beulah's purse. She overlooked what he took, it was never that much, and when he did, she told herself that the coins he took were small compared to what a lot of men did to their women.

Then one day, when she had closed the cafe early because of the trouble the musician's union was giving the Honeysuckle Rose Hotel, she had found Archie at home . . . in bed . . . their bed . . . adding insult to injury he was in bed with another man. She had witnessed what she considered to be a most foul and vulgar deed. If only it had been another woman; she could understand that. Not forgive. That was when Archie had broken her heart. She drove both men out with the threat of a meat cleaver naked onto the street. After they had stopped pounding on the door, she had thrown their shoes out the door burning the rest of their clothes in the fireplace. Archie never returned to claim what little else he had. Whatever happened to him she neither cared nor heard as she fed her wrath with gin and packs of cigarettes one after another. She was angry at the world and the more she drank the angrier she became.

Beulah lit a cigarette from the still hot end of the one she had just finished, took a long pull directly from the bottle, any glasses lost in a mountain of unwashed dishes that littered the kitchen. She then dialed the first number from a list of numbers that sat on the table in front of her. The first was the fish monger who did most of the fish deliveries for the Grotto at the Honeysuckle Rose Hotel. "Antonio, am I too late to add a few more items for today's delivery to the Grotto?"

"It's okay, your order is just being loaded onto the truck now." He called out to someone across the warehouse. "Harry, aspetta un momento, ho un ulteriore ordine per la Grotta. Si . . . Si, the driver will wait. What is it you want?"

The normal weekday order for fresh salmon was twelve to fifteen pounds. She added forty more plus six large bags of fresh oysters. Finishing with: 'Don't worry about the ice, hon, we have plenty. We'll put it to good use as soon as it gets here."

She hung up the phone then lit another cigarette, even though the one she had just lit a moment prior still burned in the nearby ashtray. She dialed the number to the butcher shop where she planned on ordering two hundred of their best and most expensive streaks. She was going to drown the Grotto with excessive orders that would break the bank. The only person to blame would be their food and beverage manager—Stub Wilcox.

19
Bruised Gin and Flounder

Rusty pretended not to listen to Stella talk with Stub as he introduced Thaddeus to the art of martini making. "Now this is important, one doesn't just pour a martini. The pour is slow and easy, so you do not bruise the gin. The same is true when it is made with vodka or shaken with ice. Gentle. Gentle. Me, I never use vodka. If someone asks, ignore them. Our martinis are made with Holy Mother Gin, with no substitutions." He poured a martini hard, if not barbaric. "Now you taste this, then we'll make one the right way."

Bruised? Thaddeus didn't get it. *How do you bruise booze?* He tasted the first, it tasted like a perfectly good martini to him. He hadn't drunk too many martinis in his day and didn't care much for the taste. But Stella needed him to learn how make them, so he would give it his best effort. Not true, he did not want the job, but under the circumstances what choice did he have. He would give it a couple of days, once Stella figured out that he couldn't mix a martini worth a damn, that would be that.

What next? Stella thought. *Another martini, a hot bath, and lock the door behind me.* Her most urgent desire was to go upstairs to see how Earl was doing.

He would sleep for some time. If there was a change, she trusted that Henry would call. Which reminded her that Henry was AWOL; that too could wait. She needed to talk to the band. She looked in their direction. Rosemary was absent, as was Mollie who was at reception replacing Thaddeus. She would give Rosemary a moment. She set her martini down as she turned towards the kitchen. The changes in the kitchen and food service would impact Roane, their newly promoted head chef, before anyone else.

Hearing the chef come in Rosemary slipped out a side door of the kitchen having done as much damage to the wooden marimba keys as she could.

Everyone's eyes were on Elsie, Sy's violin, as they waited for Stella to dump whatever news she had on them. Ray was sitting at just the right angle to catch a slight movement as someone appeared to have left the kitchen slipping quietly behind the stage. Kitchen staff would have no business going back there, which is what caused him to be curious. A moment later he saw that it had been Rosemary as she returned to her seat. He did not say anything because it wasn't his nature. Still, she was the one member of the group that made him uncomfortable. If she knew anything about his secret, she was just mean enough to spill it to the world. He turned his eyes away, not wanting to give her cause for anything. *What was she hiding? And why?*

She saw that Ray had seen her, her eyes guarded, careful not to look back, she debated whether or not he was a threat. Ray a threat, hardly. She normally considered him as a non-entity, left him in that space, as she retraced her steps in sabotaging the marimba and if that would be enough to stop Rusty. She had no idea what it would cost to fix it, but it had to be more than he could afford.

It did not take long for Ivory to figure out that something of importance was happening and he was out of the loop. He looked around for Henry or Less, then remembered that one or both of them had been hurt. *Earl! Where is Mr. C? What is Rusty doing with Thaddeus? Thaddeus doesn't bartend.*

Everyone else gloomily silent, which is what brought him back to a heightened concern for Earl. He called out after Stella as she and Stub disappeared behind the kitchen doors.

Roane knew from the previous night's near fiasco that outside of staff meals they would not be open to the public today. He needed to talk to Eva Marie, who he wanted as his new Sous Chef, and pass her promotion through Stub as soon as possible. The good news was that Lola Chiapello, his best prep-worker, was already busy putting together a waffle, bacon, and scrabbled egg breakfast for the band and resident staff. Everyone else had the day off. Hotel guests would have to fend for themselves somewhere in the neighborhood.

———

"Roane, good morning, I'm glad you are here," Stella said as the kitchen doors swung shut behind her.

The bacon smelled good. She grabbed a crispy slice as she practically dragged the chef towards the elevator. "I need you and Eva to inventory all foods left in the grill as well as the Martini Room and see that it is properly stowed here in the kitchen. Move staff around as you see fit, then give notice to anyone who doesn't fit into the plan."

Roane nodded knowingly seeing to need to interrupt or add anything as he nibbled on some bacon while taking in her every word.

—

A delivery truck pulled up in the alley. The driver hopped up onto the delivery platform and punched the call-button bell then opened the back of the truck to unload the fish as he waited for someone to slid open the delivery door to the Honeysuckle Rose Hotel and Grotto.

Stella continued her monologue, much of which Stub and Roane already knew, as the service elevator door closed behind them. "We will be closed to the public both today and tomorrow which should give you enough time to come up with a new menu; your way. You know what works and what hasn't. If the New York Steak has been marginal than strip it out. We will have to talk about the pricing. You and Stub get together this afternoon about what equipment you want to keep from the grill and Martini Room. The grill is up for sell. The Martini Room will be closed until we decide otherwise. Make sure you get orders based on the new menu out before the end of the day."

The elevator door opened as Stella continued barely taking

a breath.

Ivory arrived too late. "Where is Stella?"

"She, Stub, and the chef just went up to the grill.

The delivery bell buzzed.

"Ivory can you get that, I've got waffles on." Lola asked. "It's most likely our regular delivery. Stub will check it in as soon as he can."

While the band was still waiting for word from Stella, she was beginning to feel that things were slowly finding their own level of normalcy. Panic and crisis no longer seemed to be their sole guiding force.

—

The only way to reach the receiving dock was the service elevator from the kitchen which took him up to street level. Ivory slid open the delivery door to find buckets overflowing with fish waiting to be received. And a hell of a lot of it too. He did not know where the house order list was to match the delivery bill. He hadn't a clue that the salmon had been changed to flounder. The Grotto had never served flounder, which without being on ice, would spoil quicker than salmon. Beulah had called back and switched the fishes giving the fish monger no time to realize this was a peculiar order. Ivory eyeballed the buckets to see that the numbers matched the driver's delivery manifest and signed off leaving the fish on the loading dock—sans ice. He had never been involved in orders or deliveries that was Stub's responsibility. The driver seemed okay with everything. After signing for the delivery, Ivory was off to the grill to find Stella.

The first piece of news he received was about Earl and Les. That was enough to put everything else on second burner as he hurried off to Stella and Earl's suite to see for himself.

20
A Tornado of Swirling Darkness

Henry sat by Earl's side waiting. Waiting for what? For Earl to wake; that might be for hours. He might not wake at all. He suspected that Earl had some sort of a concussion, perhaps a stroke. If he awoke to the pain and hysteria, he had experienced, then perhaps it would be best if he passed away more peacefully. God knows what his mind was experiencing even now as he slept the medication preventing him from screaming out for help. Henry had had enough battlefield experience with head injuries to know that all he could do was wait. A doctor would only tell him the same.

He had said nothing about his suspicions to Stella, only that he would wait by Earl's side and call her if there was any change for the better—or worse. He was hungry but had no appetite. Thoughts outside this room were irrelevant, not needed, or wanted. The power of love and prayer was all he had, and he had no wish to break that concentration.

When you are blind and medicated it is sometimes difficult to tell if you are awake or dreaming. Earl's last thoughts had been trapped in a horrid nightmare which was not a dream. His only connection were his own screams as he was thrown about in a tornado of swirling darkness. The last thought he tried to grasp and call his own was Stella's voice. He did not know if he was dead, alive, or somewhere in-between. If only he could grasp and hold onto her hand. No Stella. At the moment he has no thoughts, his heart and mind empty for once of thought, his music silent. There was only swirling darkness and a barely audible wind that came from nowhere taking him to the same place. He had a sudden sense of falling as those microscopic little lights that he had seen before returning, dancing, laughing at his helplessness.

Earl's hands flayed the air, searching. His mouth open, with no words coming out. The look that came from a blind man's eyes were enough to tear Henry's heart out as he grasped both of Earl's hand, not knowing if his grasp was of any comfort.

Earl felt Henry's grasp just for a moment. Henry had leaned in the best he could cradling him as a concerned father might an injured child. Earl did not know who it was, only that it wasn't Stella's. He called out for her, but that cry could only be heard in his mind.

Henry held on.

21
Right Hug At The Wrong Time

The door partially open Ivory cautiously peeked in at the moment Henry enveloped Earl in a deeply emotional hug. Ivory's feet grew roots into the old hall runner and floor beneath—until that moment he could not have guessed how bad Earl's condition was. From where he stood, he could not help but wonder if he had just seen his beloved Mr. C. die. It was the way Henry held him and the way Earl hung loose in his arms. Ivory's face tightened with pain as he slowly grasped the doorway so as not to fall to his knees. He stared wordlessly at the scene before him with deep sadness, loneliness, and fear. There was not a word he could utter that would describe . . .

Henry had seen his reflection in a glass picture frame that set upright on a dresser near the window. His words were soft and meant to be reassuring to Ivory and to Earl. "He is still with us, but I don't know where. He is grasping through drug induced sleep for help. There is nothing more I can do but hold him to let him know that I am here. Ivory, would you please go and tell Stella that she is needed by his side. Be careful not to alarm her, just tell her that he is not resting easy and needs her reassurance."

Ivory had been there, close to where Earl was now.

It had been Earl who had lifted him from that dark place closest to death without tasting its bittersweet wine. Ivory thought as he stood frozen in place trying to grasp a difficult reality. What? He suddenly felt lost; helpless. Afraid, more for himself than Earl. Earl was his rock, when Ivory's own sanity teetered on the edge.

"Now, please." This time Henry's voice was less reassuring, more urgent.

Exhausted, whatever color Stella had left in her alabaster skin paled, when she caught the look on Ivory's face as he came into the room.

"Stella, its Earl . . ." Ivory said uneasily. The news ominous, Stub dropped a glass. Ivory's words fell hard. Stella's world, the moment in time, her heart, everything that mattered, stumbled, then stopped on that thought. She leaned back on a counter for support as her legs almost went out from beneath her. At that moment she saw nothing but Ivory's face. She hated him for fear of what he was about to say. Her words came deep from her inner soul as they slipped out at the same time as those, she whispered allowed. *Please God, NO! Not now, anything but my Earl.* The word that came out said it all; "Earl?" She shook her head from side to side as if that could erase what she desperately did not want to hear. *No, don't you dare . . .*

Ivory realized when he heard the anguish in Stella's voice that he had somehow brought great sadness and pain.

"Is he . . . gone?" Where her words.

"Gone?" Ivory didn't know. Anything could have happened in the short time he had left Henry holding his mentor and best friend. Earl and Stella were his family, more so than his parents had ever been. The reason he had joined the marines was to get away from his pathetic home where his father, a good-for- nothing alcoholic, berated him as a good for nothing little shit on a daily basis. He had come out of the marines a beaten man—a dead man barely walking. His physical being wasting as his will to live sought the door to oblivion; that was until Earl and Stella had given him their unconditional love, support and friendship. He did not know what had happened to Earl to put him in such desperate straits.

Ivory did not want to be the bearer of bad news especially since he had no news. Now Stella looked at him with the deepest anguish he could ever imagine. His mouth opened and closed wordlessly as he searched in vain for something remotely appropriate to say before he finally gasped: "No! No, Earl is . . ." He didn't know. "Henry sent for you because . . . damn my soul, what am I supposed to say?"

Taking Stella's hands in his, Stub also thought that Ivory had become the unwitting bearer of the Grim Reaper's hateful passage.

"Henry said that Earl is waking and thought you might want to be there." Ivory gasped; but not before Stella slapped him so hard, she practically knocked his words right back down his throat.

She faltered as she raised her hand to strike him again.

"Stella . . . stah . . . stop." She had pulled her hand from Stub's so fast he had had no time to stop her.

Chef Roane, aghast and troubled by the mind-numbing turn of events, stepped back as far as he could go until his way was blocked by a prep-sink. He was a good- natured man who had never found a way to deal easily with his own emotions yet alone others. He squeezed his right hand shut, as if that motion alone could capture and render everything that was bad as harmless as a trapped fly. This time the fly painfully bit back as the paring knife he had been holding sliced deeply into his palm. "God damn," he yelped with an airy gasp of pain. The knife slicing through his flesh hadn't hurt at that moment as it did when he opened his closed first dripping dark red blood.

Stella took the same hand which she had used to slap Ivory to cover her lips to block other hateful angry words, that were hard to choke back. Her eyes squeezed shut as she realized what she had done. Her heart steadied as she came to terms with why she had been angry; and most importantly that her husband needed her. Her most urgent need was to run to her husband's side, but not before she managed to get herself together long enough to say she was sorry.

Ivory saved her the moment, her eyes said enough.

"No harm done, Stella," Ivory said, his cheek still stinging. "You go to Earl. Stub, would you fill me in here. I feel like an empty hat. What has happened to Mr. C.?"

He got no answer.

22

The Beat, Beat, Beat
of The Tom-Tom

Sy put a cupped hand to his ear. "Listen. Do you hear it? The damned silence is enough to make this old hotel weep." He pronounced with a soft but provoking voice as if everyone were waiting for a coffin to be lowered into the ground. He brought his hand down slowly as he let the silence speak for itself. Wakened from their doldrums everyone looked at the old man each with their own individual face of curiosity.

"You youngsters know that I'm the new kid here." He chuckled. "But, like it or not, I'm going to throw in my two cents worth under the presumption that we will be playing together tonight, tomorrow night, and the night after that." His facial expression suggested that they would be together for a long time to come. "The other day Stella was telling me that the first thing Earl did when they bought The Honeysuckle Rose Hotel was to fling open every door to let the music course through each hallway, every room, and even her god-damned plumbing. Well, that is what we are going to do right now.

We are going to open all the doors, and we are going to play until it reaches and courses right through Earl's veins until it touches his heart."

Everyone looked at each other as the misery on their faces shape-shifted into purposeful smiles.

"Yes . . . s," the word was long and drawn out. Sy's aged and crackled voice seemed to reach out from somewhere in the great beyond and drew them in. "We are going to have to improvise. Each one of you has the heart and the experience to bring it together." Sy picked up his violin and began to play, but this time it was his voice that led.

> *'Like the beat, beat. beat of the tom-tom*
> *When the jungle shadows fall . . .'*

"Ray you come in soft then bring up the tempo.

> *'As it stands against the wall . . .'*

He brought down his violin. "Rosemary, you come in with your cello, deep, rich, and mysterious. Play through the stanza twice. Cello and drum, that's it."

> *'Like the drip . . . drip . . . drip . . .'*

"Vocal again here, bass, drums, and tenor sax." Sy pointed lightly towards Michael O'Dea. "You come in here, like the sun rising to warm the frosty morning dew. Imogene you take the vocals from here."

'So, a voice within me . . . '

Thaddeus was not going to learn to make a great martini. He didn't care and was just going through the motions. As he heard Sy's voice Rusty made the decision to cut the martini lesson and tend to the music. For the moment he would not say anything about his role as the band's new leader. It was more important that they were moving, wanting to play, to get out of their premature mourner's clothes. The elderly violinist continued to surprise him. "Thaddeus," he said as he excused himself to join the band, "you're doing fine. Will take it up again later."

Sy paused.

Sometimes it took a moment or two for his thoughts to catch up with him; or was it the other way around. *Damn they needed a better piano.* He couldn't hear Mollie coming up with the magic needed here. He had almost forgotten the marimba. There was no question the marimba was needed, but he wasn't sure if Rusty had a place here. No one had any idea why Rusty was here, or if he was joining the group. God knows without a piano they needed the marimba. *Well,* he thought, *until told differently the marimba is in.* "Mr. Mayer, you come in with Imogene."

While everyone gathered on stage and positioned their instruments Rusty hurried backstage to bring out the marimba. He would need several different mallets testing one on the wooden keys. 'Ouch,' several weren't sounding true—real clinkers. Upon further inspection he discovered the cracks, man-made, beneath. For a moment his thoughts grew dark, disappointed, then desperate. God must have heard him for on the floor was a musician's case marked marimba. Inside were spare parts including replacement keys for most of the marimba.

Someone did this deliberately, he thought. Not wanting to waste a moment he placed the case on top of the marimba and rolled it out to his place in front of the stage. Without looking up at his fellow musicians he rumbled through the case finding all but one of the damaged keys, that one he left off knowing he could play around it.

You are doing great old timer, Sy thought to himself, *I'll just sit in for now and see where this is all going.* Ready, he glanced up at the stage where everyone was thoughtfully going over their parts in an improvisation of a popular and well-known tune. No one paid him any notice but Rosemary who apparently had been watching his every move; while perhaps pretending not to.

Sy set his sights thoughtfully on the ceiling. *Why he had stepped up and taken the leadership he couldn't quite fathom. He should just stick to dancing the dance with Elsie, his violin. He was too old and tired for anything else. He was after all, the new kid—well maybe not as new as Rusty. Still, he should have asked. Stella? She might be their employer, but she wasn't a musician. Oscar?*

Stella had told him that in the beginning Oscar and Earl had played and sang together. As did Henry, but for now the army has him. His thoughts came back to Oscar. *No,* Stella had told him how he and Earl had bellowed and brawled like two bull sea lions during rutting season. *One day and one song at a time, we've got a hell of a lot of improvising to do without*

Earl at his piano. His eyes set on Oscar who had been sitting quietly—just waiting of someone to clue him in.

"Ready?" Michael asked.

Startled from his thoughts Sy turned with a slightly awkward motion. "What? Oh, yes . . . give me one moment." Without Mollie's assistance, Sy needed almost as much help as Oscar did as he left the stage to bring Oscar up. He sat Oscar where he normally sat when delivering his poetry. "Oscar," he announced, "has agreed to opening the set with his marvelous poetic verse."

"I did?" Oscar said with obvious delight.

"You do know the lyrics?" Sy asked.

"Yes, just as well as I know the sun will come up tomorrow." The laugh returned was friendly and contagious.

"Fine, would you please begin at my first note." Readying his violin Sy took in each of the musicians. Rusty raised a mallet to let Sy know that he was ready.

Oscar repeated his part over and over in his mind so as not to forget any of the words.

"Elsie, my dear, shall we begin," he whispered to his beloved violin as he tucked her close to his chin and began to play.

"Like the beat-beat-beat . . ." Oscar's rich voice caressed the semi-darkened room with words that brought memories, mysteries, and romance opening to a universe of powerful musically induced emotions. Each instrument joined in as if they had played exactly this way until it was easy perfection.

Imogene stole the moment challenging the musicians—their instruments—to sing with her:

'Night and day, you are . . . .'

Thaddeus went to open up all the doors around the hotel as the music began to break the death grip Earl's accident had brought to every nook and cranny.

Rosemary missed a few notes as she switched between the cello and her bass.

The marimba played with perfection.

"With the beat-beat beat ...."

Upstairs, Mollie's eyes rolled softly as Oscar's voice and the first stands of music drifted up from the Grotto. She was one who always wore her emotions close to the surface. Today's reservoir of tears flowed easily as she knew what no one else did; that everything would be all right . . .

23
Nothing To Do But Wait

Stella knelt by her husband's side taking his hand in hers searching for a pulse. There was a hesitancy here for she feared she wouldn't find what she needed most. She gave his hand a loving squeeze followed by a lingering soft kiss to his palm. She could feel his heartbeat but doubted that he knew she was there.

If there was any good news it might be that he was in a deep enough medicated sleep that he most likely would not be troubled by the vertigo and the powerful headache that had brought him to the point of screaming from the pain. As she hurried upstairs, it had sounded from Henry's message that Earl was waking. She now looked at Henry who shook his head and nodded. "For a moment I thought that he might be waking up prematurely from under the meds." Both he and Stella knew that if that happened the shock of waking back into the disorienting vertigo and pain could cause immediate stress on his blood pressure and heart. The only thing worse would be for her Earl to wake up under those same conditions in a hospital; that was why she had not called a doctor. Stella would rather give her own life than lose her husband. For Earl to lose his mind would be something far worse than death. She sat there quietly stroking his forehead and hair. "Oh, my darling blues man, whatever are we to do?" She whispered; the whisper unnecessary.

"Any word on Les?" Henry asked, his words neither a whisper nor a conversation. They sat quietly, neither sharing their thoughts or pained glances. Their silence thickened as they listened to Earl breath with little conscious effort. "Not much," Stella finally answered. She had not been told anything, but as a nurse she could pretty much guess Les' prognosis. "He will need a few surgeries and mending will take some time. The army won't be needing him now."

"Bastards!"

Stella heard the rage and anger tied up into a knot within that one-word Henry had uttered. "Yes, those god-damned fucking bastards," she replied her hand shaking as she released Earl.

Henry almost smiled at Stella's verbiage. Language like that was just something Stella did not do, but this time it was so true.

Tears glistened in her eyes, as they did Henry's as she fought to keep her deep well of anguish from spilling over. She blinked three times as the first strands of music drifted up from the Grotto reaching out to them. They exchanged small smiles as she rose. "Earl may not be hearing our words," she said. "He surely will hear the music and love coming his way."

"I'll stay," Henry said, not that there was ever a question.

"I know," Stella whispered barely loud enough for him to hear as she left the room. The music grew clearer with each step that separated her from her cantankerous bluesman, the love of her life.

His mind set on his bed-ridden best friend it hadn't occurred to Henry that he and the United States Army were going to have to have a serious conversation.

24
Everyone Needs A Nightingale

It all sounded good; the music. Sure, their hearts were not into it. Earl was the glue that held them all together. Music was their very heart and soul and they didn't need a psychic to tell them that that was where their healing had to begin. What they had just played sounded good, but it was lacking heart and soul.

While he would not admit it Sy knew that there were more troubles knocking on their door than Earl's dire condition. If the musicians who now looked to him for guidance didn't each find their own hearts than the dark buzzards who circled overhead would peck away at them until their hearts all burst like so many balloons.

One of the buzzards was flying a bit low for his comfort and he wondered if anyone else had noticed Rosemary's fumble. While he had not been at the Honeysuckle Rose for long, he understood that Rosemary was the bloated ego in the room.

Each of these people carried a burden when they had arrived at the Rose. Les Moore was a poor black man from the South.

Stub stuttered. Michael was ugly. Sy was more likely counting the hours rather than days before his ticket expired. Each, in their own way had put these handy-caps aside and given to Earl the only thing he asked—the music that flowed straight from their hearts shared without reservation; an unselfish blending of the amazing talent God had given them.

Then there was Rosemary. She did not share easily anything with anyone. Rosemary wanted—needed—to be better. She was more than a perfectionist and thus unforgiving of anything less than perfection in herself. The problem being that no one is perfect and there was an anger growing within her because she wasn't and thus not getting her just due. For now, she directed her self-perpetuating wrath at Mollie, the sweetest gal in the whole damn town. But that was changing and soon venting on Mollie would not be enough.

Sy nodded at Rusty as if he expected him to say something. Rusty smiled back leaving Sy with the baton. For a brief second Sy's eyes locked on the vacant space where a key went missing from the Marimba. An accident? He did not think so.

"It sounded good," Sy said with honest appraisal. "Shall we do it again? Oscar, you ready?" He shouldered his violin as he intentionally stole a glance at Rosemary whose rage buzzed like so many angry yellow jackets around her.

Thaddeus had no qualms in retreating back to the registration desk. If he stayed at the bar the next thing Stella would be wanting him to learn is how to make gimlets.

Mollie looked at Thaddeus with expectations that he had

something to tell her.

Thaddeus knew what she was looking for. A lot had happened this morning, changes were coming that would shake the old hotel and everyone in it right down to its foundation. Would their family hold together or was this the beginning of the end?

Mollie knew that she had already lost Rosemary and the thought of losing everyone else almost too much to bear. She knew that Thaddeus could be cantankerous and stubborn. Everyone knew that his mind was slowly slipping away. But this cold indifference . . . it just made her want to slap him.

What kept Thaddeus from saying anything was that his thoughts—so . . . so many of them were all jumbled together, and he couldn't sort them out. Embarrassed by his own silence he finally found a word. "Martinis."

Mollie was as confused by what he had said as he was by its utterance. "Martinis?" The thought slipped away as abruptly as a dust devil on a warm summer's day. He really has lost his mind, she thought as her lips quivered with frustration.

"I'm not going to make them." His rummy hound-dog eyes turned away from the mail and key boxes as he positioned himself behind the registration desk. "Martinis. Stella will just have to find someone else. This is where I belong. This . . ." He looked sheepishly into Mollie's eyes. "Child, it will all be explained in time. You had better go down with the others. Stella, she . . . she . . . you just go on down to the Grotto."

The phone rang.

Thaddeus, who preferred to not want to deal with anything else for the moment, let it ring. It rang four times before Mollie, who was about to take the stairs down to the Grotto, turned about. "Damn it, Thaddeus, answer the phone. It could be news about Les." Thaddeus ignored the phone and Mollie as he checked the mail that had already been sorted and placed in their proper boxes. She answered. "This is the Honeysuckle Rose Hotel. Mollie speaking."

"Mollie, why is you answering the phone? Never mind, this is Lloyd William Jones over at the Alley Cat. Tell me it's not true, girl. Earl? Word is that the cops have nearly beat him to death. I hear Les is in the hospital too."

—

Not wanting anyone to see herself fall into a catatonic self-pitying tear fest, Stella stopped the elevator between floors. She was as close as one could get to that overwhelming tear fest as she pounded her fist on the inside of the elevator's door. It wasn't hard enough to hurt her hand. It was a soft tap, almost afraid to be heard, as she knocked on the door to her heart. "Please God, give me the strength . . . it's all I ask, just . . ." Her plea, a whisper, she remembers herself pounding on the metal bed frame, asking the same, when the first critical burn patients arrived from Pearl Harbor. How helpless she had felt. How small and unprepared. Her pounding faded to a tap; her fist opened as it slowly fell once more down to her side.

If there is a God, she sent Stella a simple answer to her prayer, as she one again heard the music they were playing for Earl; the music that bound them all together. Closing her eyes tightly, she let out a long slow breath, then tapped the start button lightly once. As the elevator began to move, she stepped back into the center of this slowly moving metal box, patted her hair down the best she could as she straightened her posture hoping to appear poised—if not in control.

Thankfully there was no mirror.

"Mollie, wait up, please." Stella had deliberately stopped the elevator at the lobby floor catching Mollie just before she would have taken the stairs down to the Grotto.

Still feeling some angst from her not-so conversation with Thaddeus, Mollie pushed her own problems aside. Stella was carrying everyone's load while at the same time needing a lot more support than she would ever admit. As they stood in front of the stairwell each embraced the other. "Earl?" Mollie inquired with a caring younger woman's heart.

Stella softly broke their embrace keeping Mollie's hands in hers. "No change, perhaps that is a good thing." She answered. "For now, no more questions, there is a lot to be done, and quite a bit I must ask of you."

Mollie nodded that she understood, although being told not to ask any questions was tough. She freed one hand as she tossed back her hair the way she did when she was caught in an awkward situation and did not want the confusion written in her face and eyes to show.

Stella knew this as she gave Mollie's remaining hand a squeeze that said *don't worry; everything will be all right.* "I'm about to share what has, or is, about to change for everyone in the Grotto, so I won't duplicate everything here. What I need from you—dearest Mollie is for you to continue giving what you do best—sharing your heart and positive spirit. First, I want you to move out of your room with Rosemary today; as soon as soon as you can, we need to cut the tension. I'll take care of Rosemary. Your new room will be next to Oscar's. Sy will move out of the room he is sharing with Henry to one near you and Oscar. When Les returns he will be in a room between you and Sy. These all have a private bath. Each of our wounded birds need their own nightingale as you must be for each. Keep the connecting guest doors between each unlocked so you can see to each as needed."

"When Les returns I suspect that he will be in a whole leg caste for some time and you will both have to get used to your nurse-like empathy as you help him dress and other matters sometimes more delicate."

Mollie's eyes glistened as she gladly accepted her charges. *Gosh, it's wonderful to feel needed.*

"As of Monday, everyone is going to be paid for the work they do around here. The pay is the same for everyone; I'll explain downstairs. If you need anything to help Sy, Oscar, and Les, you let me know and we'll find a way to make it happen. Okay?"

Mollie started to nod . . .

"Next. I know that you are classically trained. You have done a wonderful job backing Oscar's poetry. Rusty's Mayer is going to take Earl's place as the band's leader. His marimba playing is what we need without Earl on the piano Rusty's brilliant marimba is what we are going to need. I don't expect you to even try to fill Earl's shoes, but I need you to try to figure out how you can adapt your piano playing into the sound that Rusty is going to move towards. Can you do that? For me; please?"

Mollie brushed back her hair. "You just get Earl back to us. I'll do my part." Her words were brave, cloaked with a great deal of self-doubt wrapped around them.

Stella mouthed a thank you as she let go of Mollie's hand. As Mollie opened the stairwell door to the Grotto Stella said one last thing before following her down. "Don't worry about Rosemary. I have not figured out yet what to do about here, but I will; I promise." Stella did not follow. Along as she was here, she needed to have a word with Thaddeus. The old man had enough thrown at him today, so she wrote him a note that he could take his time to digest:

Dear Thaddeus,

I appreciate all you are doing. Please help me out by completing this list and then let me know as soon as it has been done.

1. Have housekeeping make sure the rooms next to Oscar are made ready for Les, Mollie, and Sy. Move Sy and Les' belongings. Mollie will do her own.

2. You are released from any bar keeping duties.

3. As the cafe is closing choose and train someone

from the staff to help at registration.

4. Put a sign on the front door that the hotel will have no food service until Monday. No new hotel guests until Monday.

5. If the army sends military police to pick up Henry tell them that as far as you know he has already reported in. Say nothing more.

6. Stop sorting the mail, you are mixing everything up. Everything will be Okay

- Stella

Thaddeus was sorting the mail; again. His back to her, she left the note on the counter, preferring not to have a long-drawn-out conversation explaining everything. She tapped the registration bell to get his attention, then headed down to the Grotto.

25
Passing The Baton

Ray raised a stick to let Sy know that he needed a quick break. It was not the men's room he was interested in. He had grown suspicious of Rosemary sometime earlier and now his curiosity had gotten the better of him. It only took him a few minutes to find the knife and meat mallet that Rosemary had left behind. While this alone was not evidence of foul-play there was no reason for these kitchen tools to be there. He had gone in the same direction he had seen Rosemary go and there they were. He put two and two together deciding that he had enough to raise the question: Had the marimba been sabotaged by Rosemary? She didn't need a reason. She was venomous to anyone in the band who threatened her which would automatically make Rusty a target.

He was thin blooded, and mornings were always cool in the Grotto—especially when the kitchen was not working up a steam. He put the mallet and knife in his coat pocket and returned to his drum set, careful not to show the bulge in his pocket to Rosemary. He doubted she would have any reason to suspect him—he is the quiet little mouse she thought him to be.

Lola rolled a kitchen cart out, with everyone's breakfast, checked the coffee, then retreated back to the kitchen. There would be no lunch or dinner prep and breakfast clean-up could wait until she got back, and the band had finished with theirs. The musicians were notorious for taking their own time on when to eat. She left a note for the chef that she had some errands to run and would be back in a couple of hours. She was glad to get out, even for just a few hours, the day felt wrong for so many reasons. The air itself was heavy and tasted of . . . what, she couldn't quite discern.

The chef, busy with inventory with Stub down in the cafe, gave no thought to deliveries. He hadn't placed any and neither had Stub. If there had been any deliveries someone would have called him or Stub to check it in.

It was a pleasant 74 degrees in receiving.

—

There were plenty enough to go around.

"Okay everyone," Rusty said, "it looks like breakfast has been served."

I guess the cat is out of the bag, Stella thought as she descended the stairwell. From all appearances it looked like Rusty had taken charge with no big rift developing. At least that is one less thing to worry about. *If there is going to be a problem it will be Rosemary,* she thought as she gave the bass player a careful look, detecting nothing of concern. *Still I will have to keep a close eye on her,* she thought as the aroma of bacon and eggs drew them all towards the serving cart.

26
A Secret Exchanged

Ivory digested the news about Earl and everything else that was happening until, like Stub, he too almost had a stutter. He did not drink anymore, and for damn good reason; however, if he ever needed a drink, it was now. His ability to handle stress was thin-skinned as he was reminded by pain in his feet and legs from his panicked excursion up and down the steep hills of San Francisco. Now he was beginning to understand Stella's emotional state. That Earl might be dying was almost impossible to contemplate.

The tears that would not quite flow blinded him as he unconsciously sucked in all his personal hurt, fear and anguish, as it became clear that most everyone at the Rose had more important needs than him. Right now, he needed to be present, to make sure no further harm came to anyone. He could smell trouble coming from a mile away. This time trouble was close. Who? What, he didn't know, but sure enough it was here. Without saying another word Ivory fetched the baseball bat he kept in his room and took up his post in front of the hotel. With the bat tucked into a corner near the front door, he blocked the entrance to the Rose. If you did not already have a room or worked at the Honeysuckle Rose Hotel you were not getting in; not even the postman. No one was going to disturb Earl. No one was going to add extra stress for Stella. The army goons would not be going anywhere near Henry until he was damn well ready, and he wouldn't be until Earl recovered or passed on.

So far Stella had let things flow, everyone had a lot to chew on and she did not want to force feed them. Now it was time for her to seize the moment. "Ladies, gentlemen, everyone, fill your plates and gather around, we have a lot to discuss and now is as good a time as ever."

Plates and mouths full there was little conversation as everyone waited on Stella. She did not take a plate herself. She had much to say—little appetite—and no idea where to begin. She did not know it, but she was about to make her first mistake—her presumption that Rusty had already introduced himself as their new conductor. She had no idea that Sy had fallen into that spot by proxy.

Everyone's lovable old granddad knew a lot about music, had a good ear, and was far more patient than anyone else. That strange sixth sense of his somehow gave them reassurance. Until, and if Earl returned everyone was comfortable with Sy as their conductor; except for Rusty who wanted—needed the job. Sy who did not want it. And Rosemary, whose growing paranoia was rapidly eating away at any common ground there was between her and everyone else. She yearned for the baton, regardless that no one else wanted her to have it.

So far Stella had failed to see how dangerously close Rosemary was to a mental breakdown.

Sy's premonitions rarely got him in trouble. As he sat down for breakfast, he sensed trouble—danger close by. There was no question in his mind that this was coming from Rosemary, and, for some reason he did not yet comprehend, needed to talk to Ray in the next few minutes. "Stella, before you start, please give an old man a chance to do what we do more often than we like to admit." Sy asked with a good-natured sheepish grin. He had been seated next to Rosemary. As he rose, he placed his napkin over his plate to keep it warm, said nothing, nor glanced at Rosemary as he passed behind her, giving Ray a slight nod for him to join him.

Ray was as anxious as a newly housebroken pup needing to go outside with no one to take him. He assumed that Sy was now the band's leader. He needed to tell someone his suspicions about Rosemary's sabotaging of Rusty's Marimba.

Like Sy, Oscar had a sixth sense about trouble which came from years of rancor between he and Earl before the Honey-suckle Rose had become sweet. Where they all sat was not their usual spot. "Mollie, would you please." he asked, his silk mask waving just a little from his breath. He preferred going upstairs to his own room versus using the public bathroom. It only takes one little gift left behind for a blind man to be acutely uncomfortable about public toilets. As he rose, he felt her hand on his elbow as she guided him towards the elevator.

—

It soon became obvious that this was not going to be one of those great breakfasts they shared over hot coffee, good food, and long-winded stories of cabbages and kings. Concerned about how Les' operation was going Imogene decided to take the opportunity to go the phone booth which was on the far side of the elevator and restrooms.

Michael went with her. He also did not want to be left alone obligated to exchange small talk with Rusty Mayer. The Marimba player was not really one of them yet. Michael usually said little to nothing to strangers. Because of his disfigurement he did not want to call attention to himself. Far too often a simple hello from him brought out the usual rude comments about his looks; least said the better.

There was nothing unusual about half of the group needing to take a bathroom break. It gave Stella a chance to exchange a few thoughts with Rusty before they got back. She saw but thought nothing strange about Sy picking up Elsie from a nearby table and taking the violin with him.

Mollie, who had been sitting next to Rosemary lost her appetite. As Rosemary's, once upon a time best friend, Mollie could see the stress building and did not want to be the victim of her rage that threatened to erupt now at the slightest provocation. Mollie rose, set her plate on a neighboring table as if she was done, then, at Oscar's request, escorted him on the heels of Sy and Ray leaving only Rusty and Rosemary with Stella.

Rusty chewed thoughtfully on some bacon as he waited for Stella to pass the baton his way. Personal time was going to be at a premium today. At some point he was going to have to slip away and pick up his stuff from his old apartment without the landlord seeing him. He was past due on the rent, and it wasn't the first time. A room here at the Rose would solve a lot of problems.

Rosemary chewed on a mouthful of bacon as a cow would masticate a mouthful of sticks it had mistaken for sweet grass. It did not take much guessing for her to deduce that it was Rusty, not Sy, who had been chosen. Her mind was overwhelmed with thoughts on how to change that. She trusted Stella no more than Rusty.

If the baton was to be hers, she would have to eliminate Rusty herself. How, was the question. She had immediately thought him to be a womanizer without a brain above his waistline. She could goad him into insulting her, then take it from there. No one would blame her for defending herself against a vile sex predator. First, she needed her purse.

With Rosemary now away from the table Stella wanted to ask Rusty how everything went when he told them the news.

Loyal William Jones appeared at the top of the stairs. "Stella, I came as fast as I could. What is this I am hearing about Earl?" Jones started down the stairs, eyes moving back and forth from the steps to Stella.

"No William, you stay there." Stella practically leapt from her seat not wanting any of their conversation to be overheard by any of the band as they came back to their breakfasts.

Loyal William Jones was comfortable staying right there. He

was a big man whose balance had been off for years. He had always taken the elevator in the past; the stairs getting the best of him.

27

Elsie

Rosemary nervously glanced around the room as she retrieved her purse from its usual spot on the floor next to her cello. She hesitated for a fraction of a second when her fingers first touched the purse's strap. Until this moment she had been confident that no one knew about the gun in her purse she had stolen from Beulah a few weeks prior. She could have just taken the gun, but then Beulah would have looked for that. Purses being stolen were more commonplace. When your purse is stolen you get mad as hell, search with frustrating exhaustion, then blame yourself for leaving it out for easy pickings. The loss of any money and favorite keepsakes the hard part. At the time, she hadn't known there was a gun in the purse. She had just wanted a little payback for Beulah being such a bitch.

Now that she had the gun, she knew how she was going to use it. She would goad Rusty into a verbal donnybrook and then shot in self-defense. As her fingers tightened around the purse strap, she could not get over the idea that someone else knew that she had it and was watching her every move. That feeling of being watched, of imminent betrayal, rose along with her blood pressure, as she, with purse in hand headed towards the women's restroom. Her building paranoia sparked on everything. Stella was practically running towards the stairs. *Had Earl died? Loyal William Jones had suddenly appeared; was he going to take over the band? That bastard Rusty Numb Nuts is just sitting there too damned smug and self-confident. Does Mollie know something and is getting Oscar out of harm's way? Well, Miss know-it-all, maybe I should take you out to?* She passed Sy and Ray, afraid to even blink, her tension rising. *There were so many enemies . . . so many enemies. In a few moments she would show them all that she was a woman who was not to be trifled with.*

In the restroom Rosemary peeked in each of the stalls to make sure no one was lurking to spy on her. A touch of madness built within her, just as Sy stopping Ray a few feet outside the restroom's door.

"Son," Sy said, "I know you have something to say. You are holding back something as hot as a brand new hundred-dollar bill burning a hole in your pocket. Tell me about it? It's got something to do with the trouble brewing with Rosemary, doesn't it?" His voice lowered as he looked Ray straight in the eye. "We both know that there something terrible is about to happen, don't we?"

Ray looked back with rapid eye blinks and a bob of his Adam's apple, as he slowly lowered his eyes to watch his own hand reach into his coat pocket. Nervous, his eyes darted here and there, as he searched for danger—Rosemary—it did not cross his mind that she was just on the other side of the door behind them. "I found these . . ."

—

Stella had to catch her breath as she met Loyal William Jones on the stairwell.

"Take it easy girl, catch your breath, then give me the bottom line on my friend Earl?" He and Stella had been close friends since Earl had challenged the racial barriers in San Francisco encouraging black musicians to perform at the Honeysuckle Rose. Earl and Oscar, two blind men had stood up against the pickets and union thugs breaking the back of the closed-door musician's union. That had been two years ago, and black musicians had performed, dined, and danced at the Rose, right alongside the white men, on a nightly basis.

Lloyd William Jones' large dark hands took hers in his, friend to caring friend, as he said: "If Earl is as bad off as I hear, I know one thing to be true, and that is that just as sure as the moon will rise tonight and cast its great white shadow over everything that is earthly borne, Earl will want the music to go on with or without him."

"Now, hear me out, girl. I've talked it over with my partner back at the Alley Cat and I am here to sit in at Earl's piano until he returns, or we find someone to fill that seat on a regular basis." A broad smile lit up his face, his teeth and eyes beacons in the night. "Not that anyone could ever replace Earl at that there piano of his. Now tell me about Earl. Tell me it isn't so bad?"

—

"And that's all I know, Sy. I am as certain that Rosemary used these to scar the back of the marimba keys as I would be if I had been there to see her do it, myself. I saw her come and go. No one else could have done it." Ray Said.

"You are a conniving, slimy liar . . . I did no such thing!" Rosemary had come out of the bathroom as Ray was still holding up the treacherous tools for Sy to see. Shoulder butting Sy aside, the towel she had been using to cover the gun slipped to the floor as she raised it threateningly towards the now terrified drummer.

Ray back pedaled as she continued to press the gun closer. "I . . . I . . ."

"Those are your last words; more than you deserve." She hissed as her finger tightened down on the trigger.

"No, Please . . ."

She pulled the trigger with a queer little satisfied expression on her face. That smile was lost as . . .

Sy, while usually not quick on his feet, moved to stop her by raising Elsie high enough to come crashing down on the back of Rosemary's head.

The shot missed by barely an inch as she collapsed with a surprised shriek, the gun letting off a second round before it fell from her hand.

Outside of peeing his pants, Ray went unscathed, as he hopped backwards until he upended a chair falling to the floor. His breath caught, his eyes wide with disbelief that he was still alive; he had just stared straight down the gun's barrel as it fired and hadn't even been wounded.

Sy's violin looked like a lumber jack had stomped on it the base crushed in, several large splinters on the floor, its neck broken, held loosely together by strings that would never play another note. "I'm sorry," Sy whispered to his beloved violin. It came from deep within, a heartfelt numbing prayer for forgiveness as he slowly leaned up against the wall bringing the shattered instrument into a 'Dear God, what have I done,' grasp close to his heart. "Oh, my dearest Elsie, how can you ever forgive me?"

The old musician's face turned gray as he seemed to age well beyond his years as he slumped back against the wall. There, he held what was left of his treasured violin; their music forever silenced. As his last breath passed, his face took on a profound look of sadness.

Michael stood inside the phone booth behind Imogene as she dialed the phone.

Two insanely loud gun shots came from close behind them. Without thought he knocked the phone from Imogene's hand as he pulled her down the best, he could in the cramped space of the booth shielding her with his body.

"William, I don't know what to say. I know that Earl . . ." Her head could not have turned any faster as two shots rolled like angry thunder throughout the ballroom. A shriek mixed with the baroom-oom-ooming of the echoing shots until the rumblings faded away into an expectant silence.

Loyal William Jones sunk to his knees awkwardly on the stairs pulling Stella down with him in fear that whoever had fired the shots was not done yet. "What the hell? Who? Are you all right?" He searched the room for further danger. Who had fired the shots and from where? It was difficult for the big man to duck down low enough on the stairs to feel any element of safety. There was some activity across the hall near the restrooms. Someone was down, but he couldn't see who. The next four seconds weighed heavily with an echoing silence.

"I don't know. What happened?" Stella asked as she tried to get up. Is everyone all right?" In trying to get up she slipped down a step, grasping the railing so as to not slide further down the stairs. "William?" She had a bewildered expression on her face, her eyes searching his for an explanation. "I . . . I think I've been shot."

William turned his full attention to Stella. At first, he could not see where, or if, she had been shot. She was pale sliding slightly into shock, more afraid than in pain. She held out her right hand, her fingers dark red and slippery with blood. No longer fearing for his own safety, he rose giving Stella some support as leaned over her to check her left side, the side that had been facing the banister, and the direction the shots had come from. The light wasn't good, there was an obvious hole in her left bicep that was oozing blood. There did not appear to be an exit wound, so the bullet was most likely still in the wound. Lodged, the bullet, might be the reason there wasn't any heavier bleeding. He took out a handkerchief as he looked out across the ballroom. "Someone, I need help here, Stella has been shot!"

—

Rusty turned in the direction of arguing voices. It sounded as if Rosemary . . . He choked on a mouthful of scrambled eggs at the sound of the first shot. The sensation of swallowing food the wrong way more alarming than the realization of the shot. He reached for his coffee, the second shot causing him to spill it as he tumbled from his chair in search of shelter. In life-threatening circumstances, it is amazing how long a couple of seconds can seem to last.

There were other cries of alarm.

The next thing he heard was the hollow wooden thunk with the twang of violin strings springing apart; followed by a pained shriek. He pounded his chest a couple of times to clear the blockage. Coughed. Spit up a yellow blob. Then continued to hunker down for another few seconds. Who shot who, and why? *Was that Rosemary?* He peeked back in their direction as he rose to his knees.

Rosemary was prostate on the floor. Had she been shot? Ray sat by an overturned chair motionless.

Sy leaning up against a wall. Who shot who, is there another shooter?

He was about to call out when he heard a deep-set male voice coming from the stairs. "Someone, I need help, Stella has been shot!"

—

Thaddeus cringed as the two quick shots caused his heart to jump. The shock of the sudden deafening POPS unnerved him. At this point in his life he was not about to charge out, risking life and limb, to only get shot himself. What he would do is get the hell out of harm's way. Leave it to the young bulls like Ivory. He couldn't tell if the shots had come from the street or somewhere in the hotel. Keeping as low the ground as his bursitis would allow, he scurried to the front door locking it without so much as a glance outside. Retracing his steps, he ducked back behind the counter, opened the door to Ivory's room and locked himself inside. "Okay, get ahold of yourself old boy," he tried to reassure himself. "Ivory will be here in a moment."

There was a phone in the room which he used. "Operator, this is an emergency, give me the police!"

Locked outside the hotel, Ivory remained vigilant against any oncoming threats. A passing bus and the thick walls and sturdy windows of the hotel had muffled any sounds of the shots leaving him ignorant of the events taking place inside.

Michael and Imogene looked at each other as they untangled themselves in the telephone booth. At first it was hard to admit that what they had just witnessed had in fact happened.

Rosemary had just tried to murder Ray. Sy's quick action

had saved him, sacrificing his beloved violin. Now Sy wasn't looking so good. Rosemary was down for the count while Ray was momentarily frozen in place having come within a hare's breath close to being murdered. The gun was lying on the floor within Rosemary's reach should she wake.

Michael did a Houdini act in liberating himself from the phone booth, then dashed, skidding to a stop as he scooped up the weapon. *What now?* He pointed the gun at the motionless woman. Even though she was unconscious, he was afraid. She had just tried to commit murder and from everything he had witnessed she would do it again. "Ray, give me a hand here, we've got . . ."

Ray didn't move.

Imogene was now at his side, open-mouthed, not as fearful, more awestruck by the ferocity of events that had just occurred. Her eyes locked on the gun pointed at Rosemary.

"Now what," he said, more a statement than a question.

The two musicians looked at each other as Rosemary stirred just a little. Both knew that when Rosemary woke Michael could threaten her with the gun, but he would never use it.

"Ray give me your shoelaces," she demanded. She didn't wait for him to decide as she quickly untied the laces practically yanking the shoes of his feet. The shoelaces free she tied them into one long lace and bound Rosemary's wrists together tying the ends into an impossible knot. It would have been better if her hands had been secured behind her back, but Rosemary had been afraid to try to roll her over.

Michael lowered the gun feeling a little safer.

"Now yours." Imogene repeated as she began to untie his right shoe as he opted on one foot as she forcefully removed his shoe.

With both laces tied together as she had done with Rosemary's wrists, she bound her feet together.

Michael tucked the handgun in his waistband as he started to go to Sy's aid. After two steps he turned and placed the gun on the floor near where it had initially fallen. "That's for the police," he said as he turned back towards Sy who still leaned up against the wall. Why he had not slid down to the floor was one of those odd things that never has an answer. "Imogene, please you call the police while I check on Sy."

"Wait," he stopped in place, then turned to look back towards the stairs on the far side of the room. "Did someone say that Stella is hurt?" He called out hoping that no one would answer with words he did not want to hear.

While he strained to hear, Imogene went to check on Sy.

Loyal William Jones answered as Rusty started up the stairs to help. "Yeah, she's hit in the arm. I don't think there is any serious damage, but there is a lot of blood. We need to get the bleeding stopped." He called back. "Anyone hurt there?" He spotted Rusty, delegating him to grab a pile of linen napkins they could use as a tourniquet.

Michael called back. "Unbelievable! It was Rosemary, she just tried to shoot Ray. She's down for the count, but we've got her hog-tied for now. If it hadn't been for Sy . . ." He turned towards Imogene who was checking Sy's pulse. After a moment she turned as she nodded the sad news. Cracking from both anger and sudden grief Michael's voice reached across the room. "Sy, he . . . he's dead. It must have been a heart attack."

Ray swallowed his heart, if one could do such a thing, as he blamed himself for Sy's death. Without a word, nor a glance to say how much he needed to reach out. No one missed him as the elevator door slid shut behind him.

Stella squeezed her eyes tightly shut. Her arm was beginning to hurt, but it was the news of Sy's death that that impacted her most. While she had only known Sy a short time he had endeared himself to everyone at the Rose. How he managed to do everything, so well, at his age was a mystery in itself. Her eyes shut she could almost hear his voice: *Don't grieve Stella, I'm fine. It's been a long time coming. Good-bye, and thanks for your kindness. Your Earl, he will . . .* his voice faded trailing off into the heavens.

She grimaced, biting her lip as a sharp pain pecked around her gunshot wound. Opening her eyes, she could see old Sy still leaning up against the wall holding Elsie tight. She whispered "Good-bye."

"What was that? Asked Loyal William Jones.

---

*911 was not established in San Francisco until the late 1960s.

She didn't answer.

"Brace yourself girl, this might hurt a little. I'm going to use these napkins to help staunch the bleeding, then we will get you up to the couch in the lobby." He took the napkins from Rusty, asking: "I didn't catch the name. Folks call me Loyal William Jones."

Rusty gave him the same look most folks did when Loyal William Jones gave his name.

"I know . . . I know. It's okay by me if you just call me Bill, or William, or Loyal; but for some reason folks insist on calling me Loyal William Jones." He chuckled. "One would think that if one part was left out, they'd be missing something." He tightened down the tourniquet.

"Ouch!"

28
Sy's Last Deed

The sound of the shots, muffled and distant, broke the silence of Henry's bedside vigil. Stiff, he had not been out of his bedside chair for hours. Needing to stretch, and curious about the shots, he rose, stretched, and went to the window opening it just enough for a breath of fresh air to seep in. The city outside looked, smelled, and had not changed much since his bedside vigil had begun. He glanced back at the bed where Earl appeared to be the same; unaware of the world and his own condition. Henry turned back to the window opening it wider appreciating the cool outside air. His day had started out just south of fair to middling, taking a short cut to shitty day shortly thereafter. Never-the-less he braced himself for what might come next. Whatever might come, the shots must have come from somewhere out there, no threat to anyone here.

The sound of the sliding window and the street noise were the first things Earl heard as he woke with a jerk. He knew that he was in his own bed, nothing about how he got there. He was awake, still blind, those little fireflies of light that darted around his mind as if they were trapped in an old mason jar were gone leaving barely a fluttering memory. The spinning, his vertigo, was mostly gone. But, ohhh, he had a bad headache, and an uneasy feeling that he was caught in a nasty Irish bog bubbling straight upwards from hell—while his head was clear, his knees were trapped deep enough for the devil to tickle his toes. "Henry, that you?"

Both startled and relieved Henry spun around. "Earl, dear God, you gave us a scare."

Earl tried to rise, finding out quickly that his legs were as wobbly as flat bicycle tires on a rock covered ancient riverbed. "I'm fine, fine . . . , never mind about me, it's Stella."

"Stella?"

"You heard me. Stella, she's been hurt, and I have got to get to her right now." He tried to rise again and failed. "Henry, get me that damned wheelchair."

"Slow down now," Henry answered, "you're still dizzy and shouldn't try to get out of bed yet." His hands were now on Earl's shoulders gently holding him down; reassuring.

"The hell you say, I'm not dizzy. Now get me that wheelchair or I will get up and kick your ass down the hallway and clean down the stairs. I've got to get to Stella I tell you. Now!"

"Stella's not hurt; you most likely had a dream."

"Listen to me, old friend," begged Earl, "Stella has been shot . . ."

Shot? But that came from somewhere outside and there is no way that—Henry thought as Earl's mounting concern caused his own concern to become rise alarmingly. "What makes you so certain that Stella . .?"

"Because Sy told me," Earl shouted in anger and frustration. "Now fetch me that wheelchair." He took a breath. "Please."

29
Reassurances

Mollie left Oscar in the privacy of his own bathroom after telling him that she would be back in a couple of minutes. She had heard the shots and needed to know that her charges were all alright. Oscar was safe in his room. Sy and Michael were down in the Grotto as far as she knew, and that was where she was headed now.

She had heard the shots just as the elevator door had opened. She did not know if Oscar had heard anything, his attention was on not letting his bladder empty prematurely.

For the moment the Rose was bereft of music, camaraderie, and joy. All the droopy pouting lips and shared woe-is-me-ings are not going to do a thing to help Earl. All he can do is wait and see; or pray, if he was a believer. Oscar was not; often joking that he had not yet seen the light. He had a tape recorder to which Mollie had been reading selected poems he had requested. These he listened to over and over until he knew and could recite them without error. This was a good moment to leave other human beings on the outside of his black veil and be with his poetry.

Loyal William Jones and Rusty got Stella to the lobby coach, redressing her wound with fresh napkins the second she was comfortable.

Rusty tapped on the window motioning for Ivory for help. Seeing Stella prostrate on the couch with blood stained table linens wrapped around her arm caused him to almost go berserk.

Ivory's pounding on the door echoed across the lobby added extra stress and confusion to the chaos that seemed to have swallowed everyone whole. Rusty made the mistake of standing in the wrong place as he opened the door. Ivory's fist, which was intended for the door, struck Rusty dead-on leaving his left eye with a promising shiner and a potential broken nose for an ambulance attendant to look after.

Ivory froze in place, his arm and closed fist still extended, his other arm slightly behind him, a knee cocked in a running position, stalled in time. His facial expression changed from that of desperate rage, to a sheepish grin as he watched the blood gush from Rusty's nose as Loyal William Jones quickly stepped behind him, tipping his head back as he applied one of the linens. "Whoa, it's not this fellow who shot Stella, she's downstairs," barked William as he eased Rusty into a nearby chair.

Stella did see the humor in the moment, her chuckle ending with a lip pinched ouch as she unintentionally moved her arm.

Ivory dropped to his knees by Stella's side, his eyes beseeching her to tell him that she was alright. Which she did.

Thaddeus peeked out from his hiding place.

The sound of wailing sirens grew nearer.

"Her?" Ivory looked at William with eyes that read—tell me it ain't so?

"Your bass player tried to shoot your drummer. The tall grandpa character bashed her over the head with his violin. The bullet hit Stella instead." Loyal William Jones looked at Rusty for confirmation. Rusty, keeping his head up with a bloody linen pasted to his nose mumbled, his words meshed, back "Rosemary shot Stella is all I know."

Stella took a breath. "Guys, I'll be fine, the ambulance is almost here. Ivory, I need you to go down and make sure Rosemary can do no more harm. See if Michael and Imogene need any help?"

"Thaddeus," she asked, just loud enough for him to hear, I need you to go into the Martini Bar and make me a double martini just the way Rusty showed you. And please be quick. I could use a good strong belt before the ambulance whisks me away. Rusty you stay right here. You're bleeding worse than I am."

"I'll be right here by your side," Loyal William Jones promised.

She smiled extending her good hand just enough for him to touch it. "I'll be fine, the ambulance will be here soon. Right now, I need help on a couple of things. Would you be kind enough to go next door to the cafe and get Stub. He'll be in charge until I get back." She thought for just a moment. "Ivory, as soon as you have seen to Rosemary please go around and open the delivery door to the back alley. I think it would be better to have the police arrest and take her out the back way. The less the neighborhood knows the better. I'm sure the gossip party line is already burning hot with speculation.

Loyal William Jones, knowing that it wouldn't do any good to argue, smiled that he understood.

"William, just go around to the front door of the cafe and bang on the door. It will be a lot quicker, the connecting door to the lobby is locked tight. But first, my dearest friend, please lite me a cigarette, will yah."

30
Grand Duchess of The Grotto

While the elevator descended Mollie finger-tidied her hair as she worried about nothing at all, and everything both large and small—where does one begin. It stopped on the second floor letting on four of the hotel's guests. All men, all musicians, all grumping that for some reason there would be no food service for the day. With the cafe closed they would be forced to walk to one of the ritzy hotels where the cost of a meal was pricey on musician wages. The door slid open to let them off as their conversations changed to the shots, they had all heard and speculation as to where they had come from. Over-hearing their knowing speculations left Mollie to wonder the same as she was taken down to the Grotto. It never occurred to her that all the ruckus had something to do with Rosemary.

—

Stub followed Loyal William Jones back to the lobby beating him to the front door as he hurried to make sure Stella had not been seriously hurt. There, he found Stella perched on the couch, her arm in a makeshift linen sling, resting on a pillow. Queen of the Nile as she puffed on a cigarette while holding a large ice frosted martini glass.

The elevator opened and closed as another load of the curious disembarked to find Stella, Grand Duchess of the Grotto, the center of attention. At this point her enthusiasts, all men, each fawning over their wounded queen. made what a few moments prior had been a mood both somber and worrisome, to one of revelry and instant camaraderie. Many of the musicians brought out their own instruments and began to play. The only blood to be seen was around Rusty's bruised and swollen nose which seemed somewhat comical as he came out of the Martini Bar with a tray of martinis, which to his surprise Thaddeus actually seemed to have enjoyed making.

Stub pushed through the serenading musicians to get close to Stella.

Damn, that was fast, Loyal William Jones thought as he took in the crowd, the party atmosphere, as the ambulance arrived immediately behind him. He chuckled at the ambulance, whispering "party-pooper" as he took one of the martinis in hand. *This place is nuts,* he thought as his mind shifted back to why he was there in the first place. He still did not know a damn thing about Earl. *Maybe I should go upstairs and have a look-see myself, but not before Stella is on the way to the hospital. Say, wouldn't this be a good time for Earl to get checked out too?* His mouth opened and closed as he was about to ask, checking the question because he knew that if he were able. Earl would kick and scream all the way to the hospital and hail a cab for home as soon as the ambulance doors opened.

Following Stella's wishes Stub went out to the ambulance

and directed the driver to take it to the service entrance in the back alley while the attendant prepped Stella for the ride to the hospital.

A police patrol car arrived a moment later, the officer stating that he would not move it until he had secured the crime scene.

All Stub knew was what he had been told, that Rosemary had shot Stella, and was still down in the Grotto. The officer called for backup, assuming that there still might be an armed felon, possibly with hostages, laying siege to the ballroom in the basement of the Honeysuckle Rose Hotel. The ambulance attendant was ordered to stay out of the Grotto until it had been cleared of threat.

Stub did not stick around to correct the information that would soon bring a number of armed officers to what they thought was still an active shooter situation. His friends were being held at gun point by a mentally deranged woman, and he needed to open the door to the alley for the ambulance and the police before Rosemary shot anyone else.

Chef Roane took the service elevator from the back of the cafe's kitchen down to the Grotto. There he found the larger kitchen empty and a note saying why.

He was about to check the Grotto for breakfast cleanup when something triggered his 'oh shit' alarm. Retracing his steps back to the service elevator he was beginning to get an idea on what it was. He hadn't paid any attention to the smell on the short trip down. Now, as he approached the elevator, he knew what that odoriferous stench was, and where it might be coming from.

The elevator's door opened on the receiving dock five seconds before the door connected to the Martini Bar opened. "Stub, we've got a problem." Roane understated the obvious as Stub opened the door.

"That I can smell," Stub replied before he actually got an eyeful. "Jesus, what is that?"

"That, my friend, is about two weeks' worth of fish—no ice—and my guess is that it has been here for four or more hours. Worse, its flounder. We never serve flounder, too many bones, and spoils too quickly." He shook his head with humorous despair. *How the hell are we going to get rid of this much bad fish. Trash pickup wouldn't be for four more days.* "Two bits this is Beulah's doing. It has to be Beulah, there was no way the fishmonger and the butcher would know that she has been fired."

The door still open, the delivery room felt warmer than the

Martini Bar just on the other side. They both felt it. "The sliding door to the alley is drafty so heat from the rest of the hotel is drawn down here."

Stub's nose wrinkled. "That would be . . . be why it smells more la . . . like two-day ol . . . old fish. What, Steak too? This . . . this is going to kah . . . cost an arm and a la . . . leg."

There were three hard knuckle raps on the delivery door followed by a prolonged buzz from the delivery call button.

"That would be the am . . am . . .bulance. And I sus . . . sis .
. . pect the police will not be far behind. Roane, we'll have
to deal with the fish on Fri . . . day; no pah . . pun intended.
Would you mind op . . op . . . opening the delivery door while
I ga . . . go down to . . . to the Grot . . . otto to and see what's
uhh . . . up?"

A police officer, gun drawn, stepped out of the elevator, swivel-
ing left to right to make sure there was no other threat present.
"Not just yet, please identify yourselves." Three more officers
burst through the entryway from the Martini Bar, guns drawn,
each exchanging odd faces as they stepped around the rotting
surf and turf. "Who is in charge here?" One of the officers
asked, directing his question to the chef."

"I . . . I am." Stubs stuttered.

"How many ways in and out of here are there?"

Roane answered. "The service elevator will take you down to
the main kitchen serving the Grotto. There are three ways in
and out of the main kitchen. The main service door will take
you out to the main ballroom. There is a set of stairs located
just off the storage room which connects back up to the Martini
Bar, and a second service door at the far end of the kitchen to
the left which comes out behind the stage. Out in the ballroom
the main staircase is to the left across from the bandstand. To
the right, down a hallway past the bars is the public elevator
and restrooms."

The ranking officer, staring with disgust at the rotting fish,
wanted to ask, but there was no time. "If you gentlemen would

please return to the lobby—and stay there—we will be wanting statements from you later. "Floyd, he addressed another officer, "please escort these gentlemen back to the lobby, then lock off the public elevator. You three go with Floyd and be prepared to enter the ballroom via the staircase. You four with me, we'll take the back stairs that leads down from the Martini Bar. From there, two through the door behind the stage, and three, including myself, through the main service doors off the kitchen. Time?"

All of the officers looked at their watches. "In three we go in. Here's what we know. We have an active shooter, female, no description, with one down—possibly female, and two or more hostages. The suspect has shot two people that we know of, so if you are given cause to shoot, do so."

They did not ask for any additional input.

"GO!"

—

Quiet can be unnerving.

Ivory tucked himself close up against the wall as he peeked around a corner into the grotto. He knew the room well, but at the moment he felt the stranger about to walk into a trap. The room was not well lit with islands of brightness around the stage and a group table where breakfast dishes still sat. The bar area and hallway beyond were lit up as if it were a Saturday night. The only people who should be there were all friends. Except Rosemary, who had proven two ways to Sunday to be both dangerous and creepy. Creepy, that was what the Grotto felt like, both dangerous and creepy.

—

Michael O'Dea sat backwards in a dinning chair with his arms resting on the chair's back as he kept watch over Rosemary. She had not moved since Sy had clobbered her with his violin.

Imogene had just pumped a dime into the payphone calling the hospital for the second time as she tried to find anything out about Les' condition. Sy remained where he was. The gun lay on the floor near, but out of reach by Rosemary should she free herself—being bound the way she was that was not very likely.

Satisfied that there wasn't anyone else who could be a threat in the room Ivory entered as if he was still the ex-marine tough guy everyone could count on; not that he felt that way this morning—not by a long shot. "Stella is okay, the ambulance just got here," he announced as he reached Michael gratified to see that Rosemary's restraints were secure. "You okay?"

Michael nodded. "Good as can be expected, but I can't see any good coming from anything that has happened so far this sad day." He turned his head as he pointed slightly. "Sy," was all he had time to say before the elevator door opened.

Mollie, innocent as to everything that had occurred so far in the Grotto, entered as if she were planning on finishing her breakfast. Her face went white when she saw her once best friend and now evil stepsister Rosemary bound and motionless on the floor, a gun on the floor next to her. Michael, his disfigured face made even more appalling by the forlorn expression on his face as he pointed Ivory towards Sy. As if watching an old noir style black and white film she stared numbly as she followed Michael's gesture towards were Sy still leaned up against a wall, his hands cradling Eloise, broken and battered, against his lifeless chest. The hiss of the elevator's door closing behind her made her jump as she tried to register what she was seeing.

"It most likely was his heart," Michael said to both Ivory and Mollie. "It all happened so fast. Sy stopped Rosemary from shooting Ray, with Eloise."

Imogene's back was to them as she finally got someone on the line who knew something about how Les' operation was going.

Mollie's grief was instantaneous as she tried to grasp that Sy was gone. He had died standing there, just as he was now. She had come to think of him as her beloved grandfather. Ivory no longer registered on her conscious. He was not there as their so-called head of security but rather as one more confused, if not scared member of the Rose's extended family.

"She tried to kill Ray. When Sy's violin struck Rosemary the gun went off, the bullet striking Stella."

"She'll be alright. It struck her in the arm, what they call a flesh wound. The ambulance is here now." Ivory added with an odd catch in his voice as he heard the sarge whisper in his ear reminding him of his duty.

Mollie had a fleeting thought that came and went with nowhere to land. *Where is Ray?*

A tear caught in a wrinkled scar on Michael's face. "Thank God." He shifted in the chair, nervous of Ivory's demeanor, as Ivory stared at the gun.

If anyone ever needed shooting, the sarge whispered, encouraging Ivory to shoot Rosemary, to punish her betrayal, for all the grief and harm she had done. As far as Ivory was concerned, Earl in his bed upstairs, was as much her fault as everything else. He did not see Rosemary as being a woman, now bound and helpless. She is evil and has just tried to bring the Honeysuckle Rose down and bringing harm to everyone here. Going to jail for killing Rosemary would be easy, compared to the POW camp he should not have survived. He had long felt guilty for never having fired a shot against the enemy back in the war. The sarge egged him on, that he was a marine; that it was time to be a man. He looked at the gun as a sense of release came to him. He knelt down and picked it up. This time he would not cower, perhaps he had been saved for this moment.

Michael rose. "Ivory, no!"

Imogene hung up the phone, turned as she came out of the phone booth. Her words—good news—never made it to her lips as she saw Ivory raise and point the weapon at Rosemary.

"Ivory, don't!" Mollie screamed.

It was too late for Sy to say anything.

The only thing Ivory heard was his own heartbeat as his finger slowly tightened down on the trigger.

"Police! Put the gun down."

Police, all with guns drawn, seemed to appear from each and every nook and doorway. "I said, drop the gun. Release the trigger, and slowly put it on the floor in front of you, then take three steps back as your hands are raised above your head where we can see them." The officers noted the woman on the ground, perhaps a victim of the shooter. They had been told the shooter was a woman. But it was a man who now held a gun pointed at a woman.

Ivory did not want to die in a hail of bullets. He wanted revenge, but not at that price. The serge told him differently.

The elevator door suddenly opened changing the equation as half of the police guns moved instantaneously towards the opening door.

Wheelchair bound, Earl, guided by Henry, drew everyone's attention, including Ivory, causing him to slowly point the gun away from Rosemary.

The police did not know if the victim on the floor was alive or dead. She was the only one bound; why? There was no way they could know that she was not a victim to anything other than Sy's violin. They also did not know that old man holding a broken violin was deceased.

The officer in command used the name he had heard one of

the presumed hostages use. "Ivory, we don't want any more shooting here today. Put the gun down."

Earl sat up straight, ears cocked. This was the second time he had to deal with the unwelcome presence of the police in one day and it angered him mightily. When he heard a policeman use Ivory's name the hackles of his hair stood on end. "What the hell is going on here?" He roared as he tried to stand on wobbly legs. His voice a rusty pipe. "Ivory? Who has a gun and why?" He was wobbly because the vertigo, while being better, had not disappeared.

"Ivory." Mollie answered with a squeak.

"Ivory, put the gun down," This time it was Henry.

"Stella, sweetheart are you . . .?" Earl called out, remembering what Sy had told him

Michael answered. "Stella, she's upstairs, Earl. Rosemary shot her in the arm when Sy stopped her from shooting Ray. Rosemary is bound and unconscious on the floor. Sy had a heart attack and has passed on."

The actors were changing roles too fast for the police officers to keep up with. The woman upstairs had been shot by the woman on the floor who is not shot—that they knew of—but bound and restrained. The old man is deceased of natural causes. It had been the old man who had knocked out the woman before she could shoot anyone else. Why did Ivory have a gun, and why was he threatening to shoot the woman, who was already restrained? If the woman upstairs had been shot accidentally, where, and what was, the crime?

Sy, dead? Earl's feet nearly went out from beneath him. Stella had been hurt just as Sy had told him. Somehow, he needed to remain on his feet. "Ivory, talk to me, son. Where are you?" Earl asked.

"Here," Ivory answered. The gun was no longer pointed threateningly at anyone, but neither had he put it down.

"Say again, son. I'm coming to get you."

"I'm sorry, Mr. C., I didn't mean to cause you any more hurt."

Earl tried to follow Ivory's voice. His wobbly legs not making the task easy.

Michael, aware that the police might take his slightest movement wrong, kept his hands raised shoulder high as he stepped towards Ivory. "Easy pal. Please don't move. Your hand is shaking, and we don't want you to accidentally shoot anyone—especially Earl, now do we?" He was four steps away. "On the count of four I want you to give me the gun. Just let it ease into my hands."

Earl stood where he was. "Easy son, just do as Michael asks." Henry slowly edged the wheelchair behind Earl allowing him to slide back into it.

The police grew more tense as Michael started to count. There were too many civilians, too close to a loaded gun.

Michael's looks left the question open that once he had the gun he might turn and use it. The police had dealt with some ugly characters. There was no foundation for this except that someone that ugly just might be crazy. "You have two seconds to put the gun on the ground or we will shoot." The officer ordered. He moved his gun just for a fraction of a second towards Michael. "You, freeze."

All guns, except the one, remained on Ivory. With the one officer's gun pointed directly at his heart Michael began to count with each step that drew him closer to an increasingly nervous war traumatized ex-marine. "One . . ."

The officer began his own count. "One . . ."

"Jesus enough is enough. I want all you god-damned cops out of here." There was no strength left in Earl's attempted bark.

"Please," Mollie pleaded.

Imogene brought both hands to her face, fingers to her lips, as she watched Michael take the next step.

"Two."

"Two." That was the officer's final count.

No one fired.

"Three." Michael slowly brought one hand down to the same height Ivory held the gun.

Ivory's hands shook, tears visibly flowed down his face as Michael counted four, his fingers gently taking the weapon from him. Ivory had been certain that Michael was too late, that they would both perish—death by cop—before he could blink away another stinging salty tear.

All the police briskly brought their full attention to Michael who was now the man in the room with the gun and whose true intentions remained uncertain?

Ashamed and terrified, Ivory dropped to his knees.

Regardless of the number of guns pointed in their direction Henry pushed Earl's wheelchair to where he could now reach Ivory. Ivory had been a man haunted by too many ghosts, too much guilt, and the false courage of a marine who had become that last man left behind. Wherever that pride had come from it was gone leaving a shell of a man who was now reaching out for sustenance for his soul.

Earl reached out and took Ivory's face in his hands as he leaned forward and whispered into his ear: "Ivory, I . . ." Words failed him as his vertigo took him for another wild ride.

Ivory listened, wanting Earl's wisdom to guide him as his words had helped so often when he needed them.

In his churning black reality Earl could find no firm ground to steady him, find no words that weren't jumbled nonsense. He knew Ivory needed him, but right now he couldn't help himself.

Marine, you listen up. It was the Sarge. *If you want to remain*

*a coward in flesh, then leave your mortal remains behind and
take your rightful place with the platoon. We've had one man
missing for too long. I ain't got nothing to say to you than I
haven't before. But I will give you one cracker-jack piece of
advice. You listen to the old Jew with the fancy fiddle—for a
Jew he's a pretty smart guy.*

Michael held the gun by its barrel high above his head. "Officer," he said, "as you can see my friend is now as harmless as
an old tabby satisfied after gorging itself on a bowl of milk.
His best friend and mentor, Earl, has him, and I must ask you
to leave him be. If you are to slap handcuffs on him now you
will forever destroy the soul of this once great China Marine."

The officer looked at the broken weeping man in Earl's hands.

Rosemary stirred.

"Now, for god's sake, will you take this gun before I drop it
and accidentally shoot myself in the foot."

Several of the officer's laughed.

Michael turned as he slowly extended the weapon to the
officer in charge. All weapons were lowered as the bad air
left the room.

Earl let his hands slip from Ivory's face. "I'mth aurry." His
words broken, his voice sounding as if it were coming from
an old Gramophone; His Master's voice painful to the poor
dog's ears.

An officer stepped up behind Ivory with handcuffs.

"Is that necessary?" Henry asked, the humanity in his voice beseeching justice—though so far this day he had seen little justice or heart from the men on the other side of the badge.

The officer looked back at his commanding officer who had just relieved Michael of the gun. "It's your call," he was told. He turned back towards Henry touching his hand momentarily to his forehead tipping an imaginary hat, then turned and placed the handcuffs on Rosemary's already bound wrists.

With emotional tears flowing Mollie rushed across the room to Michael—kissed his face as she said: "I love you." Words he had never heard before. No one in the room could believe that she had kissed that face. Mollie knew that ugliness is not catching—her lips and breath warmed his cheek. Her kiss the loveliest, most pleasurable, sweetest touch, that beauty, the ugliest man had ever experienced.

"Michael, you were a witness. Best you be the one to press charges." Henry said, helping Earl with what he wanted to say.

Earl tilted his dark glasses to the bridge of his nose as if perhaps he was looking over them, his eyelids and the scars around his eyes vivid. He would know Imogene's perfume in the middle of an onion field. The fragrance as exquisite as he thought her to be.

Imogene answered. "Ummm . . .umm. Me, I'm still shaking like a little old fox treed and scared to death." She rolled her eyes as she tried to shake off the dark images that still stuck to her mind. "Damnedest morning, I have ever done seen," she said to no one in particular. "Mr. C., I just got off the phone with the hospital. Les is still in surgery but doing as well as can be expected. He should be home in a day or so. You had best set your mind on getting well and on your feet Mr. C. because Les is going to be needing that wheelchair for quite some time."

Earl's churning darkness had slowed to a much more pleasant shallow whirlpool allowing him to collect some thoughts and a word or two. He loved Imogene's voice, which sounded as if it could bring the beauty and fragrance of a spring meadow to melt away the filth and grudge of an old farm pigsty. He smiled. *You have got to sing something for us, songbird, we've all got a case of the blues riding hard over our hearts today. But first, I've got to find Stella*. He thought.

"Stella?" He managed to say.

Mollie had surprised him. Earl had always known that she was a strong girl with a heart made of solid gold. She had just professed her love for the ugliest man in town. There was no way he was going to steal a second of that moment.

Henry was not comfortable with leaving Earl in Ivory's care. Ivory was anything but stable. Neither was Earl.

An officer told them the medics would be taking Stella to a waiting ambulance out back in the alley. Without hesitation Henry asked Ivory to take him there. Everything else could wait. As Ivory pushed Earl towards the service elevator in the kitchen Earl tried to bark at the cops "Finish your business here and get the hell out of the Rose!" Ivory did not understand what Earl had just tried to say.

Henry did.

Earl tried to sound like the old Earl, he no longer was. If anything, Henry was amazed at the act Earl was putting on. As a former battlefield medic Henry was fairly certain that Earl still suffered from vertigo or dizziness. His skin was pale, his breath slightly labored, with beads of sweat around his neck and forehead. He had observed Earl massaging his left hand where he had some trouble opening and closing his fingers. If Henry could have his way he would go along with Ivory and force Earl into the ambulance with Stella. But he couldn't do that because Earl had sworn to him that the day he entered a hospital would be his last. "When my time comes it will be here at home in my own bed with Stella by my side and our music wishing me bon- voyage."

Henry shook his head in awe. How does Earl keep up this charade?

Earl rode the rest of the way to the elevator quiet and exhausted. The drugs that not so long ago had put him into medically induced deep sleep still floated in his system. The stress exhausting him, his thoughts befuddled by the vertigo, leaving little in his mind to suggest he still had a grasp on his sanity - and that scared him worse than the dark that had always terrified him.

Single minded in his task, Ivory pushed Earl past Elsie where she remained cradled in Sy's loving hands. Earl turned his head without comment. He and Sy were not done yet. With sad, emotionally drained eyes, Ivory looked at Sy as if he expected the old man to come back to life.

As the kitchen door swung shut behind Earl and Ivory Henry carefully took the mangled violin from Sy's death grip. A policeman then helped him lay Sy gently on the floor. A white table linen respectfully dropped over him as if that simple gesture would release him to heaven.

31
To Party in Hard Times

The reek of spoiling fish assaulted their nostrils before the elevator's doors even opened.

Earl turned his head to address Ivory wanting to say - 'get me to my Stella, just get me to my Stella'—but couldn't. "Stella." Ivory said it before Earl could. Stella was on the way to the hospital without her telling Earl that she was okay.

Ivory had never been good at finding words that might mean something when someone is hurting inside. "Don't be afraid, Mr. C., she'll be fine. The bullet hardly touched her. She'll be home in no time at all."

Earl reached back and found where Ivory's hand was on the chair leaving it there for a moment of mutual comfort. He sighed, wanting to call a cab and follow her, then his fear of being in a hospital got the better of him. He tried to flex the fingers on his left hand. Tried. He was beginning to think that he could live with the vertigo now, just as long as it got no worse than it was now. But losing the use of his left hand—that was something else entirely. What good was a one-handed blind pianist. That's like asking a Chinaman to eat a bowl of spring peas with one chop stick.

—

Loyal William Jone's eyes lit up as bright as two full moons as Earl and Ivory reached the lobby. Stella had not really given him an answer regarding Earl. It was hard to answer everyone's questions especially since she really did not know. Avoidance is sometimes the easiest way to avoid the truth you are afraid to face it.

The party was still in full swing.

The guests and residents of the hotel had come to support Stella and to exchange grave concerns and rumors about Earl and the future of the Honeysuckle Rose amongst each other. One rumor that had been floating around was that Earl had died; and here he was looking almost alive. Most of the hotel's guests had seen and heard Earl play, but few knew the man, which made him even more the legend.

Annoyed with the frivolity after everything that had happened Earl's first thought was to kick everyone out, close the hotel, and to hell with each and everyone else. It's easy to feel that way when you are being battered by bad winds and feel as if the devil himself is taking personal interest in your declining health.

Earl cursed himself for being a damned fool. This was his Honeysuckle Rose and the very air; the heart of the old hotel was in sync with their music. "The devil can go back to hell, I will, not surrender the beauty of this place." His voice barely a whisper, his words too scrambled for Ivory to understand.

Loyal William Jones clapped his hands together making three loud claps. "People . . . people, make way for," he interrupted himself with a deep incredulous laugh, "our King of the Blues, Mr. Earl Crier, who the good Lord this day has chosen to raise from the dead. Sweet Jesus, if anyone here needs proof that there are miracles, search no further."

The music stopped as a cheer rose loud enough to rattle the cables that keep the Golden Gate Bridge clinging to the sky.

Everyone wanted to shake Earl's hand and pat him on the back as Ivory wheeled him into the Martini Bar parking his chair near the piano. In his weakened condition the back slaps nearly knocked him from his chair. He did his best to not allow anyone to shake his left hand—which was impossible. He could only wish that no one noticed. The wish was honest, the prayer he reserved, that no one would ask him to play the piano. It was beginning to hit him that he might never play again.

Loyal William Jones stole a martini right out of Thaddeus' hands placing it in Earl's right hand before sitting on the piano bench next to him. Ivory moved Earl closer to the keyboard. Earl pushed himself away with a foot then tried to guide himself over to the bar. With his left hand almost useless he dropped the martini glass. That was when Loyal William Jones spotted Earl's attempt to hide his left hand.

Earl's presence was a surprise that Stub had not quite digested when Earl propelled himself away from the piano. Concerned,

Stub took a closer look, spotting Earl's malady, its cause unknown, it was obvious that Earl desperately wanted to hide it. Stub grabbed a bar towel drying Earl as he whispered to Ivory to move their boss farther away from the piano. A second towel Stub used to dry Earl's left hand which was not wet leaving it draped there.

The sudden movement and excess stress jump-started Earl's vertigo to the point of helpless terror. When the first seizure had come, he had been scared. Now he could feel his own blood pressure rise along with it. The numbness which so far had been isolated to his fingers had moved to his wrist leaving most of his hand unable to respond to what his brain told it to do. His first concern had been to keep the issue private—no one needed to know. He and Stella would figure this thing out soon as she got back. Now Loyal William Jones, Ivory, and Stub knew; that was three too many.

Loyal William Jones spotted Henry as he came into the bar, clarinet in hand; Michael and Imogene shortly behind. Something was wrong with Earl that was impacting more than just his left hand. Henry, being a former medic needed to know, especially since it looked like Earl's condition was worsening. He and Stub needed to get Earl out of the chaos into quite surroundings where Henry could take a look at him.

Jones' fingers touched the keyboard. The first notes of *Stella By Starlight* drifted across the room. Henry's clarinet soon followed as did other instruments forming an impromptu jazz orchestra providing just the medicine Earl needed—his love song to Stella.

No one knew how helpless he felt, nor how weak and dizzy he was. A tear ran unchecked down his cheek as he took to heart the music he so loved. He held a second martini that Ivory gave him firmly in his right hand. He never took a sip. Earl had never been more scared since he had been with Merchant Marine, and his ship had gone down in the Murmansk Sea in a bitter cold sea. He had been the only survivor. This time he was beginning to understand that the odds were far greater against him. He tried to smile.

Ivory understood taking Earl back to his room. He would make sure that Earl was not disturbed until Stella came home.

32
Loyal

Fortunately, Stella's wound was a flesh wound with no major vessels damaged. Once cleaned and dressed she was given the option of going home or staying overnight at the hospital for observation. This was a conundrum. She had no idea that Earl had risen, tried, and gone back to bed. She knew that if she tried to sleep in their bed now, she wouldn't get any rest. Sure, there were other beds in the hotel. There were so many problems piling up she would worry herself awake. The spoiled fish she had smelled and seen in the delivery dock was going to cost her money they did not have, and it was added to a list of issues she did not want to deal with. This was Earl's turf and he was good at it. Now it was all being dumped in her lap. A night of pampering and rest in a clean hospital bed sounded pretty damn good at the moment.

The Grotto was deadly quiet with all of the activity in the lobby and Martini Bar. Loyal William Jones, talking over martinis with Rusty, found out that Earl had left Stella in charge and she in turn hired Rusty as their new band leader. William needed to take a long hard look at his involvement. It was obvious to him that this Rusty character was not used to working with people of color. That alone did not make him a bigot, but until proven different the question would remain on the table. It was going to take some time to help Mollie make the move from classical to jazz and bebop. He wondered if she had the life's experience to bring her heart to the piano keys. Was there enough left of the band to put out a good sound; Rusty played the marimba, Michael the tenor sax, Ray the drums, Les Moore was in the hospital, so his trombone was out for the time being. Henry was AWOL. He had advised Henry to report in before he got into any deeper in trouble. Earl and Imogene had provided voice and vocals. There it was, plain and simple. They no longer had the musicians or instruments to play many of the numbers they had performed so well with Earl at the helm. That, and most of the musicians knew—yet—that Rusty was now their appointed leader.

For friendship's sake, Loyal William Jones had come offering his help with all the best intentions, but now as far as he was concerned the Honeysuckle Rose for all intent and purposes lacked a functional jazz band. Both he and Rusty had eye-balled the musicians jamming around them and it was difficult to determine if any of them had the depth of talent needed to join the band. Earl found exceptional musicians and drew them in with charisma; not just his, the bands. He was only interested in exceptionally talented musicians, then raised the bar from the first moment they picked up their instruments. Rusty had never done this and hadn't the first clue as to how to go about it. Auditions were going to be needed and if the talent wasn't there—what then?

The Earl Crier Sextet was broken. Loyal William Jones had not anticipated the level of commitment it would take to put everything back together again. It would take weeks, perhaps months to make this group stage worthy. He had his own business to run. He might as well move into the hotel for all the time and effort it would take; his wife would not be happy with that.

He and Rusty agreed to take a break for the rest of the day and get together the next morning for a long thinking session before calling the rest of the musicians together again. Loyal William Jones left disheartened to say the least. With Earl gone there wasn't any real chance of putting Humpty Dumpty back together again. Regardless of what he had promised Rusty he had no intention of coming back tomorrow. He did have one thought rolling around in the back of his brain. Imogene. His thought about Imogene was enticing; unforgivable betrayal, yes—but opportunities like this don't come around that often. Vocalists like her come along once, maybe twice in a lifetime. While this band was failing perhaps, he could persuade her to come over and elevate his at the Alley Cat.

Rusty poured off the last of the martinis, closed off the bar, allowing the musicians to continue with their jam session to see if he could spot any potential talent. There was no question that he had some serious soul-searching to do. In truth the job did not pay well, even with the trade-off for room and board; especially since the band's continued existence was now very much in doubt. He needed a paycheck and he was beginning to doubt there would be one around here for much longer.

—

When Michael is sad, he plays his horn. When he is glad, he

plays his horn; the melancholy put aside. When confused he will lay on his bed, close his eyes, and try to un-clutter his mind. Needing no excuse, he left the Martini Bar and went to his room, lay on his bed, closed his eyes and played his horn, with Mollie on his mind.

Mollie let him go knowing that sometimes a man needs his space—especially when that soft spot in his comfort space is threatened.

Michael did not understand that this was one of those moments when a woman needs to be held, but then again, he had never held or been held by a woman, and that was both threatening and arousing all wrapped up together.

Having a moment to herself was not something Mollie needed now. There were so many emotions she was afraid to catch hold of any one of them. Her newly discovered feelings for Michael kept trying to run all other thoughts out of her head; only they wouldn't leave. Sy's death was going to hit her like a falling brick; that brick was still in the air. Rosemary brought out feelings of both anger and worry. They had been best friends for so long, and then she had turned on her like a cornered feral cat. Then there was Earl, Stella, Ray, and poor Ivory. Learning to play the jazz piano was not something she wanted to do. There were too many other things more important. Oscar, oh my gosh, she had forgotten all about Oscar.

Oscar sat in a chair near an open window catching a little fresh air as Mollie tapped on his door and came into his room. "Mollie," he said, "I'd like to change my mask. This one is getting a bit fusty. perhaps something bright, everyone is in such a dark mood, lets brighten it up a bit, shall we."

With Oscar this meant a complete wardrobe change. Around the hotel he usually wore a black or white tuxedo which she color—coordinated with his many silk head masks. She knew just the tux needed and laid it out for him only on special occasions. It was the tux Imogene had picked out and shown to Stella who purchased all of Oscar's clothes. In his quail eggshell blue tuxedo Oscar was stunning. She laid out the blue tux matching it with a glossy dark blue mask adorned with a white slash that covered where his eye holes should be, then thinned out, disappearing entirely just above where the mask covered his ears. That look and his poetry always brought a standing ovation.

Satisfied with her clothing picks Mollie's lips quivered as she started to cry. She was an emotional wreak. Today had to be the saddest day in her life. The Earl Crier Band was floundering without leadership or direction. She could see that each of the musicians were losing it, and without Earl to guide them there was nowhere to go but down. It was beginning to look as if they would never play again. and if that happened the Honeysuckle Rose, her home—their home—would close. So yes, this was a special occasion when everyone ought to look their best, be their best, with smiles that lit up the world. She had read somewhere that the Titanic's orchestra went down with the ship, their music bringing a surreal calm in the final death throes as the mighty liner slipped beneath the waves.

Mollie was caught in an emotional quagmire. She could stay and flounder or find a path to walk. Yet, like a ball of yarn, the thread must be pulled soft and slow. *Well, so be it . . . if the Rose were to go down its music will be its heart until the last musician closes the door behind them,* Mollie thought as she finished laying out Oscar's clothes.

As Oscar dressed, she went to her own room to find something appropriate for the occasion. She had just the dress, which she had brought with her to wear the first time Rosemary played with the San Francisco Symphony. Now she would wear it on an occasion she had never dreamed would happen. The dress, ballerina style in length with robin's egg blue Chantilly lace over white satin, cap sleeves and subtle boat neckline with double-strand white-marble necklace grazes. It had a gracious formal hemline falling between mid-calf and ankle, a very sensual look, the fabric fairly kissing the skin. Finished with a wide white satin sash tied in a sweet feminine bow just over the gentle roundness of her belly. After dressing she looked in the mirror and purred "I think Michael will like this."

33

Many Questions, Few Answers

Henry told Stub that he was fairly certain that Earl had suffered more than just a concussion. He had every sign of having had a mild stroke, perhaps a more serious one, and could be suffering from first states of heart failure. Earl's sedentary lifestyle hadn't been exactly healthy. Earl looked and sounded as if Henry's diagnosis was right. He needed to be in a hospital, but those were words he refused to hear. He and Ivory got Earl back into bed. As soon as Earl was asleep Stub left Ivory to sit by his side telling him that he was going to the hospital to check on Stella; if possible, to get her home where she was needed.

Before he left, Stub checked in with Roane who was pondering his own future as he finished inventory in the cafe. The chef had a lot of questions. Stub had few answers, nor the time to try to answer the one's he could. Outside of basic meals for the band the kitchen would be closed for the foreseeable future. For lack of a paycheck most of the kitchen staff would be giving notice which would make starting up again that much more difficult. While he did not have the authority Stub promised Roane, and Eva Marie, a paycheck for the next thirty days—after that, who knows.

They both knew that the bartenders and waiters would bolt like a pack of greyhounds at the starting gate. The waiters would be out the door two minutes after they heard the kitchen was closed. If and when the band got its act together, they wouldn't have the staff to move enough booze to make the payroll Stella intended to pay them. One or two bartenders working their asses off would never be able to pick up the difference. Stub did not say anything, but without a paycheck, Rusty would have to seek other options before the Honeysuckle Rose musicians had a chance to even get a start.

Bleak was becoming an understatement.

The last thing Stub asked Roane to do as he left for the hospital was to get rid of the rotting fish before it closed down the Rose prematurely. This was no easy task with the trash pick-up five days away. A special pick up, especially since it was all rotting surf, and turf, would cost an arm and a leg; if the sanitation company would even pick it up.

Roane went back up to the delivery dock to get a better idea of what needed to be done. There was no question that they would have to get rid of it today. The stench was far worse than the first time he had seen it. If they waited any longer the stench would spread throughout the hotel. Once the old drapes and carpets soaked in the vile odors, they might never get rid of it.

The door to the alley was still open as the police were finishing up downstairs. Roane stepped out onto the loading ramp to catch a taste of fresh air. *How . . . how?* He asked himself over and over until it came to him. *But of course, return to sender. Didn't Wiggy own a pick-up truck?*

Time to make a phone call.

34
Ray

Mollie took Oscar by the elbow as she gently him along a well-known path between his room and the elevator. As the elevator door slid shut, she remembered that there was one more person hurting that most everyone had forgotten. Ray.

Ray was a quiet, shy, sensitive, man, who rarely shared his feeling with anyone. He was bound to be shook-up; Rosemary had just tried to kill him. While Ray had survived without a mark on him, Sy had died saving his life.

Tears welled up in her own eyes as she thought of Sy and the guilt Ray must be feeling. She checked her tears, not wanting to ruin the mascara she had just put on. Ray loved it when people dressed well, especially women. She pushed the button for the floor Ray's room was on telling Oscar that they were going to make a short side trip. Maybe this isn't such a good idea. Perhaps I should get Oscar down to the lobby and come back up for Ray. The door slid open.

"Where are we going, girl?" Oscar asked.

"Going to see a friend in need," she answered.

Oscar was oblivious to everything that had just happened down in the Grotto. Sy's death. Rosemary's arrest. Earl's condition. Stella shot. Well, he was about to get an abbreviated tale. She couldn't tell it all even if she the wanted to.

—

Using Stella's car Stub dropped Henry off at the Presidio before going to the hospital to check on Stella.

Henry had called a number listed on his call—up papers, spoke to a duty officer, and inquired about the chances for emergency leave. The answer was an emphatic "NO!" The unit he was assigned to had just taken off with a refueling stop in Hawaii before preceding to Japan. The North Koreans were kicking the hell out of us on the Korean Peninsula with the news getting grimmer by the hour. Technically Henry was absent without leave, detached from his unit as they were now on their way to a theater of war. Henry was to report to a Colonel Bedford for his disposition and reassignment. None of this was good, and Henry knew that he needed to get in front of this Colonel no sooner than the Duty Officer hung up the phone. That meant he had no time for good-byes. Not being able to see Earl or Stella was worse than being on an airplane flying straight into the heated winds of war. Especially since both were hurt and in need of him.

Stub promised to give Henry's best to Stella as he left the frazzled Nisei army medic at the Presidio's front gate. It wasn't until Stub parked at the hospital that he saw Henry's Clarinet case sitting on the passenger seat floor.

—

Mollie knocked lightly on Ray's door. Twice. There was no answer. "Ray, its Mollie, can I come in?" No answer. She guided Oscar to a chair that sat by a hallway window two doors down. "You wait here, I won't be long," she whispered as if closed doors had ears.

Oscar nodded. He heard the music coming up from the lobby. "Say, that's not our people is it? Nope, not our sound. Take me down there will you, hon?"

Mollie did not hear Oscar as she tapped once again on Ray's door—than turned the doorknob. It opened into a darkened room; the curtain closed. There was a small candle sputtering by the bed side. "Ray?" She was afraid to wake him. Sensing that something wasn't right she turned on the overhead light. There was a woman in Ray's bed, her back to the door. The woman was dressed in a sheer cantaloupe chiffon nightgown, her long strawberry blond air draped over her shoulder as if it had been staged for a Hollywood movie set. "Ray?" She looked around the room. The only one in Ray's room was the blond who had not stirred. She moved closer to the bed, slightly embarrassed for the intrusion. "Excuse me, but where is Ray?"

Mollie had never seen Ray with a woman. Was he on the other side of her where she couldn't see him? Not wanting to startle her Mollie nudged the pillow to wake the woman. The woman did not wake. Mollie was now close enough to see the astonishing truth—the woman was in-fact a man—it was

Ray dressed in a women's nightgown; complete with eye gloss and lipstick. More than surprised, Mollie staggered backwards until she was stopped by the small table where the sudden flicker of the candle highlighted the empty pill box that lay open and empty next to it. She did not know how many of the pills he had taken but the awful truth was plain to see. "Ray, wake up," she shouted. "Ray? No . . . ooo!" The tears flowed unchecked down her cheeks and dripped from her chin. She was too sad to cry out or wail. She just stood there as still as a statue while the magnitude of what Ray had done swept over her. Ray, the quiet little mouse of a man, was finally able to reveal his true self, which finally had driven him to seek that place where he would no longer hurt; his guilt and loneliness guiding him towards the peace found only in death.

Oscar, hearing Mollie's cry, retraced the steps he had counted back to Ray's room. "Mollie, you need help?"

Closing the door behind them it was Oscar's turn to escort Mollie down to the lobby where Michael took her in his arms. For a moment she never felt so alone. So, lost ... So incapable of doing even the smallest of tasks. And this was only the beginning, the beginning of the pain, the suffering and the endless conga line of emotions that were in store for her. Stella had asked her to be strong for everyone else. How? She looked at Michael and found her answer.

Michael kissed her softly, tenderly, his lips speaking volumes. She returned the kiss, never wanting it to end, tasting her own salty tears knowing that she would never forget this moment. She would never forget Ray, Sy, and yes, Rosemary too. She opened her eyes looking close into Michael eyes, his incredible face. She finally found the words to tell him that their drummer would play no more.

———

Rusty took Ray's death with a silent introspective. One moment he had been a poorly paid bartender wanting a job as a musician. Before he had time to say it aloud, he had his own jazz band. Poof! His dream of having his own band was now dying, as an unwanted, unforgiving wind swept everyone into harm's way. He had not had the time to build any real connection with any of the musicians. He had barely known Ray, pondering the loss of the drum more than the loss of the man. For a bit of animal skin stretched over a wooden cylinder a drum sounded pretty awesome. It could be as quiet as a tiptoe through autumn leaves, or as loud as a roll of booming thunder just overhead. It could keep the beat of any song as steady as a clock, but with a reverberating sound that echoed to the very heart and soul of the song. The music of the drum brought the rhythm of life to the music everyone gathered in their hearts.

Rusty tried but could not hear the ghostly rhythm that had beat . . . drummm . . . rummm . . . alongside Ray's heart.

The one musician Rusty truly appreciated was Imogene whose luscious vocal talent blended with a voice that melted all other thoughts that the rich memories her song brought out. He needed her, for without her, they wouldn't be able to match a Salvation Army Band. He drew his eyes away from Mollie and Michael searching the faces of the musicians who mostly felt awkward as they couldn't tear their own eyes away from the young lover's self-discovered moment.

The tiniest of smiles crossed his lips as he raised his hands high bringing them together as if they were a pair of orchestra's cymbals bringing everything to a new beginning. As thirty sets of eyes left Michael and Mollie they turned their attention to Rusty Mayer who wasted no time in establishing his authority.

"Gentlemen, if you are interested in trying out for the new Honeysuckle Rose Jazz Orchestra meet me in the Grotto in twenty minutes. We will start as a group to discover which of you and work well and play together. Before we are done, we will have found our voice; those who can't will be eliminated. If you are not currently staying in the hotel, I doubt there will be a place for you. We do not have the time for commuters. We have some extra rooms if you are interested, if not the door is right there. Who is not registered here at the Rose?"

Three sets of hands went up.

A brief silence overshadowed ambition as Rusty waited for their decisions. Two of the musicians wished everyone well as they chose the door to other opportunities.

Everyone talked at once as the excitement of building a new band spread like fire amongst them. "Twenty minutes, gentlemen." Rusty caught Imogene and began to whisper earnestly in her ear as they hurried down to the Grotto.

Michael was caught between two lovers. One, he was just beginning to know. Up to this moment music had always been his only lover. Now, he was scared of these new feelings he was experiencing with Mollie, and he was scared that he was going to have to compete for his own place in the band.

It would take some time for Thaddeus to figure all this out. After the two non-resident musicians left, he posted a hand-written note on the front door. *'Closed until I Decide Differently,'* poured himself a chilled martini and went up to his room. On the way up Oscar reached out to him with an old friend's chuckle. "Earl would really appreciate that kid's chutzpah."

"Stella gave him the job," Thaddeus answered. "I didn't figure he had the balls."

"I'll be damned." Oscar said. "I've lost my way towards the elevator. You going that way?

Thaddeus offered his forearm. "What's Mollie so upset about?"

"Oh, nothing much to speak of. You know how young women are." Oscar answered. Thaddeus did not need the burden of one more bad news in his hotel. Once in the Grotto he and Oscar found a table where they could take in the competition.

As Mollie and Michael entered Mollie saw the two police officers who were just finishing up with the crime scene. She left Michael to his music as she brought Ray's suicide to their attention.

35
Not as Expected

The staff sergeant looked up from his desk with obvious disdain. Henry had met many like him, no nonsense career men, lifers who had first put on their army boots to escape the Great Depression, had put in their thirty years and knew no other way of life. Most were disgruntled because they did not like being desk bound while they waited to be mustered out. They really had nowhere to go, if they were married, they wouldn't be for much longer. This one would have given his pension to have been on the plane Henry had missed. Sure, war is hell, but he liked it there. He was going to miss out on Korea, and it pissed him off to be told that he was too old to soldier.

Sergeant MacNamera took measure of Henry and did not like what he saw. He saw a smug Nisei dressed in civilian clothes who was AWOL. MacNamera's war had been in the Pacific Theater. He had been trained and conditioned to hate the Japs. He knew the brutality of the enemy and it irked him to have a god-damned nip standing in front got him now. "There ain't noth'en you can say that will make a shit difference to me. As far as I'm concerned, we should have sent you all back to nip-land finished you all off with nukes."

"That will be quite enough, Sergeant." The Colonel barked from where he now stood in the open door to his office. If you want to be mustered out short of your thirty-year benefit than I suggest you keep your mouth shut. Is that clear?"

Dressed in civilian clothes Henry, who had been standing at ease, snapped to attention.

"Stand easy." The Colonel ordered, his tight-lipped, having enjoyed reaming out the bigoted sergeant. Although he had read Henry's file enough times to have memorized it, he glanced at Henry's personal file. "It says here that you were with the 442ed, a corporal and a combat medic." His look at Henry showed respect. His facial expression slipped once again to stern as he addressed the sergeant. "Sergeant, standing in front of you is a bonafide hero. In late October 1944, a battalion from the 141st Infantry Regiment, 36th Texas Division, was surrounded by the German army. Battles were fought in the densely wooded Vosges mountains located in Northern France near the German border. We were called the Lost Battalion because no one thought we'd see a single man come out alive after the fighting was over."

The Japanese American 442nd Regimental Combat Team - about 3,000 men—was ordered to rescue the Lost Battalion by General Clayton Dahlquist, Commander of the 36th Division. The German army had orders from Adolf Hitler to defend the Vosges at all costs. The rescue mission would be one of the bloodiest battles in the history of the US Army. I know because I was there."

The sergeant who was at attention braced stiffer.

"We lost a lot of good men, far too many, and we would have lost more if it had not been for that all Nisei Division. When the fighting was over General Dahlquist asked the 442nd to pass in review. Seeing them he asked, "where are all the men?" The Colonel paused for affect. "Sorry, sir... this is all we have left." replied a teary-eyed officer. After days of near constant fighting the 442nd had suffered roughly 1,000 casualties. 200 soldiers were killed in action or missing with over 800 seriously wounded. The 442nd Regiment was the most decorated unit for its size and length of service in the history of American warfare. The bravest of the brave; and few combat medics survived." The Colonel cleared his throat for affect. "Sergeant, I think you owe this man an apology."

"Yes, Sir." The sergeant did not make one. Admitting that an apology was due was enough. The sergeant had been a good soldier, served his country well. He was old school, and nothing would change that.

The Colonel listened to Henry's reason for reporting late.

"Well son, as far as I'm concerned you have carried the weight of ten men and the army owes you a debt of gratitude. If you want to go to Korea, I'll see that you are on the next plane out. God knows we need men with your experience." He could see the look in Henry's eyes. "No. I didn't think so." For the moment our position on the tip of the Korean peninsula is such that we have no MASH units yet in the field. When possible, urgent cases are being taken by the aircraft carrier USS Valley Forge and the Heavy Cruiser USS Rochester. Because of the immediate combat situation most of our wounded are being flown directly to Japan."

The look on Henry's face had not changed.

"I'm told that Japan is not that receptive to you Nisei." The Colonel glanced one more time at the file. Tapping it with a fingernail he said. "Well, this may take some sorting out. Sergeant get Lieutenant. Akita a temporary billet in the Bachelor Officer Quarters while I see what I can do."

Both the Sergeant and Henry's jaws dropped when they heard the word Lieutenant.

"The Korean conflict has caught us undermanned and short of resources. Your recall comes with a field promotion. Make it happen sergeant and see that he gets a proper uniform and officer bars." The Colonel tapped Henry's personnel file once more for emphasis. "I'll keep this for the time being. You are restricted to base; however, I'm confident I can have your new orders within twenty-four hours.

The Colonel snapped the personnel file shut as he partially turned back to his office. He stopped halfway then turning back towards Lieutenant Henry Akita. "If you are not otherwise busy would you be kind enough to join me at the Officer's Club at seventeen hundred hours. I would like to buy you a drink."

36
Their Gifted Skylark

Rusty Mayer was not a gambler, he could not afford the risk. His luck had never drawn the right cards or roll of the dice. This time he couldn't afford not to. This would not be about a roll of the dice—it would be for the life or death of the Honeysuckle Rose.

The next time Stella peeked into the Grotto there had to be the beginnings of a good jazz band—no orchestra. A small jazz band, no matter how good, would always be under the shadow of Earl Crier, the blues man, who did it his way. An orchestra—big band—call it what you may, has a different voice. Rusty had one chance to do this, and probably would never get another chance like this again.

Rusty was tempted to let himself drown in the impossible. He hadn't the experience, wasn't good enough a musician himself, surrounded by mediocracy, and rapidly losing the talent that Earl had so closely honed. With the loss of their drummer, trombone, and clarinet, the Earl Crier Quintet was hemorrhaging its heart—soon there would be no reason to hang onto a failing dream.

He had already made the decision to say—"thanks, but no thanks"—to Loyal William Jones. Loyal William Jones is a black blues musician whose music has been very much part of the Earl Crier story. Earl had challenged the prejudicial status quo in San Francisco breaking through the racial barriers that limited black musicians to the Fillmore. Earl had stood fast against a corrupt and closed-door musician's union. Jazz, blues, and bebop would never be the same. San Francisco was slowly changing for the better. Rusty did not know much about Earl and Loyal William Jones' history, but when it came to Loyal William Jones, he was beginning to question the word Loyal.

From the get-go The Honeysuckle Rose Orchestra had to have a focus point all of the musicians could unit around. That would be their songbird Imogene. Rusty might be their appointed leader. Imogene was to be their anointed voice, the voice that would capture the hearts of music lovers the moment the first breath of song passed through her lips. He knew that in the beginning each musician would be struggling to find their own voice, the musician next to them a stranger to be wary of. It would take time for the orchestra to find its voice while the musician's egos continued to hit divisive flat notes that could very well limit the future of music at the Rose. They would have to unite around Imogene and be willing to do anything and everything for this gorgeous, young, gifted skylark.

While *Stella By Starlight* had been Earl's song, they needed their own. Imogene's signature song would be *Skylark;* her choice. Now, from the depth of her heart she had to make *Skylark* her own.

Imogene bought into Rusty's vision; her loyalty true; except for one small secret that Loyal William Jones had tried to steal her away. She had not yet said no to Loyal William Jones, but neither was she giving it much thought.

In the Grotto, as the musicians gathered, Rusty and Imogene prepared for the chaos of the tryouts soon to come. The long dormant orchestra platform would now be center stage as the musicians took their places, most not where a good conductor would want them. The first adjustment would be to rearrange the stage for the marimba along with a piano which needed to be placed across from the marimba with the orchestra in-between.

Hopefully they would find a good pianist. Because of Earl's genius their new pianist might become be their weakest link. There was no room for weak links. Sorry Mollie, it's just not in the cards right now.

Imogene remembered a poem Oscar had once recited. Oscar recited the poem to her with ease:

> 'To A Skylark
> Hail to thee, blithe spirit!
> Bird thou never wert,
> That from heaven, or near it,
> Pourest thy full heart
> In profuse strains of unmediated art.' *

As soon as the marimba was placed on stage, while the hopeful musicians cat-danced for their places, each wanting center stage, Imogene led Oscar to the stage giving him the seat between her microphone and Rusty's marimba. She whispered her intent to Rusty who nodded enthusiastically.

Rusty's first glance at the disorganized gaggle of musicians gave him his second taste of heartburn—the first when Stella had offered him the job.

There were three men jockeying for the piano bench.

He clapped his hands until he had everyone's attention. "Alright, quiet down everyone. My name is Rusty Mayer, and I am your conductor and the sole decision maker of your fate. This is Imogene," he bowed in her direction, "and you will all soon learn why she is the voice, heart and soul of the orchestra we hope to give life to starting here, and now. This is a group tryout. Solos will be held after we weed out those of you that don't quite fit the bill.

"You three," he waved his hand towards the piano, "Take a seat down there. Earl's voice and his genius on the piano we will never be able to replace. So, we won't try. After we have selected our first round of musicians for the Honeysuckle Rose Orchestra, we will find out who has the gift we will be looking for on the keyboard. So, listen well, gentlemen, when called upon, you had better be damned good. We will work around three well known tunes. If you do not know them, please quietly exit with our best wishes for your success . . . somewhere else." Rusty reversed the handle of a mallet to use as a baton. "Gentlemen, follow my lead."

The baton rose, then hovered in the air as it pointed not towards the musicians but rather to a blind man oddly wearing a head mask. No one but Oscar and Mollie knew what to expect.

Oscar opened with the poem Skylark by Percy Bysshe Shelly, which Rusty, at first, found a bit confusing.

'Higher still and higher
from the earth thou springiest
Like a cloud of fire;
The blue deep thou wingest,'

As his rich deep august voice fell silent the musicians were both expectant and unsure as Rusty moved the baton where it remained motionless as Imogene began to sing the Johnny Mercer tune:

'Skylark
Have you anything to say . . .'

The baton spoke, the musicians jumped in. It wasn't rehearsed and it sounded like it. He reversed the mallet allowing his instrument to stand in for both the piano and drums while listening to find the musicians who knew how to find their place.

Imogene took the mike in hand, gave Rusty a reassuring smile, as she turned towards the bandstand giving each musician in turn her smile as she brought that musician's sound in tune with hers. As she did this with each musician and instrument their sound came together as an extension of Imogene herself.

It got better as Imogene helped them find their heart. It was she that rolled the dice—Luck, a lady tonight.

37
Doing a Man's Job

Disappointed, somewhere on the third floor of the hospital, Stub tried to stretch out in an empty waiting room. Upon arrival he had learned that Stella had opted to spend the night. A nurse had given her something to help her sleep and there would be no waking her until the morning. He was restless, finding it impossible to sit more than a few minutes at a time. He too had been tempted to spend the night there, life back at the Rose right now wasn't exactly rosy.

He walked the long corridors of the hospital, twice being turned back by hospital staff. He had passed a cafeteria. He was hungry but ruled the cafeteria out—no wonder there were so many sick people at a hospital—it could be the food that made people ill.

He checked on Les. The good news that he might—might—be able to come home with Stella. After wondering and pondering for an hour Stub decided to go home. What else could go

---

◆ "To a Skylark" is a poem completed by Percy Bysshe Shelley in late June 1820 and published accompanying his lyrical drama Prometheus.

wrong? He thought as he mirthfully glanced up at a pale-yellow ceiling—not exactly a portal to heaven. "Dah . . .Don't answer thah . . . that."

—

Mollie told the policeman cleaning up the crime scene about Ray's suicide then took them up to Ray's room. There had been enough turmoil, and one thing the Honeysuckle Rose's family—what was left of it—did not need, another emotional circus call. The tragedy of Ray's death made it even more urgent to expedite the ugly removal of his body with as little sensationalism as possible. Mollie offered to stick around after the policeman closed his notebook.

"No," the policeman observed, "it's fairly obvious the man . . . woman . . . whatever was deranged, taking enough pills for a quick and painless exit. The morgue will take some fingerprints to establish and I.D. You have identified the body. I doubt there will be any further investigation. One more for potter's field." The officer shook his head as he pulled a sheet over Ray's body. "Nice dress."

With Michael in rehearsal, Mollie offered to relieve Ivory from Earl's bedside watch. "Thanks, I'll stay with Earl until Stella comes home." The truth being that Ivory did not trust himself to be anywhere else. Even unconscious Earl somehow would keep him walking the straight and narrow. He had made a damn fool of himself earlier and could have bought a bullet for it.

She put on a pot of coffee for him without much more conversation. "I'll be down in the Grotto with Oscar, call me if you need anything."

Ivory hadn't even noticed her dress.

—

The larger orchestra stage was filled with bustling, anxious, musicians. The Grotto itself was empty except for three men sitting near the stage. Mollie giggled to herself as she got a woof whistle—which got an evil eye from Rusty. Finally, someone had noticed her dress. She took a seat soon finding out that her company were pianists waiting for their turn to try out.

They seemed rather chummy for competitors, which was fine by her. There had been enough personality conflicts so far today than she had seen in a month of Sundays; another and she just might scream. The number of musicians on stage amazed her. She hadn't known there were that many musicians in the whole hotel. What really fascinated her was Imogene who appeared to be conducting the rehearsal rather than Rusty. Earl had always run things his way. Still this was a man's world, and here was a woman doing a man's job. And pretty damn well, if she did say so herself.

38
Returned to Sender

Stub had just reached the front entrance to the Honeysuckle Rose Hotel as Roane came out. "You're ah . . . up late." This was asked with curiosity for its own sake. It had indeed been a long day.

"Just taking care of business," Roane replied with a smirk that suggested a secret loosely held.

Stub could smell what he was up to; or had been. "You got rid of the fish?'

"Just about to," he answered as he lit a cigarette.

Stub appreciated the aromatic tobacco smoke. Roane reeked of the bad fish Beulah had left them as her parting gift.

"We have it all loaded up in Wiggy's pick-up truck and are about to pay the bitch a mid-night visit. We thought it would be appropriate if we returned it to her. The poor dear has no paycheck and might be hungry." Roane looked at his watch. "I know . . . it is a little late, but it has been a busy day. We thought we would just leave it on her front step—wouldn't want to wake the dear woman would we now."

Stub laughed aloud. All that spoiled fish and rotting steak blocking her front door. All the dogs and alley cats for blocks around would have a field day. He wanted to go along for the fun but being Beulah's ex-boss could be a problem if caught in the act. "I had bet . . .better nah . . . not," he said stifling a yawn.

39
Gabriel Calling

Each day, as Earl lost more of his ability to communicate, it became more difficult for Stella to reach out to him. She could see that Earl, the love of her life, was not long for this world. She focused on his needs, putting aside her own pain—she would have the rest of her life to live with that. He had had a stroke, three or four perhaps, robbing him of any normal function on his left side from his foot, which would no longer support weight, his arm—the fingers which would never play the piano again—to his face which now drooped changing forever the way her husband looked, slurring his speech to three or four sounds which never seemed to come together as a word. The sound she most recognized was a deep sob of frustration signifying that her husband wanted to let go and pass peacefully out of the dark dissolution that was all that was left of his existence.

When he first lost his ability to speak, she held up a pad and gave him a pencil. The results were negligible; his limited scrawl all but meaningless. Over the next few days she patiently asked a number of questions asking him to nod once for yes, and twice for no. That failed to. She finally found a connection by holding his right hand. There she got a squeeze once for yes, twice for no. He could hear, but Stella feared that to he might be losing his hearing as well.

Her own thoughts grew dark as she tried to imagine what it must be like for him. To be blind, now trapped in that darkness without the ability to speak, or perhaps hear, his legs and arms failing him. It had reached the point where she was beginning to wish for his passing. He was cut off, alone in the dark, his ability to reach out sliding away as each hour passed.

Earl's world was dark, but not still like death. His dark, swirled, riding an erratic wind that he could neither see, touch or feel; never-the-less, always in motion. Except for his tiny fireflies, few, but they were there. After a while Earl had come to like the skittish little white lights, swift fireflies darting here and there in his dark place. As long as they were with him, he knew that he was still alive, not dreaming, or in some kind of waiting place while the Boss determined if he were going to heaven or hell. That scared him, because where he was at now was Hell, and if that were so, then had the choice already been made for him. His vertigo had never gone away. When he stressed it got worse. And there was plenty to stress about.

One of the greatest cruelties he endured was that he no longer created or heard music in his mind. Often the only sounds he heard was his own breathing and the sound of his own blood working its way through clogged pipes. His taste was off. He knew when his mouth and throat were dry but could not ask for anything to remedy his thirst. Time passed without recognizing him in the process. Not that long ago he had felt and heard something go wrong in his head. There had been a sudden pain, which mercifully did not last long. The numbness in his left arm vanished leaving him without even a shadow memory that he had ever had a left arm in the first place. The strange noises he had managed to utter instead of words were also gone. He could turn his thoughts into words, but they never went anywhere. Stella's voice, all sound, came to him tinny, distant, as if it were coming through an old tin can with the string to his inner ear almost too short leaving him afraid that if he turned his head that string might break taking away his last contact with the outside world; Stella. The worst thing of all was that he would never be able to tell Stella how much he loved her; never to sing again their song.

He had lost his music, the dragon that had terrified him for so long had disappeared. When Stella touched his hand, he would anger and want to scream out which only brought on the vertigo powerful enough to take his breath away. When he could not feel her touch, he was afraid that whatever was slowly stealing his life had once and for all taken her away— that would be too much for him to finally bear.

He was alone—that was what he thought. The window was open letting in a quiet soft breeze. There was another sound; slight. He could hear someone breathing—distant and tinny. Most likely it was Ivory who stayed steadfastly by his side. Earl could almost feel Ivory's sad eyes as he watched over him, never saying a word. Once in a while, Ivory would fluff his pillow, lightly pressing a supportive palm on his left shoulder to let Earl know that he was there. He might as well of been patting a Moose Head mounted on a wall; the moose felt nothing, as did Earl. Nothing.

Earl kept asking where his Stella had gone, the question unable to leave his mind, as he waited and listened through that damned tin can for her return.

He also listened for Henry; worried.

His long death rattle had begun the morning he had gone down to see Henry and Les off to the army. That was when life changed, when all the joy simply blew away like so many dandelion seeds. Poof. Gone.

Stella had told him that Les was home, safe from the army, his leg in a cast. Earl had often wondered why Les had not come to see him, perhaps he had, and he didn't even know it. Time, memories, and reality were all fleeting, hard to sort out one from another. Finding himself on the slippery slope between life and death Earl reached out to Sy for reassurance that the end was not final. Sy had been psychic; perhaps, just perhaps?

Is Henry safe? The only question he continued to ask besides where his Stella was. His only answer the tinny sound of his own breathing as he listened, reaching out to a world he was no longer part of.

What's happening? Earl asked as he felt himself being lifted from his bed. His right hand was not dead, as was his left, but it took time for him to give it a command—the results often not what he wanted it to do. Recently he had been thirsty and had willed his palm and fingers to curve as if holding up a cup and then to raise it towards his head to tell Stella what he needed. He had no idea how long it took to raise his hand, but his hand did not curve until sometime later.

It was Stella and Ivory who were moving him, and he wanted to know why. This time he was able to raise his hand just enough for Stella to see.

"My darling, you need some fresh air. You need to get out of this stupid bed. Ivory and I are going to take you down to the Grotto where the band is about to have a final rehearsal before their first public performance tomorrow night." She said this slow and careful, her mouth close to his ear. As soon as he was in his wheelchair she reached for and found his hand where she was startled by his response.

No! No! Two squeezes each. *No!*

She knew that he detested the wheelchair. It embarrassed him, telling all who might see him how vulnerable, how fast he was becoming a human vegetable. He did not want everyone's pity. "Everyone is so looking forward to seeing you. The band has been . . ."

No! No! That was not what he wanted, the band he loved played in a time no longer his—as was his music. He did not want to hear any music because it tore at his soul to know how much he had lost. *No!*

She kissed his wrist letting his hand go. She was not going to argue with him; not now. Once he was in the Grotto and heard their music it would bring him some peace. It was the least she could do. She looked at his sagging face wishing that he could smile. If he could, then she would know that she was doing the right thing.

—

A sign hung in the window of the front door to the hotel read: *Closed for Private Party.* Everyone was waiting in the Grotto for The Honeysuckle Rose Orchestra's final dress rehearsal. Even the kitchen staff, which had been beefed up for their first public performance, had turned off their pots and pans and had joined this small but expectant audience.

Earl did not want to go, being taken against his will brought tremendous stress and with that the vertigo. His wheelchair ride was not quiet and peaceful. He was caught inside a tornado, a whirlpool of erratic motion that brought his blood pressure up to a roar as it surged in his veins so loudly that he could not hear Stella as she tried to sooth him.

In the elevator Stella was beginning to have second thoughts about what she had planned for Earl in the Grotto. She could feel his blood pressure through her touch. His palpitations were too erratic. She started to reach for the elevator button to go back up.

The door to the elevator opened.

The moment he heard Imogene sing he began to calm.

    '. . .We kiss, and . . .'

His reaction to the music surprised no one more than Earl himself. He knew Imogene's voice, though it sounded distant and canned, it drew him towards that special place in his heart he thought he would never feel again. His love for music. He had lived for it. It had been his life's passion until he had met Stella.

Stella understood that Earl had both a mistress and a wife—she was never jealous of his first love.

One by one the band fell silent leaving only Imogene singing. While blind, Earl's tear ducts still functioned, his tears brought the same to Stella's eyes. While he couldn't form a smile the right side of his mouth quivered as his lips tried to do what his paralyzed left side couldn't.

A space had been cleared front row center stage for his wheel-chair. All the seats next to and behind him were filled with friends including a few special guests like Loyal William Jones, and the reporter who had been there the night Michael, Earl, and Oscar had taken on the mighty musician's union.

"Earl, the angels are singing for you," Imogene purred sultrily into the mike as she finished the tune.

Earl squeezed a YES to Stella.

"The band is bigger now, more of an orchestra. We all hope you will like our sound. First, I want you to meet the boys, a few you already know." Imogene said as she put down the mike.

Les Moore rolled up next to Earl, his left leg extended full length in a cast. They had all been instructed by Stella to speak soft and clearly near his right ear. When done to place a hand momentarily on his right shoulder.

"I'm fine Mr. C., don't you worry none about old Les. My knee might not be much good, but I'm done with war. The army won't have no more to do with me." Les looked at Stella, not sure if Earl knew he was there. Stella drew his eyes down to where she held Earl's hand. There he could see Earl squeezed Stella's hand.

Earl says he's so happy to know that you are okay and still here playing that magnificent horn of yours.

"I've got something here for you Mr. C. It's a letter from Henry. He asked me to forward his clarinet, which I have done. It says here that he is in Hawaii."

> 'You tell Earl that the army is treating me swell.
> They made me an officer; can't you imagine that?
> I'm now a First Lieutenant in charge of all field
> medical supplies for the entire Pacific theater. My
> unit sees that the combat field medics have what they
> need, when they need it. When I was an army combat
> medic my medical kit frequently ran out of things.
> More than once I had to resupply my kit from that
> of another medic who had been wounded or killed
> in action. My job is to see that there are enough
> medic kits close enough by that a runner can get it
> to a combat medic even under fire. That is going to
> save a lot of lives. Enough about the army for now.
> I've met a few buddies from my old Nisei unit. We've
> started our own small jazz group. It reminds me of
> the old days at Adam's Place. Les, I wish you had
> known Gibby. He was a pretty swell guy.

Tell Mr. C. that I Miss him; Stella too. Hell, I miss all you guys. When the army is done with me, I'll becoming home. Keep the music coming.

- Henry

Les struggled with his emotions as he placed a loving hand on Earl's shoulder.

Earl squeezed a happy *YES! YES!* to Stella as tears slid down from beneath the right side of his dark glasses.

Following Les came Michael, then Mollie and Oscar. When it was Rusty's turn Stella told Earl that Rusty was the orchestra's new conductor. Rusty denied that, saying that everyone followed Imogene. He just waved a stick when the idea came to him.

One by one the musicians followed. This was difficult for most of the musicians had never performed with Earl, some hadn't even met him before. Most had never exchanged words with someone who was so visibly handicapped.

"Joe Cassinelli, slap bass, Mr. Crier."

"Angus Moneyouth, guitar."

"Oliver tucker, folks call me Owl; drums."

"Sarah Hinkley, piano."

Most of the names didn't linger long in his memory. The

instruments did. French horn, oboe, bongo, trumpet, tambourine, slide guitar. With Michael's saxophone, Les' trombone, Rusty's marimba it was becoming quite the orchestra. As the line of musician's and friends passed by Earl, Rusty played his marimba until all the musicians were back in place on stage.

The room grew quiet as Oscar delivered his opening poem, followed by Imogene and the orchestra performing *Skylark, Black Coffee, And the Angels Sing*. Oscar recited *Somewhere Over the Rainbow* mixed with Imogene's vocals of the same.

Earl struggled with his hearing, everything distant and tinny. The more he struggled to hear, the better it seemed to get. Slowly, like ear pressure releasing after coming down from a tall mountain, Earl's hearing in his right ear cleared. *YES! YES! YES!* He kept squeezing Stella's hand as his hearing became better and better.

Stella had no idea why Earl was so excited—that he was happy was all that mattered as she continued to hold his hand. The word *YES* quietly passed her own lips each time he squeezed her hand. *YES! YES! YES!* Her shared joy almost orgasmic.

The first time Earl had heard Rusty on his marimba had been the last time Earl had performed. No one could have guessed the consequences of giving Les Moore—black man—a goodbye hug on a public sidewalk in front of the Honeysuckle Rose Hotel. Earl remembered that Rusty was not only a talented musician, energetic, and a talented ballroom dancer, as Stella whispered to him what was happening.

The lights darkened around the orchestra. A moment later

a spot highlighted Michael as he sat alone on a chair in the center of the dance floor as he brought up his saxophone and began to play a rich, sultry, if not, lonely tune.

Rusty and Mollie, with wings on their shoes, danced slowly twice around the dance floor. The two parted gracefully, leaving Mollie to dance alone as Rusty returned to his marimba tucked away in the shadows. Mollie wore her robin's egg blue Chantilly dress and was absolutely stunning. She slowly stopped dancing as she came to Michael's side as he sang. That Michael was singing this song to her was profoundly evident.

> *'Love once left me cold and gray.*
> *I had almost reached heaven . . .'*

No one had ever heard Michael sing before, his voice rich with emotion, as he sang from his heart directly to her.

> *'Taste, touch, hear, see, feel me now girl*
> *and you'll know I'm so ready*
> *To exchange lifelong vows,'*

Stella gasped.

Mollie walked with Michael as a minister met them both on the dance floor just beneath the center of the orchestra's stage.

> *'cause now you've shown me how God has smiled*
> *on this chance and this moment . . .'*

The orchestra played the first few notes of the wedding song.

"Michael and Mollie are getting married," she whispered to Earl. He squeezed three strong *Yes's* as the minister began to speak.

Mollie never looked lovelier. Michael, the ugliest man in San Francisco, suddenly very handsome, very elegant. His suit was made of cashmere, vested formal, the print a muted houndstooth weave~ very beautiful, luxuriously soft like velvet. The vest was raw silk in a quiet rust tone woven in a subtle leopard's rosette print in an offsetting darker rust color. From the back the groom could have been Clark Gable, they both have big ears. A simple hat covered Michael's hair which had often been described as being cut by Oscar when he had been a lousy blind drunk.

Michael and Mollie were married with only Rusty, Imogene, and the minister knowing ahead of time that their wedding was to take place. No happier couple have ever graced that dance floor with more love and grace.

Earl squeezed Stella's hand

The band played on.

Stella cried as women universally do at weddings.

Michael and Mollie retired for a private moment behind the stage.

Imogene brought the orchestra back in focus with *I Wonder Who Is kissing Her Now.*

Earl chuckled to himself, an emotion he had almost forgotten as he listened to the music. Then . . . *What? Who's that?* He thought someone was whispering in his ear. But the voice was coming from elsewhere. *Sy?*

"I wish I could have been there. Good for Mollie," he heard Sy say. *"They make good music together. Gabriel wants you to know that he has reserved a piano right by his side. He's very fond of the Blues you know."*

For their anniversary Stella and Earl had been recording some of their songs hoping to make a record. They needed a recording studio, without one they had only managed to produce a single which Imogene now placed on a phonograph that had been set up on stage. "Earl, this is for you." The record was scratchy, tinny at best. It was the old Earl Crier Sextet with Earl playing his piano and singing:

> 'That's my Stella by starlight,
> And not a dream,

Oh my, oh my . . . he thought. He then suffered an acute tug at his heart, followed by a sharp and final pain. He squeezed Stella's hand one last time as the blues man finally found peace.

> She is everything on this earth to me.'

Stella squeezed Earl's hand just as the record ended. A scratch . . . scratch . . . scratch of the needle reading empty space followed as the orchestra moved into something to lighten the mood. It was Rusty this time who sang as he brought joyous notes from his marimba.

'Come on and blow, Gabriel, blow!
I want to join your happy band.
And play all day in the Promised Land.'

As Earl's hand fell away Stella tried to hold it for just one more moment. She knew that her Earl was gone, but he would never be silent as he played by Gabriel's side the sweetest blues you could ever imagine.

Ivory heard Sy. Sy spoke to him, just as the Sarge said he would. *"No Ivory, this is not your time. Treasure life while you have it. Earl needs you here to help Stella. She is going to need you by her side. You stay here and grow strong. I'll get back to you when it's time."*

The End.

CPSIA information can be obtained
at www.ICGtesting.com
Printed in the USA
FSHW011844170220
67150FS